TAKE A CHANCE ON LOVE

BOOK 4

VIRGINIA'DELE SMITH

BOOKS ARE UBIQUITOUS

Published by Books are Ubiquitous, Inc.
Tulsa, Oklahoma in the United States of America
booksareubiquitous.com
Books are Ubiquitous is a federally registered trademark.

This book is a work of fiction.

Names, characters, places, and incidents either are the product of the author's imagination or are used fictitiously. Any resemblance to actual persons, living or dead, business establishments, events, or locales is entirely coincidental.

Paperback ISBN: 978-1-957036-15-1

———

Titles by Virginia'dele Smith

Sadie & Sam: PART 1 - Introductory Short Story (FREE)
Book 0: My Manifesto - Short Memoir (FREE)

The Davenports
Book 1: Grocery Girl
Book 2: In the Trenches
Book 3: Three Times to Make Sure
Book 4: Take a Chance on Love
The Davenports EAT — A Green Hills Cookbook

Book 5: *Undeveloped Love* (coming fall 2023)
A Christmas Collection Novella

The Green Hills of Scotland (coming 2024)
Book 6: *Isla*
Book 7: *Ainslie*
Book 8: *Elspeth*

———

To Cannon Bailey.

You are the life of our party,
my favorite debate adversary,
and the most thoughtful, big-hearted,
chivalrous boy I've ever known.

You, SonShine, are a gift.

1

Sometimes our light goes out,
but is blown again into instant flame
by an encounter with another human being.
Albert Schweitzer

"Landry, go home," the attending physician on duty commanded as he passed the young woman in the hallway.

"Almost there," she promised, glancing at her watch. Monday morning. She'd been at the hospital since Saturday afternoon and felt *more* than ready to leave.

Doctor Landry Stark had relinquished the care of her patients to a new shift of doctors and nurses; they were in excellent hands. And yet, the tug to complete her rounds prevented her from leaving without putting eyes on each person she'd treated just one more time.

Quiet as a mouse, Landry slipped into each room, consulted the monitors, glanced over charts, adjusted lines, and smoothed blankets. Seeing her patients resting peacefully helped lift the weight of the last thirty-eight hours.

Reminding herself to put one foot in front of the other, Landry entered the doctors' locker room, swapped her lab coat for her raincoat, grabbed her purse, and closed her locker. Finally, she walked toward the doors leading out of the hospital, ready to head home.

She turned down the last corridor on her way to the staff entrance and parking lot and immediately spotted a fireman sitting in a hard plastic chair along the wall. Alone. His knees supported his elbows, which kept his hands in place to hold up his head. Landry didn't need to see his face. She didn't have to look past the grime and soot covering every inch of his clothing. She knew exactly who sat there.

"Davis?" She kneeled in front of him, slow to put a hand on his arm so she wouldn't startle him awake. "Davis, do you need to see a doctor?"

When he barely lifted his eyes to hers, Landry had the impression that picking up his head might be too heavy a task for him. Davis's expression, along with the pain and vacancy in his eyes, scared Landry. The broken shell before her bore no resemblance to her friend, so well-known for his boisterous personality, his coquettish demeanor, and his endless charm. The fun-loving facets of the man her friends adoringly dubbed "The Flirtbird" had vacated the premises.

No, he'd not been asleep, but perhaps in a trance. They'd both seen such horrific things that day. It didn't stretch the mind to imagine Davis fighting *not* to close his eyes.

"Davis, are you hurt?" Landry persisted.

"No," his voice was raw. He took a deep breath, probably shoring up whatever strength he had left. He straightened and then stood, helping her stand up with a hand under her elbow. "No, I'm fine."

He sounded more like himself. He looked more like himself — steady and solid. But he was not fine.

"Are *you* okay?" Davis searched deep into her eyes, ferreting out the truth.

"That was my first large-scale catastrophe. I hope it's my last."

"I've never seen anything like it," Davis said, his voice hollow again.

They stood in silence for a moment, neither one having the right words to help process the tragedy.

"Someone said Earl opened Triple T's early to serve breakfast to first responders. Come with me?" Sensing they both would benefit from more human contact, Landry's request came out as a plea. Besides, they needed food. Neither of them would've eaten since they were at Daisy Lake on Saturday afternoon. Almost two days ago. The distance between the peace she'd experienced at the lake and the exhaustion she felt in that moment had to be greater than a mere two days.

She hadn't planned on going to the diner before coming upon Davis in the hallway, but her gut told her to take the detour. They both needed it.

"No, but thank you. I'm waiting for word on the Cadells. Eddie Cadell and his boy, Zane. Zane would've been on one of the earlier ambulance runs, but Eddie—" His voice hitched. He cleared his throat before trying again. "Eddie stayed in the building a lot longer. He was in bad shape."

"Yes, I know—" she started to say.

"Is he dead?"

2
____

And we find at the end of a perfect day,
the soul of a friend we've made.
Carrie Jacobs-Bond

At its beginning, Saturday looked perfect. With a day off from the hospital, Landry Stark had not set an alarm. Instead, she'd gradually woken up to a sunny bedroom and birds chirping outside her window. She stretched and smiled, burrowed into her cozy sheets and heavy winter quilt, and refused to get out of bed until her stomach growled so loudly that she'd giggled in response.

Once she'd forced herself out of her cocoon, layered a heavy, flannel bathrobe over her pajamas, and slid her feet into thick cabin socks *and* her winter house shoes, Landry had taken the time to brew a macchiato latte in the fancy espresso machine. The coffee was steaming hot with the perfect balance of bitter coffee and sweet, frothy milk. She closed her eyes, savoring every sip. Her closest friend, Maree Davenport, had turned them all into tea drinkers — hot tea, iced tea, sweet tea, fruity tea — but sometimes the day called for a strong cup of coffee.

"Mmmmm," she groaned in bliss, just as Miss Sadie walked into the kitchen of her boarding house in which Landry was a long-time resident.

"I was coming in here to heat an apricot tart for you...in case you stayed in bed all morning," Miss Sadie teased with a wink.

"Breakfast in bed?" Landry stacked her hands over her heart, faking shock and dismay. "Marshall Mansion policy plainly states that all meals are to be taken at a table," she teased right back as she set down her coffee mug.

Landry's landlord felt more like a grandmother. Living in Miss Sadie's home — known as Marshall Mansion ever since Sadie's dad built the farmhouse in the 1930s — had turned out to be quite a blessing.

"One or two, Ms. Smarty Pants?" Sadie sassed, looking pointedly at the homemade pastries under the cake dome. Known for her warm and welcoming, kind and nurturing ways, Miss Sadie was also a phenomenal cook. Landry's stomach grumbled again, reminding her of — and alerting Miss Sadie to — her hunger.

"Definitely two, please," Landry answered, giving Miss Sadie a hug. "Will you have a cup of coffee with me?" Landry moved toward the cupboard, reaching for another mug.

"You'll have to work that cursed coffee maker y'all insisted we have," Sadie replied. "What happened to the days of a simple percolator?"

"What's a percolator?" Landry joked.

"I refuse to answer that," Miss Sadie said with her chin lifted, pretending haughtiness as she took Landry's plate out of the microwave. She added a dollop of clotted cream and a spoonful of fresh berries, and she carried it over to the breakfast nook as Landry set both mugs of coffee on the table.

"Thank you." Landry expressed her gratitude, reaching out to squeeze Miss Sadie's hand once they sat down.

"Well, I wouldn't want you to starve," Sadie replied. "Maree mentioned y'all are going out to Daisy Lake today. Might should go sooner rather than later... It's beautiful out now, chilly but clear. I'm afraid a storm's coming our way this evening."

After her late breakfast, Landry made up her bed, took a quick shower, and threw her wintertime lake essentials in a tote bag: a wool quilt, her favorite beanie and gloves, and two books — the one she'd already begun and a backup just in case she finished the first one too quickly. She called the hospital at Green Country Medical Center where she was in her final year of residency to tell Ruthie, the charge nurse and supervisor on duty, that she'd be away from her phone for the day but out at the lake so they could reach her via Audrie Boucher at Lakeside Yoga. Miss Sadie handed her a gigantic picnic basket filled with sandwiches, two tall thermoses of hot soup, bagged chips, fresh fruit, and still-warm peanut butter cookies.

*B*y noon, Landry had curled up in her favorite spot on Davis's dock, wrapped in a quilt and soaking up the warm sun from the comfort of a long chaise lounge.

Maree and her fiancé, Rhys Larsen, and his best friend, Daniel Davis, soon joined her.

"Is that basket from Miss Sadie?" Davis asked.

"What basket?" Landry asked, faking a confused expression.

"The one sitting next to your chair," he pointed out.

"Oh, *my* basket? Yes, Miss Sadie filled it — for me — before I left this morning. Hot soup, homemade cookies— You should've smelled them coming out of the oven." Landry closed her eyes, inhaling the crisp air and remembering the scent of fresh baked cookies with rapture.

"I can smell them now," Davis supplied. "Peanut butter, I'm guessing."

"Mmmm— Yes."

"And are you planning on sharing *your* basket?" Davis oozed charm as he smiled at Landry.

"I imagine that depends. What will you give me?" She enjoyed tossing the saucy challenge his way.

It was always this way between them: flirting and teasing and grinning, but never anything more.

Landry first met Davis over a year ago at Scooter's. She'd been desperate for a few hours away from school and studying, and Miss Sadie had forced Maree to go out with her. The girls had been having great fun dancing, singing karaoke, and acting silly. Then Rhys appeared at their pool table, asking to join their game. His buddy wasn't far behind. Within seconds, any fool could see that Rhys and Maree had eyes only for one another, so Landry and Davis paired up to dance together.

Refusing to sit out a single song, Landry had made the most of her night out and her time on the dance floor. They'd looped arms in the Cotton-Eyed Joe, stomped out numerous line dances with the crowd, and cozied up to one another during the slow songs. Chris Stapleton's cover of "Tennessee Whiskey" would forever hold a special place in her heart after being in Davis's arms while it played.

Talk about sensational!

They'd danced and danced the night they'd met. And Davis hadn't complained once, seeming perfectly happy to stay right there with her as long as the night — and the magic with it — lasted.

Landry thought they'd had some chemistry; she'd even entertained the thought of an innocent kiss in the parking lot when they left.

But Davis hadn't walked her out that night, hadn't asked for her phone number, and hadn't kissed her under the stars. Since then, Davis had never indicated he saw Landry as more than a friend — a good friend, as they were both close to the Davenports and had gone through quite a few trials with their friends over the past two years, but *just* friends, nonetheless.

Landry accepted that because a good friend beat an ex-boyfriend any day.

"Well, Doctor Stark," Davis said with exaggerated interest and insinuation. "What do you want?"

Ah, the million-dollar question, particularly where Daniel Davis was concerned.

"Play nice," Maree instructed. "I have it on good authority that Miss Sadie sent lunch to *all* of us, and I intend to dig in." With that, Maree snagged the basket, set it on the picnic table, opened the lid, and began setting out the contents.

Landry gave Davis a "what'cha gonna do" shrug, which he answered with a "you got off lucky" shake of his head. And so the dance continued.

After their late lunch, Landry snuggled under her quilt again, opened her book to read, and promptly fell asleep.

She awoke to Davis gently shaking her shoulder and looking concerned.

"Landry, you gotta wake up," he urged. "Something's happened."

Her heartbeat lurched as she shook off the remnants of sleep.

"Wha—" Davis didn't allow time for Landry to ask what was going on before he shuffled her out of the lounge chair and into the house, pushing her backpack into her arms and turning off lights.

"There's been an explosion at the City Park," he began. "We've got to get to town. I can drop you off at the hospital if you don't feel that you can drive."

"But— Wait." Still drowsy from sleep, Landry struggled to process what Davis said. She reached out to stop him from scurrying by her again, grabbing the sleeve of his Green Hills Fire Department sweatshirt. "I don't understand."

Her hand slid down his arm to grasp his hand, forcing him to stop and face her. An anxious but serious light shone in his eyes. She could tell his mind was focused elsewhere.

Davis glanced at their clasped hands and gave hers a reassuring squeeze. "I don't have much to go on," he explained. "Audrie ran over from her studio saying that the hospital called for you, asking that you come in immediately. Before she could get the words out, Rhys and I both received pages from the fire department. When Rhys called in, dispatch asked for all available responders to the City Park. Several people had called 911 to report an explosion and fire at the basketball gym. That's all I know for sure."

"Let's go," Landry replied, fully alert by then. Jumping into action, she jogged out the front door of the cabin and down the porch to her car. "I'm fine driving my car; you go on to the park. And Davis, be careful," she added over her shoulder as he locked the front door.

"You too, Landry. Take it easy on the lake road. I know how fast you like to drive," he teased. His smile didn't quite reach his eyes, but she appreciated his effort to help her remain calm when there was no telling what they faced.

*L*andry couldn't have imagined the scene.

She arrived at work to find the hospital in utter chaos. Ambulances, some of them extras called in from surrounding communities, unloaded gurneys through the emergency room entrance. EMTs helped those who could walk make their way through the main entrance. People desperate for information filled the sidewalk and parking lot.

A pop-up tent served as a command center where the police chief, fire chief, and hospital administrators huddled around folding tables that held blankets and bottles of water. Landry noticed Miss Sadie nearby, doing her best to soothe and settle a young woman on the verge of hysterics. Miss Sadie wrapped a quilt around the woman and secured her under one arm as she spoke to her in a firm yet kind voice.

Landry hustled over to them.

"Can I help?"

"Inside, dear," Miss Sadie instructed, sparing Landry only a quick look of sadness.

"You're needed inside. We'll be okay out here."

The hardness in her tone sent chills down Landry's spine.

Out of the corner of her eye, Landry saw Maree consoling a couple who appeared to need medical attention, too. She felt pulled in two directions. Ultimately, Miss Sadie's clipped directive — so out of character — won out, and Landry ran into the hospital.

The lobby looked like the triage unit in a dramatic war movie. Wheelchairs filled the room, parked frame to frame with injured bodies hunched in them, as though the waiting patients might slide out and slip to the floor at any moment. Stretchers lined the corridors with more injured bodies haphazardly covered in bloodied sheets. Some people moaned, others cried, while still others remained too silent. Most all the bodies on gurneys were small and short. Children.

Nausea gripped Landry's stomach. What in the world had happened?

"Doctor Stark, thank goodness you're here," Ruthie called from across the room as she helped a young boy roll to his side before covering him with a warm blanket. Landry rushed to the nurse's side, ready to assist. "Rachel is doing rapid assessment as they bring in patients. Tell her you'll take exam rooms six through ten so Doctor Bradford can open another operating room. Be precise, but be efficient. This is Zane; he's ready to go with you." Ruthie nodded once at the boy. Her lips pressed together in a straight line of determination, a silent message to the boy clearly showing that she believed in him, that he could handle what came next.

"Yes, ma'am," Landry responded, giving Zane a reassuring smile as she pushed the stretcher toward the exam area.

"You'll need to check his right thigh immediately," Ruthie whispered as Landry pushed the gurney past her.

"Yes, ma'am," Landry repeated, careful not to alert Zane or make him nervous.

Behind the curtain of Exam Room 6, Landry moved the sheet from Zane's right leg to reveal a rough piece of wood projecting from the boy's thigh. She surveyed the grotesque tears in his flesh and sections of exposed muscle. Like shrapnel from a bomb, the wood fragment wasn't large, but it could prove deadly, just the same. From the paint scraps she could see, Landry guessed it was a thick sliver of the old wooden bleachers. Impaled so close to Zane's femoral artery, the sharp tip created a life-threatening puncture wound. The medical staff needed to control the bleeding with external pressure while repairing the artery; otherwise, Zane risked bleeding out internally.

"It's bad, isn't it?" Zane asked, a resignation in his voice no child should experience.

"How old are you, Zane?" Landry asked while Suzanne, the nurse helping Landry, placed a loose tourniquet beside the bloodied twill belt someone had thought to secure above the wound.

"Eight," he answered. "Well, almost. I will be next week." His sweet honesty instantly endeared him to Landry.

"So, second grade, I'm guessing," Landry said, continuing to engage Zane in conversation.

"Yes, ma'am." Zane's words ended in a sudden gasp of air as Suzanne tightened the tourniquet. Together, they began cleaning around the wound.

"Well, eight years old is old enough to know what's really going on, so I'm going to tell you the truth. It's not ideal, but it's not so bad, either, Zane. A piece of wood wedged into your leg. It's kind of in a bad spot — you were brilliant to leave it there and let us take it out a certain way. Good job, there." Landry gave him a wink and a moment to catch his breath. His leg would feel as though it was on fire, burning from the bone out to the skin, the cleaning process another form of torture. "But I can't take it out here in the exam room. I'm going to give you a little medicine to ease your pain, something to make you relax. And then I'm going to ask Doctor Bradford to help me remove the splinter. I think four hands can get the job done just right."

"Will I ever walk again?"

His bravery shattered Landry's heart.

"Most definitely," she pledged. "You'll need to stay off it while it heals, and I'll prescribe some physical therapy, but once you're cleared, you'll be good to go." Then she stepped aside for Suzanne to start Zane's IV line. Landry ordered a cocktail of medicines, a strong one for sedation and pain relief with a preoperative antibiotic on the side. Suzanne administered them through Zane's IV while Landry continued to visit with him, trying to sound as normal as she could.

"So, Zane, what do you like to do? Besides go to school, of course," she added with another wink for the sweet child. "I remember second grade... Those were the days." Suzanne made a humph sound as though she might disagree, which made Zane smile.

"I like to play baseball," Zane answered, his words already

slurring. "My dad…" He drifted off for a moment. "…my coach…" Zane's eyelashes fluttered as he tried valiantly to finish his sentence. "…the best."

"Doctor Bradford has OR3 ready," Suzanne announced as she hung up the phone on the wall. Efficiently, the nurse organized Zane's IV bag, pulse sensors, and the various lines she'd attached to him. Within seconds, Suzanne had him ready to transport to the operating room. "Doctor Stark, he's asking that you assist. I'll make sure someone covers your exam rooms."

"Absolutely, and thank you." Landry walked beside Zane's gurney as Suzanne rolled him to the elevators. "I intend to see him through this ordeal and on the baseball diamond again in no time."

The surgery to repair the damage caused by the wood impaled in Zane's thigh followed simple steps, but the proximity of the puncture wound to his femoral artery added substantial risk to the procedure. Landry said a quick prayer for the boy and for their team working to save his life.

"But I will restore you to health and heal your wounds," declares the Lord… Jeremiah 30:17.

Landry repeated the scripture, both a reminder and a prayer, over and over as she scrubbed in for surgery.

She also sent up a praise of thanks for Doctor Bradford, known as a magician in the operating room.

Still undecided on her area of specialty, Landry had purposefully applied for rotations in all the program options throughout medical school and her years of residency. Continuing her training another two years to become a surgeon held a certain appeal, so she'd spent quite a bit of time in the operating room. Those hours of observing and assisting reassured Landry that Zane's future was in the best possible hands.

It took over two hours, but the surgery was a success. Barring any post-operative complications, Zane's prognosis was great. He should be back on the baseball field in a matter of months.

Landry accompanied Zane to a recovery room, but she'd barely finished checking charts and making notes when an overhead page called for her to report to the emergency room. She instructed the post-op nurse assigned to Zane to call her when he woke up or if his vitals changed, and hastened to the stairwell to run down to the emergency room.

Stunned upon opening the door to the stairwell, Landry stood in awe at the dozens of people sitting, standing, even laying along the edges of steps and landings between floors. Some appeared to be in a daze, stunned and filthy by the events of the day. Others appeared to be weeping or sleeping. Several needed medical attention.

"Ruthie?" Landry called, looking for the charge nurse as soon as she emerged from the stairwell.

"Over here, Doctor Stark."

Landry followed the voice to the waiting room, where nurses worked from rolling carts, cleaning and bandage minor wounds, while volunteers offered fruit cups, granola bars, and bottles of sports drinks to those strong enough to eat or drink.

"Ruthie, why are all those people in the stairwell? There are dozens, maybe close to fifty, people in there."

"No other place to put them, Doctor Stark. The cafeteria is full, the waiting rooms are full, and as you can see, the foyer is full."

"Where am I needed?"

Landry's question halted Ruthie's progress in wrapping a bandage around a teenager's temple. The young man wore a referee's striped pullover with black pants and black tennis shoes, which were torn, tattered, and smeared with blood. He looked to be around seventeen or eighteen. Landry thought he might've been the boy she'd met just weeks ago at a surprise wedding reception for Maree's older brother and his wife. She couldn't be sure if the boy with Ruthie had been their deejay at the party because of the nasty abrasion covering half his forehead, his right eye, and the area from his temple to his cheekbone. His injuries turned youthful skin that had been smooth and healthy into pulverized tissue. Swelling and bruising had already deformed his strong, athletic features. At least a third-degree abrasion, Landry feared the avulsion would leave permanent scars.

Ruthie stared at Landry for a second. Her red-rimmed eyes reflected haunting sadness. She scoffed and sighed, perhaps incredulous at the only answer she could find.

"Everywhere."

3

____

***With the new day
comes new strength and new thoughts.
Eleanor Roosevelt***

Ruthie had not been wrong.

The next thirty-four hours whizzed by in a blur. Landry treated several more projectile and blunt force injuries similar to Zane's, but thankfully, none were as life-threateningly close to a major artery. She set broken bones and ordered casts for the fractures. With the aid of nurses and volunteers, she treated burns, taught parents how to use nebulizers to improve their child's breathing after inhaling dust and smoke, ordered hundreds of tests for dozens of patients including x-rays, MRIs, echocardiograms, and even hearing tests for those she feared had experienced a tympanic membrane rupture from the blast.

She remembered Doctor Bradford ordering her to rest at one point; Landry recalled how her body had ached in agonizing protest when she'd stretched out on the couch in the staff lounge for half an hour. She couldn't have guessed how long ago that had been. The hours, the injuries, the blood, the tears, and the desperation fused together into one dense, sticky blob of devastation in Landry's mind.

When Doctor Jayr, the attending physician, told her to go home, her watch read 4:53 a.m.

But then, as good as home, a shower, and her bed at Marshall Mansion sounded, Davis needed her more.

"Is he dead?" Davis had asked in a vacant voice.

"Oh, Davis. No," Landry gasped, realizing he'd been assuming the worst for the Cadell family, thinking he'd failed to save Zane's dad. "No," she told him again.

Her answer didn't seem to register. The despondency in his body language startled Landry. Where was the glimmer of light ever present in his pale, powder-blue eyes? Why did his smile lines, usually framing his soft lips in a bold grin, age him unnaturally when set so deeply in worry?

"Daniel, listen to me," she urged, resorting to his rarely used first name to get his attention. His lost look remained. Framing her hands on either side of his face, Landry forced him to look at her. "Eddie is not dead. And Zane is going to be fine — better than fine. Doctor Bradford did a beautiful job repairing the puncture wound. Zane will be fielding balls and hitting home runs by summertime."

"And Eddie's okay?" Davis's voice rang hollow.

"He has a long road ahead of him. Once he's able, they'll transport him to Parkland in Dallas. Their burn unit will offer the most comprehensive care available. He's strong, and Zane needs him. That's all the motivation he'll need to navigate through the challenges of healing."

"He'll need surgeries, skin grafts?"

"Yes," she confirmed, a sour feeling in the pit of her stomach. She dropped her hands from his cheeks, looked down at her feet. "It will be a rough year, but Eddie's okay. He can do this."

"But he shouldn't have to." The bleak resentment in Davis's voice concerned Landry. He'd always been the epitome of optimistic, positive energy. She found it terribly difficult to see him so defeated.

"No, he shouldn't. But we did good here today — the past couple of days. So much trauma, and so many to treat. But we didn't lose a single patient. Think about that. Not one life lost after such a horrific event. That's something to celebrate, Davis. That's a miracle." Hot tears born of passion, fatigue, and pride streamed down Landry's face.

"You're right," Davis said in agreement, pulling himself out of the cold and distant spell she'd found him under. He exhaled and pulled Landry into his chest, wrapping her in a hug. The powerful frame of his support opened the floodgates that had been holding her pent-up emotions in check. Her body shook with sobs. Davis didn't seem to care. He tucked her into his body tighter, rested his cheek on her head, and let her cry as long as she needed. When her breathing had regulated, he moved his hands to frame her face, just as she had done to get his attention earlier. He leaned down enough to bring them eye to eye. His thumbs swiped under her eyes to clear away the moisture, and he even attempted a slight smile. "You did good, kid."

Landry nodded and sniffled. "We all did," she whispered.

"Yeah," he allowed. "Come on. I think you offered to buy me breakfast." Davis lifted her bag to one shoulder while draping his other arm over her. He held her close to his side as together they left the hospital and walked to The Three-Toed Turtle, a fabulous hole-in-the-wall diner on Main Street.

Sleep could wait, Landry decided. She could hold off her exhaustion a little longer. Being together was better for the moment.

4

---

itting in a booth along the back wall of the dining room, Maree and Rhys waved them over as soon as they walked in the restaurant. Maree slid out of her bench seat, gave Davis a quick hug, and held onto Landry much longer. Both girls had teary eyes when they released one another and Maree slid back into the booth, but next to Rhys rather than across from him, leaving the empty bench for Landry and Davis.

Filled with first responders and medical personnel, every conversation in Triple T's centered on the explosion. Snippets of speculation, comments of outrage, and shocked statements of disbelief floated in the air.

"Do we know anything?" Davis asked Rhys.

"Very little for certain," Rhys acknowledged with a grim shake of his head. "Green Hills Park & Rec was hosting a little dribblers tournament, so the gym was full of youth basketball teams and their families. At 2:50 p.m., a loud explosion occurred in the south end of the building, luckily behind the stage and not in the central area of the gym."

"That old building's been a staple of Green Hills since they built it in 1936. It's surreal to think of it as a pile of burnt rubble." A crease formed between Davis's eyebrows as he spoke. His distant gaze revealed he couldn't fathom such an idea. "It was a WPA project, funded from Roosevelt's New Deal. Its construction, along with the library building and city hall, was a really big deal. And the collection of murals in all the government buildings in town? An artist employed through the Federal Art Project created them. Did y'all know that Jackson Pollock painted for the FAP?" Davis refocused his gaze upon each friend before looking down at his plate, apparently surprised to find that someone had delivered the chicken fried steak he ordered.

"They assigned a different fellow to paint in Green Hills," Davis continued while picking up his fork and knife and attacking his meal. "His name was Carmine Frederick," he said around a large bite of steak and gravy. "He came to Green Hills in 1936, a twenty-five-year-old man desperate to make a name for himself as a professional muralist. His original contract with the WPA/FAP was for two murals: one at the post office, and one at the train depot. They had given him nine weeks to research local history, design his artwork, prep the walls, and paint both murals. At the time—" Davis shoveled in another oversized bite, this time of glazed carrots and mashed potatoes. Gulp. "...the FAP was still pretty new, so a timeline of one mural per month seemed perfectly reasonable to the bureaucratic suits running the program from Washington. It didn't take long for them to figure out that artists didn't work well on rigid deadlines.

"By 1937, the artists, tired of time restrictions on their creative process, budget decreases, and contract eliminations, had unified under their own union — Local 60 of the

Congress of Industrial Organizations — and regularly used sit-ins, strikes, and riots to make their wishes known. By 1939, the government, sick of dealing with temperamental artists and tired of being strong-armed by the union, dissolved the FAP. But in the eight years of the program, the New Deal had invested thirty-five million dollars to fund over five thousand artists who produced—" Davis stopped again. He'd been taking bites around sentences, but suddenly left his audience suspended mid-thought to slop up the gravy remnants with a buttered biscuit, savor the last bite, and wash it down with a full glass of sweet iced tea.

Sliding his plate toward the center of the table to make room for his forearms, he leaned forward and rambled on. "...close to three hundred thousand fine prints; one hundred thousand easel paintings; twenty-two thousand plates for the Index of American Design; seventeen thousand, seven hundred sculptures; and two thousand, five hundred sixty-six murals — seven of which still exist right here in Green Hills, Oklahoma." Davis waggled his eyebrows.

"Who *are* you?" Rhys questioned.

"How do you know all that?" Maree marveled.

"But I thought you said they commissioned Carmine Fred-erick to make *two* murals?" Landry argued.

"Ah, you *were* listening," Davis said with a clever gleam in his eyes. Landry couldn't help but smirk, delighted at seeing the return of his usual fervor for life and flair for dramatics. "To poor, starving, desperate Carmine, a month of housing, food, and wages per mural was pure luxury. In fact, he'd finished his first one in less than ten days. He—"

"Which one was it?" Landry interrupted. "The post office or the train depot?"

"Which one do you think?" Davis challenged right back.

"I'm guessing the landscape in the post office, with the vivid sunset streaking bright flashes of golden light and slashes of oranges, rusts, and purples over the red dirt so indicative of the Oklahoma terrain," Maree guessed.

"Nah, he'd have done the post office first," Rhys offered. "He was trying to make a name for himself, so he'd want to do the largest one immediately, and in the place that the most people would see. That mural depicts the early twentieth century version of the great American dream: husband and wife clearly in love, two perfect children — one boy, one girl — with an adorable puppy loping beside them, headed to a picnic under a huge tree on a grassy plain, hinting at a late afternoon with that Oklahoma sunset in the background. He intended for it to give hope to a country fractured by the Great Depression, remind them that good still existed in life, illustrate what they were working to achieve. That's the picture he wanted associated with his name," Rhys said, sounding rather confident in his analysis.

Davis turned to hear Landry's theory.

"Neither," she said in her sassiest tone. "Knowing he'd be out of a job if he finished the commissions too quickly, Carmine practiced on something else. I'm betting he painted the grandpa and granddaughter shopping together that still welcomes customers to the Get'n'Go. It would've been the perfect way to endear himself to the community." Landry had thrown down a gauntlet, daring Davis to correct her.

"You never cease to amaze me! Beautiful *and* brilliant," he laughed, wrapping an arm around Landry in a boisterous half-hug.

"What?" Maree drawled in dismay, her wide-eyed expression boring into Landry. "How did you know that?"

"How — and why — do either of you know *any* of that?" Rhys demanded.

"Davis essentially admitted that Carmine Frederick painted the murals in the post office and the old train depot, which makes sense, as they both have a common style and a consistent tone about them. Considering that, his other five are easy. Of course, the Get'n'Go is one — which I'm guessing was first because when Carmine arrived in 1936, food security would have been the town's first concern after their struggles and hardships during the previous seven years. The jungle-esque scenes of plants and fairies and butterflies on either side of the exit doors at the Majestic is another. The collage illustrating readers of all races, careers, and ages devouring books from every genre that takes up the entire back wall of the library is his style. The cityscape of Green Hills and her civil servants in City Hall is a no-brainer. And of course, the now-ruined painting of children at play, some jumping rope while a group threw jacks, a few kicked a ball to one another, and still others flew kites, at the Green Hills Park & Rec Gymnasium was the last."

Landry's list brought them full-circle, back to the issue at hand. A somber yet invisible cloak weighed down upon all four of them, extinguishing any lightheartedness they'd felt.

Davis removed his arm from Landry's shoulder, placing his forearm back on the table.

"I played there," he said. Landry threaded her arm through his to hug his arm and rested her temple against his shoulder — anything to offer strength. "Youth basketball every winter through elementary school. Mom dropped me off there every morning for a week during the summer for swim lessons. With my brother, sister, and every other kid in town, I ate a sack lunch sitting on the ancient wooden bleachers, while the lifeguards took their break between lessons and opening the pool to the public. Then we swam until our parents came back to take us home for dinner, just so we could return to the park for baseball in the evenings. In junior high, our district basketball tournament was there every spring. In high school, I started reffing little dribbler games to make some money. And I joined the GHPARD Swim Team."

When Davis released a nostalgic sigh, Rhys asked, "The Jee Pard Swim Team? What in the world is a jee pard?"

"Green Hills Park and Rec Department. G-H-P-A-R-D. We called ourselves the Guppies and thought we were very cool. We'd go to meets in Oklahoma City, Dallas, even Arkansas and Missouri, and hear other teams laughing, making fun of our silly name and goofy team shirts. I mean, who can't out-swim a guppy, right?" Davis resumed his talk-eat-drink pattern, scooping ice cream onto his fork with a healthy bite of the apple pie slice he'd ordered with his meal. "Turns out most people can't," he added, panting through the freezing cold heap of ice cream in his mouth.

Rhys lifted an eyebrow. Maree pressed her lips together, suppressing a giggle. Landry stared at him in wonder. They watched as he finished his dessert, in awe of the way he could vacuum up plate after plate — a large salad, the chicken fried steak with carrots and mashed potatoes, that first biscuit with gravy followed by two more with butter and jelly, and finally the quarter-pie slice of dessert topped in both vanilla ice cream and whipped cream — while never missing a beat of his story.

"Mmmm, that was good," Davis confessed after gulping an entire glass of milk. And then he dove right back into his tale...

"The Guppies darted here and darted there in the pool, streaks of light in our rainbow metallic suits, beating the Sharks and the Whales and all the other predatory sea animals week after week. I can't tell you the hours and hours I spent at the park and rec facilities, climbing on the playgrounds, playing on the baseball fields, swimming in the pool, and doing all kinds of things in the gymnasium." His gestures matched up with his story, causing his fork to swim in the air. Landry had to bobble her head to avoid it. The nostalgia in his voice revealed a deep sadness for what had been, and for what would never be again. At least not in the same way.

Seeming to run out of steam, Davis paused. Perhaps to

reminisce? Or possibly to rein in control over his grief. Either way, Davis halted the trip down memory lane, so Rhys and Maree returned to their food.

Landry wanted to soothe his pain, but she also wanted to allow Davis time to work through the magnitude of what had happened in his hometown. She'd not grown up so entrenched in her surroundings, but she imagined Davis felt the emotional impact of that explosion deeper than she and Maree and Rhys, who were newer to Green Hills. Newer, sure, yet still devastated by the destruction— Davis's pain must've been tenfold.

Her right arm still entwined with his left, Landry gave Davis's bicep a tight squeeze, prompting him to look over at her, down into her face. She dug deep to force a reassuring smile to her lips, promising him without words that everything would be okay, even when it felt like the world had fallen apart.

Davis lifted the corners of his mouth — not a smile or a grin, but an acknowledgment of her support. *Thank you,* he mouthed and gave her a wink. She released his arm to pick up the spoon in her bowl of fresh fruit, and Davis leaned back, stretching out both arms to rest upon the top of the bench seat.

"During college, I worked as a GHPARD lifeguard when I was home during the summers. For a while, I considered going into the Navy to try BUD/S, to see if I had what it takes to be a S.E.A.L. I used the pool, gym, running trails, and even the decrepit, old weight room under the offices... I put the whole place to work for me; it had everything I needed. Man, the memories just go on and on," Davis added.

"We held the annual quilt show there each spring, in the gymnasium," Maree mused.

"The annual *everything,*" Davis corrected. "The Miss Green Hills Pageant, the haunted house and festival for Halloween, an angel tree and pictures with Santa every December, a Valentine's Day dance, the high school art show—"

"Oh," Maree gasped, interrupting Davis's list. "We're

hosting our first-ever Mah Jongg tournament there next month."

"Surely the town will rebuild," Landry replied.

"This community rallies every time someone's in need. They'll do it again," Rhys said.

"I'm sure they will. *We* will," Davis allowed. "It just won't be the same. That building was special. Did you know that FDR even stopped here for the Rec Hall's ribbon cutting?"

Landry detected that they needed to be überimpressed for Davis — and she was! To be sure he noticed, she assumed an expression of dramatic disbelief. "As in Franklin Delano Roosevelt? Here? In Green Hills?"

It worked. Davis perked up, shifting back to his storytelling posture, sitting tall with his forearms on the table when he wasn't gesturing and talking with his strong hands.

"It was July 9, 1938. FDR and his son, Elliott, were traveling through Oklahoma on his special train car, Marco Polo. Their cross-country voyage had begun the week before, on June 30, when they departed from New York City. Over the next eight days, they made stops in Pennsylvania, Ohio, Louisville, Kentucky, and Arkansas. Then, on Saturday, July 9, between noon and that night, they stopped at several small towns on their way to Oklahoma City. The schedule allowed them to be in Green Hills for only seven minutes, but FDR, tremendously pleased to see the beautiful results of his New Deal programs in Carmine's mural at the new train depot, asked about other WPA and FAP projects in Green Hills. The mayor, Horace Armstrong, was a gifted storyteller."

"Like someone else we know," Maree whispered aloud to the table. Davis shook his head to deflect her compliment and forged ahead.

"Horace was also a talented manipulator — all for a good cause, of course. As he extolled the impact of Carmine Frederick's artistic endeavors on Green Hills and the wonderful works of the New Deal around town, he convinced the president of the United States to look at the Green Hills WPA projects by way of a driving tour. This was practically unheard of because FDR was very private about his polio and rarely, if ever, allowed the public to see him in transit, as he couldn't walk and had devised ways to stand with assistance when he made appearances or gave speeches. To change his plans and agree to leave the train station, be helped into a vehicle, and ride around a small town in southeast Oklahoma was simply incredible.

"First, Horace drove FDR to the edge of town to show off the rock work in structures called welcoming walls that greet visitors as they come into town from the highway. Then he drove him to the new post office where he explained that all the WPA construction projects used local limestone, creating work for an additional three hundred fifty men at the quarry, thereby necessitating housing, meals, laundry services, groceries, and more...altogether bringing over eighty thousand dollars into the local economy. Next Horace drove FDR to the City Hall building where he described Carmine's FAP mural in stunning detail, making a big deal of the patriotic way it illustrated the noble work of civil servants, so vital to a community's health. Finally, they ended up in front of the Rec Hall, where the masons would set the last stones around a gorgeous metal plaque that reads—"

Davis stopped himself, his eyes filling with sadness again. "Read, I mean. Past tense. It's likely rubble now, with the rest of the building."

"What did it say?" Landry asked, prompting him to keep going.

"*Built by Works Progress Administration. For the city of Green Hills, Oklahoma. 1938.*"

"I've seen it, aged to a beautiful patina, so strong and proud by the huge, wooden double doors at the side entrance of the building," Maree said, reaching across the table to lay her hand over Davis's.

"It was," he agreed. "And it certainly made President Roosevelt's chest fill with pride. 'It's a fine building,' he pronounced to Horace. But Horace wasn't done. To protect the president's privacy, Horace ordered the crowd at the train station to gather the stone masons and meet inside the Rec Hall. He'd told his wife to get the ceremonial ribbon and scissors from his office, and he'd instructed the local newspaper photographer to set up chairs by those fancy doors on the west side of the building and have his camera ready."

"Did it work?" Maree hounded.

"Was Horace able to keep the president from being seen as they moved him from the car to the chairs?" Landry questioned, literally on the edge of her seat as she'd shifted to face Davis in the confines of the booth bench.

"Indeed, it did, and of course he was," Davis said with robust theatrics. Landry's chest warmed with emotion. No matter how difficult the situation, Davis's good nature and zest for life couldn't be suppressed for long. She loved that about her dear friend.

"FDR cut the ribbon to open the Green Hills Park and Rec Department," Rhys stated, his head shaking in mystification.

"That he did," Davis confirmed. "Stayed in Green Hills forty-six extra minutes, for a grand total of fifty-three minutes." Landry giggled at the immense pride in Davis's voice.

"Oh my!" Maree burst out. "That's why the historical society is called the Fifty-Three Club, isn't it?"

Davis bowed his head in acknowledgment of her keen intellectual prowess.

"Let me guess," Rhys said, drawing out the words to tease his best friend. "You're a card-carrying member?"

"That I am," Davis answered with a big grin, the first genuine smile Landry had seen on him in far too many hours.

5

***No one in the world
can take the place of your mother.
Harry S. Truman***

After leaving Triple T's, Daniel Davis followed Landry to the turn down Miss Sadie's drive, just to be sure she got there all right.

Then he returned to the explosion site to help tag and photograph.

At 9:45 a.m., Chief Everett ordered him home. As bone-tired as he felt, though, Davis still didn't think he could sleep. Extreme emotional levels did that, caused utter physical fatigue while simultaneously energizing the brain to make sleep — a desperately needed respite from the weariness — unattainable.

Instead of heading to his house, a tidy 1950s Craftsman-style on Wellington Street, Davis stopped by Steep to pick up a large cup of spiced black tea with cream and a dollop of honey and an extra-large coffee — their stoutest brew with no sugar, no cream, no anything.

When he pulled into his parents' driveway, Jacqueline

Davis sat on the front porch, rocking in a wicker chair, patiently waiting for him to arrive. Davis shook his head in awe of her uncanny ability to predict her family's thoughts and activities.

"Hey, Mom," he said, handing her the hot tea before bending to give her a hug and offer his cheek for her kiss.

"Hi, sweetie."

He sat in the matching rocking chair, opened the tab on the lid to his coffee, and inhaled a healing whiff of the steam.

"Thank you for the tea. It's exactly how I like it," she praised after taking a sip.

They sat in silence, Davis's eyes closed but his foot moving to rock his chair gently. Jacqueline silently rocked her chair and drank her tea. Several minutes later, Davis let his chair still. He opened his eyes to look out over the expansive front yard of the home where he'd grown up.

"Have you eaten?" she asked.

"A few hours ago," he answered. "When she could leave the hospital, Landry asked me to go with her to Triple T's. Rhys and Maree were there when we walked in."

"It was wonderful of Earl to open early for everyone."

"Yeah, I had an entire dinner *and* dessert, but I'd take a bowl of cereal if you have milk."

"Of course. Come on." Jacqueline rose from her chair, tea in hand, and fluffed the pillow that had been behind her back. Davis mimicked her movement with a teasing glint in his eye, which made her smile. Jacqueline led the way inside. Davis walked straight to his favorite stool and plopped down at her kitchen island.

"It's gone, Mom. Just a heap of stone fragments, burnt wood, and burning embers. So much history, so many memories. Gone."

"It's almost impossible to fathom," she commiserated, setting a bowl, a spoon, a box of his favorite cereal, and the milk jug in front of him. As he fixed his cereal, Jacqueline walked to the breakfast table to retrieve a napkin from the vintage tin that held them as part of her centerpiece. She set it down next to his bowl with her left hand as her right one touched a wave of hair at his temple. When her palm cupped his cheek, he set down the spoon and leaned into her affection.

Both her arms came around him. Davis's forehead fell to her shoulder. Tears burned his eyes. She continued to hug him. The moment he relaxed his guard, tears fell down his face. His shoulders shook, and finally Davis let himself cry. For his town, for his childhood memories, for those injured, and for those working valiantly to help them.

It didn't last long, but he'd needed that moment, sheltered by the person who loved him most, to unburden the weight he carried.

Straightening from their embrace, he squeezed her hands in gratitude. And wiping his eyes with his sleeves, Davis turned back to his bowl of cereal. "I guess no matter how old we get, we never outgrow Mom's hug."

"And don't you forget it," Jacqueline said smartly, pointing a finger at him to drive home the command. She grabbed two more napkins, wiping her cheeks with one, and handing the other to her son. "I heard y'all saved every single person in the gym when it happened. What a miracle, Danny."

"It was Landry and all the doctors and nurses and volunteers that made the difference. They were amazing. Each one of them! Landry, though," he hesitated in reverence. "She was really something. You'd think she'd go on autopilot in that situation, and she did work innately and with intricate precision. But you should've seen her, Mom. She never lost her sense of humanity, never forgot to look her patients in the eyes, never forgot to treat their feelings and their fears, too. Once we'd cleared the scene, those of us firefighters who are also trained as EMTs hung around the hospital, helping with minor wounds and triage. I kept an eye on her when I could, checked on her when I couldn't. I was sure Landry would drop any moment, but she just kept on going. I can't imagine how."

"She's very special—"

*J*acqueline was going to finish with *and a talented doctor*, but Davis interrupted her.

"Yeah, one in a million," he marveled. "She's so dang smart. And not just nerdy — although she aced medical school and is considered the best resident at the hospital. Her book smarts are only the beginning. She's—" Davis halted, searching for the perfect word. "Vivacious," he supplied. "Exotic, even. Those fathomless dark eyes of hers see everything. I swear, the way she reads people and situations... The way she knows exactly what to say to guide others back to stable footing, to pull them from a pit of despair or a sinkhole of sadness, is pure magic. You've been around her; you've seen her in action, so I know you understand what I mean. To say she's special is true, yet an understatement. She's much more than that."

"Hmm, I can tell," his mother mused. She switched gears rather than dig or push for information on Doctor Landry Stark. How cute that he didn't know his own heart. She'd bide her time, at least until he acknowledged the obvious truths so clear to her, yet still unbeknownst to her precious son. More fun to watch from afar as he figured it out, anyway.

Of her three children, Daniel, their youngest, had the greatest capacity to love, but the most guarded heart. He'd been the life of the party since discovering his ability to command and entertain an audience early in toddlerhood. His entire life, boys flocked to him and girls chased after him. And he'd reciprocated their admiration: a true and faithful friend, the perfect date for special events. But not once had Daniel Davis relinquished control of his heart.

They had encouraged him to share more of himself with friends and girls he dated. Jacqueline and Elijah prayed for Daniel to invest in his relationships, to trust in the power of love.

Married almost forty years, they had a strong, successful marriage, had exemplified the devotion and adoration of two soulmates whose love grew more and reached deeper with every passing day.

Heartened by the quick bond that formed between Daniel and Rhys Larsen within months of Rhys moving to Green Hills, both Jacqueline and Elijah were delighted that their son had finally found a best friend, someone he could confide in and rely upon, a buddy for life in that stand-up-at-your-wedding way. Two peas in a pod, the boys depended upon one another time and again in their work as firefighters. They'd been there for one another during tough times, particularly the revelation of Rhys's past and the turbulent start to his romance with Maree Davenport.

The way Daniel spoke of Maree when he first met her, Jacqueline had voiced hopes that perhaps Daniel had found his one true love. Elijah had cautioned her against prying or prodding, which was a good thing. It hadn't taken long to realize that Daniel did love Maree, but exactly how fate had destined their relationship to be: as his best friend's girl.

It turned out, however, that Maree had not been the only young lady Daniel met that night at Scooter's. Maree's best friend, Landry Stark, had been there as well. And Landry's name continued to sprinkle Daniel's stories more and more as time went on.

Landry this, and *Landry that... Landry helped me pick out a silly shirt for the July 4th Fun Fair. Landry insisted I throw back every fish I caught at the lake. Landry needs a certain textbook for class tomorrow, so*

I'm going to drive her to Dallas to pick it up. Landry... Landry... Landry...

"Is she okay?" Jacqueline asked. "That's a lot for a young doctor to navigate."

"Shoot, Mom. She's stronger than I am." Daniel released a deep breath. "I thought we'd lost Eddie Cadell. I was a mess — thinking about Zane and worried about how he'd survive without his dad after his mom abandoned them. Landry saw me struggling. She pulled me out of a pit of despair when she really wanted to head home and go right to bed."

"I'd advise you *not* to assume what a young lady wants," Jacqueline offered as she refilled his cereal bowl. "From what you've told me and from the times I've been around Landry, I'd bet she was exactly where she wanted to be." Returning the cereal box to the pantry and the milk to the fridge, she again switched subjects before her son could argue. "Now, tell me what you can about Eddie and Zane. Are they both going to be okay? What do you think they need in the meantime?"

Puttering around the kitchen while Daniel shared what he knew, Jacqueline listened intently to everything Daniel said, as well as what he didn't. Like Daniel, her heart broke at the devastation and loss and the forthcoming challenges their beloved town would endure after such a tragedy. When he'd finished eating, she clucked and shooed her son upstairs to shower and find some clean clothes in his old room. She accepted that at six feet tall, he towered over her. Having just turned twenty-nine years old, he was a full-fledged adult. He owned his own place, had a grown-up job, and lived his own life. But at times, a mother hen needed to keep her chicks tucked under her wing.

After what he'd seen — after what he'd been through — she needed a few more minutes with him close at hand.

Daniel must've felt it, too; he didn't utter a word of protest, not even a grunt or a groan. When after thirty minutes he hadn't returned to the kitchen, Jacqueline tiptoed up the creaky old stairs to check on him.

The sight of him face down in a diagonal across his childhood bed, wearing a pair of old workout shorts from high school with a swim t-shirt he'd long outgrown, and snoring softly proved to be her undoing. With a hand clasped over her mouth to muffle her sobs, Jacqueline Davis wept for her baby boy.

When the crying jag passed, she covered Daniel with a lightweight summer quilt from the hallway linen closet. She smoothed his hair, careful not to wake him. And she crept back down the stairs, offering a prayer of thanks for his safety, for his strength, and for his big, beautiful heart.

6

———

Music is the soundtrack of your life.
Dick Clark

Rested from sleeping several hours at his parents' house, and wearing clothes that actually fit from his own house, Davis entered the hospital with a lighter spring to his step than he'd felt in days. Evidence of mass trauma in the aftermath of what the hospital had recently seen brought his spirit down several notches, but Davis refused to let go of his good mood.

He'd brought a gift for Zane, something special Davis had spied in the back corner of his childhood closet earlier that afternoon. Exiting the fifth-floor elevator, he tucked the large cardboard box under his left arm, giving it a fond pat. A smile bloomed on his face as he turned the corner toward the pediatric wing; he couldn't wait to watch Zane open that box.

The closer Davis walked to the patient rooms, the more excited he became. And the farther he walked, the louder the sound of music became — 80s music... Unmistakable.

Stopping outside room 516 — his destination as well as

where the music originated — Davis turned to the nurses' station.

"Do we need to call a doctor?" Davis asked with a laugh.

"That *is* the doctor," a nurse replied, nonplussed.

Davis had a good idea which doctor she spoke of, so he barely inched the door open to peek inside.

A portable speaker perched on the window ledge. Landry sat facing Zane, her back to the door. Zane watched her, listening intently to what she said.

"...it's a real thing. I promise! Keep everything below your shoulders frozen in place, especially your legs, and even your toes. Start with a tiny head bob, just a slight nod forward to find the rhythm." Landry modeled her instructions as the beginning notes to "Come on Eileen" rang out from the speaker.

"What's this called again?" Zane's hesitant voice chirped.

"Head dancing. And you're going to be totally awesome at it. We just have to get our choreography down," she assured the boy. "Now, every two beats we drop one ear toward our shoulder, so it's center, center, right, right, center, center, left, left. Try it," she encouraged.

"Like this?"

"Yes! That's perfect," Landry congratulated. "For the next verse, let's turn our chin, so it's front, front, right, right, front, front, left, left." She modeled again. "By golly, I think you've got it," she exclaimed, prompting the boy to grin from ear to ear.

"I-I like-like this-this song-song," Zane said, each word matching two beats of the music and a head movement.

"Don't tell anyone, but my middle name is Eileen, so it's my favorite," Landry agreed. "Okay, now for the grand finale. Combine the two moves, so it's ear, ear, center, center, otha'ear, otha'ear, center, center, right, right, front, front, left, left, front,

front. Then we repeat," she announced. "And remember, nothing below your shoulders can move."

Once they had the hang of their dance, Davis eased the door open, walking like an Egyptian as he entered the room, head bobbing to match theirs. And he sang. Loudly.

Zane erupted in a fit of laughter while Davis continued strutting and singing to their head dancing routine.

Landry fumbled to pause the music on her phone, clearly trying not to laugh, as she feigned indignation.

"That's not it, Daniel Davis," she accused. "You did it all wrong." Her fake pout was ridiculously adorable.

"I don't know. I think I've got it down pretty good," he bragged. "What do you think, Z Man?"

"I think you look like a wacky rooster," Zane said amidst giggles.

"That's what we'll call this amazing dance: The Wacky Rooster," Davis said, taking one last strut around the room.

"Hilarious," Landry said, visibly on the verge of losing her battle not to laugh at Davis's antics. "Just don't get Zane so excited that he moves his leg," she instructed. "That's what head dancing is all about, you know...having fun *without* flailing all about."

Her snooty, Miss Know It All voice attracted him like a magnet. He wanted to push her buttons just to be irritating, so she'd talk bossy to him again.

What kind of crazy magic does she practice?

"I'll have you know I happen to be a big fan of all dancing, so I'm all in. Let's do some more."

"I'm not sure," she hedged. "Zane probably needs to rest for a while now."

"Come on, Eileen, play us a song," he begged, overly dramatic for Zane's benefit. He received a scathing smirk for his song quote.

"Please, Doctor Stark?" Zane pleaded, hands clasped

under his chin. Following Davis's lead, he batted puppy dog eyes at Landry.

"Oh, all right. One more song, but you boys are coming up with the moves this time," Landry said, relenting to the pressure of their tag team. "What do you want to hear? You may choose from 80s classics only."

"What are those?" Zane asked, his knowledge of music useless within her parameters.

"I've got this one, Z Man. You kick back, relax, and enjoy the show. We'll do more head dancing later," Davis promised. He took Landry's phone from her hand to scroll through the playlist, wondering if she felt the spark between them when their skin touched. He found what he wanted and pressed play.

"Enjoy the show?" Landry repeated his words, questioning what they meant.

Davis didn't answer. Instead, he held a hand out to Landry, daring her to take it, knowing full well he intended to pull her into a real body-to-body dance.

With a prim and ornery shake of the smooth, mahogany-brown hair cascading down her back, she set her hand in his. He'd have won money knowing she couldn't turn away from a challenge. He tugged her close, wrapping his right arm around her waist until his hand settled on the hollow at the base of her spine. He held her in place, looking directly into her eyes, until The Police began singing "Every Little Thing She Does is Magic."

Then he held her even closer.

"Tell me again... What year you were born?" Davis whispered directly into her ear. Her muscles tensed in response. Had a shiver run through her body?

"1991. Just like you, and you know it," she answered. Her voice had dropped to a husky rumble. Holding her that tight, he felt it reverberating through her chest. He responded by leading her into a series of twists and turns in tiny circles, which was all the small space of Zane's room would allow.

I'm playing with fire. But at least it's the good kind.

The song ended. Their breath came in shortened puffs, which didn't make sense, as they hadn't really exerted themselves in the dance. Landry moved to extricate herself from his hold, but Davis didn't let her go. He stood perfectly still, holding her gaze, waiting for the next tune.

"I Want to Know What Love Is," a big-hair ballad by Foreigner, began to play.

"Come on, Eileen," Davis said again, keeping his voice soft, careful not to wake their spectator, who'd drifted to sleep in his bed. "One more."

Tucking Landry into the frame of his chest, Davis wrapped both arms around her, rested his cheek against the top of her head, and savored the silkiness of her hair. They swayed to the ballad, barely moving, yet perfectly in sync.

No wonder preachers warn against dancing. It puts thoughts in your head that shouldn't be there. Makes you want things you aren't supposed to have.

Shoving those warnings aside, Davis focused on enjoying the moment for what it was: another incidence of harmless flirting with an incredible woman. On the last note, he shifted her into a silly half-dip, lightening the mood before releasing her.

"Thank you, Doctor Stark," he said with a playful wink.

She stepped back to a safer distance. Davis pretended not to notice.

"What's in the box?" she asked, checking Zane's monitors and lines.

"A secret for Z Man. Confidential, ya know. I'd tell you, but I'd have to kill you." He gave her an innocent shrug.

"I see," she replied. Satisfied with Zane's stats, she smoothed his covers and settled back into her chair. "I guess I'll have to wait until he's ready to open it to discover the surprise with him."

"I'd like to be here for that." Davis walked to boy's bed, placed both hands on the metal rail that Landry had clicked into place on the side of the mattress of his injured leg, and watched Zane sleep. "How's he doing? Medically speaking."

"Very well."

"Really?" Davis's head snapped up to make eye contact with her. He needed to hear it again.

"Yes, really. That's why I invented head dancing. Zane was bored. He kept fidgeting, asking if he could roll over, begging to get out of bed. It's important for him to stay still for now. We have to minimize the pressure behind the incision, and even slight movement gets his femoral artery pumping more than we'd like. The surgery site will heal quickly, but it still takes time. Keeping him bed-ridden the next day or so is going to be difficult."

"I'll be here to help," Davis pledged. "What's he been told about Eddie?"

"The truth. I promised Zane I'd never lie. But not all the details. He knows his dad stayed in the building, carrying others to safety, and suffered severe burns in the process. We watched the helicopter take off to transport Eddie to Dallas, and we said a prayer for his total and smooth recovery."

"He's bound to know it's pretty bad since Eddie didn't come to see him before they took him to Parkland."

"He understands there's more to it, but he's trusting us to keep him in the loop, to help him comprehend what's going on," she explained.

Davis looked at the sleeping child. "He's endured so much in such a short life. You know, his mom took off when he was just an infant. She told Eddie that small-town life wasn't for her, said getting knocked up at seventeen and giving birth at eighteen hadn't been her plan. She packed her bags and left while Eddie was at work. He was stocking shelves at the Get'n'Go at night, going to college during the day, and working at the dairy on the weekends. Eddie went home to shower between jobs one day to find Zane sound asleep in his crib, a note from Raven, and her half of the closet empty."

"Raven. I think it means *thievery* in some cultures," Landry mused.

"Yeah, well, she stole Zane and Eddie's chance at a normal life. In Native American art, a raven often symbolizes a cunning schemer. That fits her, too." Davis's voice dripped with hatred, so he attempted to dial back his disgust.

"You knew her?"

"Eddie was a year behind me in high school. Raven was two years behind him. When I was a senior and she was a freshman, she insinuated there was something between us that never existed. She only did it to make Eddie jealous. She was petty and mean that way. I convinced Eddie that it was all in her head, just a ploy to control him. I maintained my distance to prove my point, and I hightailed it out of town as soon as I could move into my dorm for college.

"But Eddie was under Raven's spell. She led him around like a bull on a ring, twisting the truth at every turn and dragging him through the wringer any time he considered getting away. When she announced she'd be having his baby, he begged her to marry him. She refused, but she *did* encourage him to cancel his plans for college and stay home to take care of her. Luckily, his boss at the dairy outside of town threatened to fire him if he gave up on school. He helped Eddie find a hybrid program with a majority of courses online and a few in-person classes at a branch campus a couple of towns over."

"She sounds like a piece of work. I think Eddie and Zane are better off without her."

"I'm sure you're right. But it's tough to be a single parent, work multiple jobs to make ends meet, all the while studying and finishing college. A mother should put her child first. Raven should've stayed to take care of her family."

"I don't know. Sometimes no mother is better than a damaged or dangerous one." The haunting flatness of Landry's voice caused Davis to look her way. He saw unmistakable pain in her eyes. "Did Eddie make it through school?"

"He sure did. Now he's the CFO and Director of Accounting at that dairy. He coaches Zane's baseball team, serves on the PTA at the elementary school, and is an incredible dad. Hands down, Eddie Cadell is one of the strongest people I know."

"That strength will serve him well in the months to come," Landry commented, rising from her chair. "It's almost six thirty, and I'm on nights this month. I better go get ready to clock in. Will you be here a while longer?"

"Yeah, I'm going to hang around. What time do you have a dinner break?"

"Oh, not until midnight. I'll—"

"See you then," he finished for her. Then he turned the chair she'd been using toward the television and slid it next to the head of Zane's bed. He snagged the remote control from the mattress, found a basketball game to watch, and turned the volume almost all the way down. Ignoring her interrogating gaze seemed to be his best defense, so he stared at the screen, pretending to be entranced in the game, until she took the hint and left the room to begin her workday.

7

> *"It's like out of a movie. It doesn't seem real."*
> *Dallas Mavericks owner Mark Cuban,*
> *Speaking to a reporter on*
> *Wednesday, March 11, 2020*

At midnight, Landry stopped by the fifth-floor nurses' station to get a status report on the patient in room 516.

"Go see for yourself," Rachel, the night nurse, replied with a mysterious smile. "Isn't Zane asleep?"

"Like I said..."

"Go see for myself." Landry answered her own question.

Landry opened the door slowly, just in case Zane was indeed sleeping. "Hey, Zane, how ya— Oh, my. What in the world?"

Twinkling Christmas lights hung from corner to corner above the windows, draping in the middle, and casting an ethereal glow upon the room. Music hits from the 80s streamed softly from the portable speaker she'd left behind earlier in the evening. A small table, covered in a white linen cloth — perhaps in actuality a bedsheet — stood against the wall, laden with to-go boxes filled with pasta, salad, garlic bread, and slices of cheesecake. On Zane's bed tray, three place settings of paper plates, plastic silverware, and cartons of milk surrounded a vase of red roses.

Zane sat proudly in his bed, a bow tie around his neck, and his hair combed into place. Davis stood to his side, also sporting a bow tie, but over a crisp white dress shirt paired with a sharp charcoal gray suit. He, too, had smoothed his wayward waves into submission.

Wow!

Heat flushed Landry's face; her pulse raced.

"Welcome to dinner, m'lady," Davis and Zane said in unison. They shared a successful grin with one another after reciting it.

"This is for me?" Her hand splayed over her chest in disbelief. They'd gone to so much trouble. *For me?*

"Of course," Davis answered, rolling the moveable tray over Zane's bed and stepping forward to guide her to stand at her place setting. "May I fix your plate?" A cloth hung over his forearm, just like servers carried in fancy restaurants.

"Yes," she stumbled in response. "Please."

Davis winked at Zane, who lit up brighter than the lights hanging from the rafters.

"This is quite a production. Thank you! Very much." She choked up a bit, overwhelmed by their efforts to make her dinner break so special.

Zane shared every moment of his afternoon and evening, chattering and rambling with enthusiasm. Meanwhile, Landry made a show of reviewing Zane's monitors and charts, creating a moment to compose herself.

"You're worth it," Davis whispered in her ear as he reached around Landry, setting her plate back where it had been on the bed tray.

"We made a playlist for you, too," Zane announced, excited to show off their creativity.

"I'm honored. And you picked perfectly; these are all my favorite songs. Davis, is this from Luca's?" The upscale Italian restaurant topped Landry's list of favorites, but it was also the most expensive restaurant in town.

"I'm partial to Italian, and I know how much you and Maree love it."

"Y'all didn't have to wait for me to eat. It's so late," Landry said apologetically.

A conspiratorial look passed between the boys.

"We might've sampled the bread and cheesecake when they delivered the food a while ago," Davis confessed while Zane giggled.

"Is it as good as it smells?" she asked.

The boys looked at one another again before answering *better*, again in unison. "Well, let's dig in. I'm starving," Landry prompted, shining her biggest and brightest smile on the two very special, very thoughtful boys.

"*H*ands down, without a doubt, this is the best dinner I've ever had," Landry announced after scraping every bit of cheesecake from her plate.

Zane beamed. His eyelids drooped with tiredness, but he beamed all the same.

"Y'all outdid yourselves, and I can't thank you enough. Both of you. It's been a tough night; we're still filled to capacity. Our dinner party was exactly what I needed to make it through the rest of my shift. Really— Thank you," she said. Emotion thickened her voice again.

"Like I said, you deserved it," Davis reiterated. "I'll clean this up so you can head back to work. Go on, get moving," he added when she reached to help clear their plates.

"Davis, this was the kindest thing anyone has ever done for me. Truly." Landry took the used plates from his hand, tossed them in the trash can, and wrapped her arms around his ribs to envelop him in a hug. "Thank you."

Then she stepped away, tucked-in Zane to say good night, and left room 516.

Landry floated through the early morning hours, her spirits buoyed by the wonderful surprise from the boys.

When she clocked out, she called home to check on Miss Sadie and couldn't help smiling as she retold the story of the amazing dinner party. Then she showered in the locker room, put on a clean set of scrubs, grabbed a pillow and blanket, and returned to Zane's room to assess his progress and steal a catnap on the sofa-bed intended for parents staying with pediatric patients.

*L*andry awoke to find the world falling apart.

The hospital staff buzzed with reports that in his testimony before the House Committee on Oversight and Reform, Doctor Anthony Fauci, director of the National Institute of Allergy and Infectious Diseases, decreed that the worst of the COVID-19 virus they'd heard about from afar was yet to come. And it was no longer safely afar. Unbelievably, more than a thousand people in forty different states had tested positive for the virus. Schools were closing around the country, affecting an estimated 850,000 children and their parents, who now needed childcare to go to their jobs. The nurses panicked that Green Hills schools might be next.

By mid-afternoon, the World Health Organization had officially declared the "global health emergency" a pandemic.

By the time the closing bell rang on Wall Street, the stock market had plummeted with the Dow Jones Industrial Average down over 1,200 points. News anchors kept saying, "An eleven-year bull market has ended," and while Landry didn't completely understand what that meant, she knew it wasn't good.

At seven o'clock that evening, just moments before tipoff in Oklahoma City, a Utah Jazz basketball player tested positive for the virus. They canceled the game.

An hour and forty-six minutes later, the National Basketball Association announced the suspension of their entire season because of COVID-19 concerns.

At 9:02 p.m., President Trump addressed the nation, announcing a thirty-day ban on travel to the United States from European countries. Maree's sister and brother-in-law, M'Kenzee and Brennigan, had just arrived in Scotland a few days earlier to visit his family there. What would happen? Were they stuck? Would they be able to come home? Surely, as American citizens, they'd be allowed back in the country.

Around that same time, actor Tom Hanks announced that he and his wife, actress Rita Wilson, were sick with COVID-19. The coronavirus knew no discrimination; no matter financial standing, gender, or race, everyone was at risk.

Landry received a text from Davis at 9:22:

- This is wild. Are you okay? Call me when you can.

She replied with a heart emoji. What could she say? Davis was right. The world had gone crazy.

*B*efore Landry found time to call him, another round of drama struck.

8

———

Nothing makes a woman more beautiful
than the belief that she is beautiful.
Sophia Loren

*M*ere minutes after hearing the dispatch over the radio, Davis stormed down the hospital corridor looking for her.

Walter Armstrong, the man thought to be responsible for the random arson fires over the past two years, possibly the culprit who'd caused the explosion at the Rec Hall Gymnasium, was at the hospital. After tearing through an exam room, tossing aside an orderly, and wreaking overall havoc in the emergency room, Mr. Armstrong had taken Doctor Stark hostage.

"Landry!" Davis bellowed down the hallway, ignoring the onlookers, including the Green Hills police officers systematically clearing rooms, one at a time. "Landry?" He yelled her name again and again.

"Davis, let us do our job," Sergeant Miles Crockett said, attempting to sound authoritative and in command.

"By all means, Miles, do your job. In the meantime, I'm going to keep looking for Landry."

The two men, similar in size and age, continued doing their individual tasks while walking together from door to door.

"Mr. Armstrong might be dangerous. He tore up all kinds of stuff when he got here."

"You and I both know he's confused, been struggling with PTSD and emotional trauma since we were kids. He would've naturally responded like a caged animal, injured and defensive, with people coming at him from all directions. He's scared and possibly hurt," Davis pointed out.

"And capable of hurting Doctor Stark, as well as every other person in this building," the officer argued.

"Exactly why I've got to find her." With that, Davis left the policeman behind and opened the door to the stairwell, ready to run up to the next floor. Upon hearing a commotion in the basement, he switched direction and flew down the stairs, calling Landry's name.

"I'm down here," she called back, sending a surge of relief through Davis's nerves.

Davis almost knocked Landry down when he exited the stairwell at full throttle, slamming the brakes on his forward momentum half a step before colliding into her. He gripped her forearms to steady them both while scanning her from head to toe for cuts or bruises.

"Are you hurt?"

"No. No, I'm fine," she answered, although Davis hesitated to believe her and continued to look for evidence to the contrary. "I promise, Davis. I'm okay."

"Where is he?"

"He took off. He was out of his mind, so scared and agitated. I tried to calm him down, tried to help him recenter. He let me tend to the burns on his arms and hands, even sat still while I cleaned the wounds, which had to be quite painful.

But the moment I finished applying the ointment, his agitation resumed. I opened the supply closet to get a box of gauze for his arms, and before I knew what he was doing, he pushed me down to the closet floor, then pulled the shelves off balance, trapping me beneath the metal racks while paper goods showered over me. While I was trying to shove that mess aside and stand up, he shut the door on me, and took off."

"He shoved you? Are you—"

"I'm fine. I'm sure. I promise," she assured him a second time. "Davis, Mr. Armstrong is covered in burns."

"You think he set the gym explosion?"

"I don't know. I only know what I saw: lots of burned flesh and a look of lost, vacant distance in his eyes. He wasn't even verbal. He made sounds, guttural grunts really, but he didn't say a single word."

The sadness in her eyes tore at Davis's heart.

By then, Miles and the other officers had reached them. They shuffled Landry back upstairs where they had her repeat what had happened time and again.

"I've got to run back to the station; don't let her leave before I get back. Please," Davis asked Rachel after stopping by the fifth floor to look in on Zane, who was sound asleep.

"I'll try," she pledged. "But you know she's awfully head-strong when she wants to be."

His shift at the fire station ended at 8 a.m., an hour after her night shift at the hospital should have been over. He said a quick prayer that Rachel would keep Landry busy for that hour.

He planned on taking her to breakfast, just to discuss the insane news reports that had come out during the day. The events with Mr. Armstrong only solidified Davis's determination to spend some time with her as soon as he could get back to the hospital.

Despite all the chaos of the world around them, the thought of breakfast with Landry brought a spark of optimism. He enjoyed talking with her; it was easy to share his thoughts with her, and he valued her opinions. Flirting with Landry had become a treat he looked forward to on a daily basis.

Since meeting her at Scooter's two years earlier, Landry had become a comfortable addition to Davis's life. He considered her one of his closest friends, hence the reason he needed to be there for her after the horrendous few days she'd just had.

"Is Chief Everett here?" Davis asked Rhys when he arrived at Station #2.

"In his office," Rhys said with a nod. "He was at home when he heard the same radio dispatch we did. He came straight here. How's Landry?"

"Other than pushing her into a supply closet and throwing rolls of toilet paper on her, Walter Armstrong didn't touch her. Didn't harm a hair on her head."

"But the dispatcher said he was on a tirade, injured a security guard or someone, shattered a glass wall in the emergency room. He sounded completely out of control," Rhys said, doubtful of Davis's news.

"I think that radio call sounded worse than it really was. Landry said Mr. Armstrong had the look of a cornered animal. He pushed away an elderly orderly who tried to grab him; the older man stumbled and fell. In his attempt to escape the orderly, Mr. Armstrong pulled down a curtain that divided two exam areas, but no windows or glass walls were broken. The commotion of the metal curtain frame clanking to the ground alerted Landry, who was with a patient down the hall. She ran to see what was happening and found Mr. Armstrong huddled against the wall. Again, she kept repeating that he was simply an injured animal, over-stimulated, and terribly afraid. Counterproductive to Landry's calming conversation with him, more and more people tried pushing their way into the exam room to see what was going on."

"I imagine several of them wanted to take control of the situation, tried strong-arming and forcing their command," Rhys commented.

"The crowd only made things worse. When he couldn't take anymore, Mr. Armstrong pushed past everyone and ran for the stairs. Everyone stood frozen in shock. Except for—"

"Landry," Rhys said, finishing Davis's sentence. "Of course, Landry went after the madman."

"She caught up to him in the basement, spoke gently until he'd calmed down. And then she used her keys to open an overflow treatment room that was included in the hospital renovation a few years ago, but never needed until last week-end. Landry convinced Mr. Armstrong to sit still while she cleaned some pretty serious burns on his arms, hands, and face."

Davis paused for that information to sink in. A look balanced in understanding and uncertainty passed between the two firemen.

"As Landry finished applying ointment to the burns on his arms, something spooked Mr. Armstrong again — probably me hollering her name loud enough to wake the dead." Davis shook his head in frustration at possibly being the reason Mr. Armstrong had escaped the hospital.

"And that's when he ran again?"

"Yeah, Landry had stepped into a small supply closet to get gauze for his burns. He shoved her in, trapped her under shelving and paper goods, and slammed the door to close her in."

"And she's okay? You're sure?"

"She promised she was," Davis answered. "But I'm headed

back as soon as our shift is over. Rachel's going to keep her occupied until I get there."

"Let Chief Everett know you need to go. We're good here. Simon worked yesterday, and he's covering for someone else tomorrow, so he stayed in town between shifts and spent the night instead of driving home to his place on Daisy Lake. If we get a call, he can roll out with us."

"I'll talk to Chief Everett. Then I'll check with Simon, make sure he's good before I go. I haven't wanted to believe Mr. Armstrong was the firebug. He's got mental health struggles, but he's never harmed a soul. I didn't want it to be him," Davis said, hearing the sadness of a broken-hearted little boy in his voice.

"And it might not be. We don't know." Rhys tried to reassure him, but they both knew the burns Landry had treated were more than a coincidence.

"Yeah, I hope you're right. Let Maree know Landry's okay?" Rhys stood as Davis approached. They did their "best buddy" handshake, ending with a big, manly hug, but neither tried to hide their feelings. They loved and cared for one another. The blessing of that friendship brought a burning moisture to Davis's eyes as he entered Chief Everett's office to share the story all over again.

"We have to stop meeting this way," Landry said, standing in front of the chair Davis had occupied the past hour and a half as he waited for her, the same chair she'd found him in after the explosion. She'd tried to sound flirty and clever, but Davis heard only frazzled weariness in her voice. That same fatigue, along with a hint of despondency, cast a shadow over the ever-present sparkle in Landry's deep brown eyes.

"My dad always warned me about waiting around for a pretty lady…said it's both a curse and a blessing," Davis teased as he stood and lifted her tote bag from her shoulder to carry on his own.

"I can carry that," she protested.

"So can I," he stated.

"I'm fine. I told you that earlier," she insisted.

"I know," he said flatly.

"Then why are you here?"

They'd walked out into the early hours of the morning, and Landry turned on him. The snap in her voice reassured Davis, as did a slightly demanding glint in her eyes.

"Because I want to be," Davis replied simply.

In a huff, Landry turned and resumed walking toward her car.

"How long did you sit in the waiting room?" She couldn't leave it alone, a fact that made Davis grin.

"Just a while," he hedged.

"Why?"

"You already asked that," he reminded her.

"True, but you didn't actually answer me." Testiness in her voice tinged the air.

He'd pushed intentionally, to remind Landry of her unending strength, to pull her out of the pit she'd found herself in lately. He'd purposefully poked the proverbial backbone supporting the spitfire opponent who unfailingly gave as much as she took.

"I believe I owe you breakfast," he said, dishing out charm.

"You owe me breakfast?" She'd stopped again to look up at him, incredulity in one raised eyebrow.

"I do."

"Davis, I must look awful," she said, trying to dismiss him.

"Landry, you're beautiful," he replied, hitching her bag

higher on his shoulder while resting his other forearm against the roof of her car. "Always."

What began as an effort to re-establish her self-esteem turned to something entirely different by the way he said *always*.

Standing under the parking lot light, Davis saw the questions in her gaze. But he couldn't make it easy on her. They'd tiptoed and danced around, evading this moment for two full years. They both knew what it meant.

Davis feared what could happen if they agreed to step beyond their friendship. He guessed she had the exact same concerns. Yet, he couldn't back down.

Looking directly into her eyes in a way she could only interpret as a challenge, Davis tilted his chin and lifted one eyebrow in question, throwing down a gauntlet.

With the ball securely in her court, whatever happened next was completely up to Landry.

9

Music was my refuge.
I could crawl into the space between the notes
and curl my back to loneliness.
Maya Angelou

Head buzzing, Landry questioned her sanity.

She'd been curious since the night they met. If she was being honest, she'd wanted to sample Davis's kiss every time they were together since then.

The gleam in his eyes and the jut of his chin left no room for misconstruing his challenge.

Standing under the soft glow of lamplight, Davis dared her to go for it. Landry gulped, licked her lips.

She noticed his jaw clench. *Hmmm, not so indifferent after all.* That knowledge bred power.

Stepping closer, she ran her hands up his chest.

His heart pounded. Just like hers.

Landry slid one hand behind his neck while the other reached up to smooth a wave from his forehead. His thick, dirty blond curls mesmerized her for a moment. Variations of sandy tan, golden blond, and light brown reminded her of the beach. The blue of his irises was as vibrant as a crystal sky over shimmering water.

A purr from deep in his throat caught her attention, drawing her focus to his mouth.

Such kissable lips, full and just the perfect shade of pink. Perfect lips — like his thick, long eyelashes — shouldn't be wasted on boys.

Moving her hands to frame his face, Landry pulled his lips toward hers.

She hesitated only a breath before lifting onto her toes to close the gap, placing her lips on his.

Not wasted at all. Those lips were exactly where Landry wanted them.

Wrapping her arms around his neck, she deepened their kiss.

Davis continued to let Landry lead, but it cost him. She felt his restraint in the steel-like hardness of his muscles.

She nibbled at his lips, absorbing their warmth a little longer.

Then she released the vice grip her arms had locked around his neck as she lifted her lips from his.

Landry slid her hands down to his chest, splaying her fingers to cover his collarbones before dropping her arms to her sides.

Gathering her gumption, she looked up at him, right into his eyes. Fire burned in them.

Oh, dear.

Landry gulped again.

Davis's hands, warm and strong, remained on either side of her waist. *When had he set them there?*

He stepped forward, gently guiding Landry until her back met the side of her car.

Her heart hummed in her ears.

He lifted her arms to place them back where she'd had them around his neck just moments before.

Then, with only his thumb and forefinger, he lifted her chin to look into her eyes. "Now it's my turn," he said on a pledge.

"What'll y'all have?"

The waitress at Triple T's did not know the earth had shifted, the stars had realigned, and the tides had turned. She thought they were living in a normal Thursday morning, that Davis and Landry were just two normal people ordering a normal breakfast.

"I'll take the tall stack of pancakes, extra butter please, a side of bacon, and a cup of coffee," Davis said with a smile that caused their server to beam under his favor.

Landry watched them, realizing when they both looked at her expectantly that she needed to decide. She stared at the menu, but the letters didn't form words. He'd rocked her world completely off its axis, rendering her useless. Prosaically selecting what to eat for breakfast seemed beyond her current abilities. She looked to Davis for help.

He winked at her, which made her heart skip a beat. She swore the man couldn't blink without winking.

"She wants the Greek yogurt with extra berries and the granola on the side, her *own* side of bacon, a small orange juice, and a cup of Earl Grey tea with cream and honey, please."

"Very good," the waitress replied. "I'll have it right out."

"How did you know that?" Landry asked when the woman had walked away.

"How did I know what?" Davis countered.

"What I like to order." She felt dumbfounded.

"It's what you always order when you're tired."

"When I'm tired? What do I order for breakfast when I'm *not* tired?" Landry asked, crossing her arms and leaning back to see what he'd come up with.

"Let's see... French toast sprinkled with powdered sugar — no syrup — when you're excited to have a day off and there's nothing scheduled that you have to do. An omelet with two eggs, ham, mushrooms, diced onions, and bell pepper — no cheese — when you have a lot of studying planned for the day. And when breakfast turns into brunch, avocado toast with a fried egg on top — over easy — with a side salad and cranberry juice instead of hot tea." On that note, he crossed his arms, leaning back to mimic her posture.

She didn't know how to respond.

Luckily, their waitress brought Davis's coffee, promising to be right back with Landry's drinks.

Waiting for her to return provided a quiet moment, one that allowed Landry's mind to catch up.

Even after her juice and tea had been delivered, and after Landry had fixed her tea with cream and honey, they enjoyed the silence, comfortable together without needing to fill the space.

Landry savored a soothing sip of her hot tea. She set the mug on the table and wrapped both hands around the warm ceramic. Davis shifted in his seat, and Landry looked up to meet his gaze.

Her thoughts circled back to his keen knowledge of her habits and preferences. Since when had he been paying such close attention to her?

"You seem to think you know a lot about me," Landry half allowed and half sassed, putting great stress on the *to think* part. She was starting to feel much more like herself again.

"I like to think I'm pretty observant," Davis replied, emphasizing *to think* just as she had. "I didn't, however, have any idea about your obsession with 80s music," he allowed, dipping his head in acknowledgment. "Where did that come from?"

"My childhood, I guess. My mother—"

"Here we go," their waitress announced. "Pancakes, extra butter, and bacon for the gentleman. Her own order of bacon, yogurt, extra berries, and granola on the side for the young lady. Anything else I can get y'all?"

Davis looked at Landry with both eyebrows lifted.

"Nothing for me. Thanks," Landry told the waitress before she walked away.

"You were saying? Something about your mom," Davis nudged. Landry had hoped the arrival of their food would make him forget the topic.

"Yeah, I think we had very different childhoods," she began. "Your parents are great. I imagine your older siblings picked on you, but only in love. It's probably safe to say days around your house were happy, stable. I'm sure you have lots of great memories of being a kid."

Davis didn't answer, but he agreed with a single nod while eating.

"Well, fading into the background when my mother played her records is the one good memory I have of being a kid. The best times were when I hid behind the sofa or under a table-cloth, listening to music when no one knew I was around. She loved the 80s — the clothes, the movies, and the music. I guess keeping those things front and center provided an escape, took her back to a time when she was happy."

"She was in high school or college during the 80s?"

"Ha," Landry guffawed. "No, she was in elementary school in the 80s. We became a textbook case of babies having babies when I came along the week of her sixteenth birthday."

"That had to be tough," Davis said without judgment. "Did she have help?"

"No." Landry really didn't want to get into her dysfunctional family history, particularly with someone who grew up with a perfect family, in a perfect house, living a perfect life.

"Where was your dad?" Davis asked, setting down his fork and focusing on Landry.

"Gone." Landry cringed at the clipped tone of her voice. Davis didn't deserve her short temper, but again, she really, *really* didn't want to get into it. She refilled the hot water in her mug and stirred cream and honey into it, a little more aggressively than was necessary.

"And your grandparents?"

"Disowned her when she refused to abort the baby."

"Land—"

"Listen, my birth ruined a sweet girl's life. It's a sordid tale, and I'd just as soon not share it. In fact, a long time ago, I chose not to think about it or talk about it. Ever. Just so people wouldn't look at me in the exact way you're looking at me right now. I don't need pity. Not everyone has a picture-book childhood, and that's okay. I worked my way to being something worthwhile. Every single day, I do my best to help others live safe, healthy lives. That's good enough for me. Please let it be enough for you, too."

Davis didn't move for a long moment, but his eyes scanned hers. She saw his thoughts swirling as he decided if he would — *could* — let it go.

Thankfully, he picked up his fork and returned to his breakfast, and Landry did the same.

"What's the hospital saying about the coronavirus?" Davis asked, changing the subject to something safer, yet equally dark and ominous.

Grateful for his cooperation, Landry exhaled to release the cramping tension gripping her shoulders. "The administrators are following the lead set by the larger hospitals in Tulsa. They've tried ordering personal protective equipment sets for the doctors and nurses— masks, clothing, gloves, and shields — but the supply companies are already running out."

"Do you have a set?" Davis asked.

"Yes, I bought a set when I began my surgical rotation. And when they confirmed the first case in Tulsa a few days ago, Miss Sadie made a cloth mask for me. You should see it: extra thick layers and a work of art. It even has a pocket for a coffee filter. After reading the CDC recommendations, I'm not sure if they even help. Opinions — even at the highest levels of specialists — seem to differ right now. But it makes Miss Sadie feel better that I have it, and after all the negative news today, I'm happy to wear it with my PPE."

"That's a good idea," Davis agreed. "I don't see it coming to a place like Green Hills, but I also think it's bigger than what the government and media are letting on. They wouldn't have suspended the entire NBA season if there wasn't something to worry about."

"I got an email earlier today from the university that all Oklahoma schools are extending this week's Spring Break for another seven days to give the virus time to dissipate. What if they close longer, like schools on the east and west coasts are doing? I'm supposed to complete my training rotations this semester and finish residency in May. Surely all this won't affect licensing exam schedules." Just voicing the possibility soured Landry's stomach and caused great concern.

"Let's not borrow trouble," Davis said, reaching across the table to hold her hand. "Like I said, it'll probably never arrive in Green Hills. Like the latest blockbuster movies, small towns in remote areas don't always see what the cities do, at least not in the same way. Nothing will stop you from finishing your residency."

"I hope you're right," Landry wished aloud. "I think I'll ask Miss Sadie and Maree to make a few more masks in case some nurses and volunteers need one. It's better to be safe than sorry, right?"

"Absolutely," Davis agreed with a smile. "In fact, I'll ask my mom to make a few for the station. She has plenty of fabric with firetrucks, firefighters, and firedogs."

With their conversation back on solid ground, Landry relaxed, dove into her breakfast, and thoroughly enjoyed her morning.

Of course, she always had fun with Davis.

Thinking back on the interaction in the hospital parking lot, she relished the way she'd felt in his arms. Indeed, he'd opened her eyes to the wonder of truly amazing kisses. But even those incredible sensations paled at her relief that she hadn't ruined their friendship by initiating those kisses.

10

Parties are the nightly ritual
of the sophisticated society.
Dominick Dunne

"Hey, Z Man!" Davis entered Zane's room a few days later wearing a huge smile that dropped the moment he saw the sad frown on the boy's face. He was further alarmed to see the downtrodden expression reflected on Landry's face as she stared out the window.

Zane's recovery continued to progress as Landry and Doctor Bradford had hoped; just that morning, Landry had mentioned that Zane was up and walking with help.

No one had seen Mr. Armstrong again, but neither had there been any more fires or explosions.

And while he'd not identified another opportunity for additional kisses with Landry, Davis *had* found ways for them to share either dinner in the hospital or breakfast at Triple T's every day since the explosion.

They'd also spoken on the phone each day as he'd taken to

checking on her when she arrived at Miss Sadie's house after her shifts. He'd text to see if she'd arrived yet, and she'd call back once she'd showered, brushed her teeth, and climbed into bed. They talked about COVID updates, M'Kenzee and Bren's decision to stay in Scotland for the time being, Maree and Rhys's wedding plans, Max and Janie Lyn's announcement that they were expecting a baby, Miss Sadie's plans for Marshall Mansion, and everything else that popped up in conversations.

They only spoke for a few minutes each call, but the calls were consistent. The regularity became something Davis relied on to start his day.

Life was pretty good, all things considered, so why the long faces?

"What's going on, buddy?" Davis set the gift bag he'd been carrying on the floor and walked to Zane's bed.

"Today's my birthday," Zane replied, in the most depressing rendition of *today's my birthday* that Davis had ever heard.

"I know," Davis said, reaching for the birthday present to set it on Zane's bed. "Isn't that a good thing?"

"I thought maybe my dad would call," Zane whispered. "And I have to leave."

"Your dad's going through a lot of tough treatments, working hard to get home to be with you. I'm sure he'll call tonight if there's any way possible. And if you don't hear from him today, I know he'll be eager to celebrate your birthday as soon as he's back from Dallas. Eddie's always up for a fun birthday dinner," Davis said, ruffling the boy's hair in camaraderie. "Now, what's this about leaving?"

At that, Landry turned from the window and faced the boys.

"Zane's doing so well that he's ready to go home." Landry's voice fell short of sounding upbeat.

"But I don't have anywhere to go," Zane added. His chin dropped to his chest, and his voice quivered.

Davis's gaze darted to Landry.

"We're working on that, Zane," she promised. "You're going to be just fine, sweetie. Don't you worry about a thing." Her voice quivered, too. And Davis caught her swiping her cheek before she walked to the opposite side of Zane's bed. "I've got rounds on the fourth floor, and then I'll be back with your special order: cheeseburger, curly fries, plenty of ketchup, and a strawberry milkshake," she said with a fake smile plastered on her face. "Davis, will you be joining us for dinner tonight?"

"There's nowhere else I'd rather be," he exclaimed. "How about I set this present over there — *out* of reach of curious birthday boys — and pick up the to-go order? I can be back before Doctor Stark finishes with her rounds, and we'll all meet here to sing, blow out candles, and make birthday wishes."

Zane brightened, and a genuine grin blossomed across his face.

"I'm halfway through a new baseball movie," the boy announced. "I'll finish it while y'all are gone."

Landry fussed over him a little more, adjusting his blanket, and glancing one last time at his monitors, although nurses had removed the bulk of them one at a time throughout the previous couple of days.

"Sounds like a plan, Z Man. We'll be back soon," Davis promised before following Landry into the corridor.

"What's going on?" Davis asked the moment they were out of Zane's earshot.

"Exactly what Zane said," Landry said, rubbing her forehead as worry lines descended on her brow. "Medically, he's ready to leave the hospital. Insurance refused my request to continue in-patient care because all Zane needs at this point is physical therapy daily and home health checking on his surgical site twice a week."

"With his only guardian fighting for his life and enduring skin graft surgeries daily, the insurance company thinks a seven-year-old boy should go home alone?" Davis's temper rose with the ludicrous point he made.

"Eight. An eight-year-old boy," Landry interjected despondently.

"And it's his birthday!" Davis was livid, pacing and running his hand through his hair repetitively.

On his fifth or sixth pass in front of her, Landry grasped his arm, sliding her hand into his, and halting his progress. He stopped by her side. She tugged him in her direction, wrapping her arms around his ribs and tucking herself into his chest. She never hesitated to take a hug when she needed one. He appreciated that. A lot.

Davis folded his arms around her, finding comfort in her warm embrace.

"It's not right," he groused.

"Child Services has already assigned a social worker to Zane. She'll be here first thing in the morning; there's a meeting set to discuss options. As part of his medical team, I'll be there. We'll figure it out." Landry tried to sound convincing, but her worry and concern were clear. "Until then," she said, lifting her head to look into his eyes, "we'll make this a birthday that doesn't stink."

"That's the best you can do? A birthday that doesn't stink?" Davis teased, his arms a tight frame holding her close.

"I wouldn't want it to be one of the best," she admitted with her typical realism.

"No, me neither," Davis agreed. "But I do know one thing that makes everything better." He waggled his eyebrows, flirting unabashedly.

"Better for whom?"

"Everyone involved," he promised, lowering his lips toward hers.

"We're in the middle of the hospital," she said, her breath heating his lips. But she didn't move away.

"I don't mind," Davis whispered, moving his hands to hold her head as his mouth settled over her lips.

What he would've given to lose himself in that kiss.

Sadly, she had a point: they were in the middle of the hospital. Added to that, she needed to get back to her rounds, and he needed to put together a birthday party that didn't stink.

So, Davis ended the kiss, rested his forehead against hers for a few heartbeats to balance his equilibrium. He struggled to let her go and ended up planting one last kiss on her lips before forcing himself to walk away.

*L*ying in bed, unable to sleep, in the wee morning hours of Saint Patrick's Day, Davis thought through his evening with Landry and Zane. Remembering the silly hats they'd constructed from newspapers found in the waiting room and the balloon bouquet they'd made from inflated surgical gloves, Davis couldn't help but smile. The wish Zane had whispered when he blew out his candle made Davis want to cry. The amazing kid had asked for only one thing: his dad to come home healthy so they could be a family again.

Davis shot up in bed. An idea hit him like a runaway freight train. Why hadn't he seen it before?

Zane needed a place to go, a temporary home and family, just until Eddie had healed enough to take over again as primary caregiver and all-around awesome dad. Davis decided right then that with a little luck on his side, he'd be the one to provide it.

Knowing he'd never be able to drift off with his mind whirling, Davis climbed out of bed.

4:17 a.m. No time like the present!

After a quick shower, Davis sat down at his computer, opened up a web browser, and put the internet to work. By 6 a.m., he'd found two firefighters to cover his shift as well as Rhys's. By 7 a.m., he'd laid out his plan— an *argument*, as it was.

At five after seven, Davis texted his parents, Miss Sadie, Chief Everett, Maree, Rhys, and Landry with the same message:

- *I need you at the courthouse at 9 a.m. — please.*

At eight forty-five, he entered the clerk's office, motion in-hand. At nine o'clock, his idea came to life.

"All rise," the bailiff announced. "The Honorable Judge Dorothy Rogers, now presiding."

With a scowl pointed directly at Davis, the judge took her seat.

"You may now be seated," the bailiff instructed.

"Except you," Judge Roberts barked, pointing a finger at Davis. "What in the world is this all about?"

Davis took a deep breath, ran the heel of his palm across his forehead to smooth his hair, and stretched his neck while straightening his green, four-leaf clover tie. "Your honor, I, Daniel Aaron Davis—"

"I know good and well who you are," the judge interrupted. "What is this petition you concocted and pitched a fit to have put on my docket today? And why is the Department of Child Services involved?"

"Well, ma'am, there's a very special boy at Green Country Medical Center who needs someone to take care of him while he finishes recuperating after injuries sustained in the explosion at the Rec Hall. He needs a place to live until his father and only guardian heals from substantial burns obtained saving the lives of over a dozen children in said explosion. That's why a social worker from Child Services is here, and I think she'll agree. The boy needs a friend to lean on for a while."

"And what's that got to do with you?"

He'd known the judge would be tough, but good gravy. He'd never seen her grumpier. Well, Davis could dig in his heels, too. Hands on his hips, he snapped right back at her...

"Aunt Dot, I intend to be that friend. I want to give him shelter and protection and help him heal. I just need you to sign that request for temporary custody to make it happen. Now, will you do it?"

11

Fight for the things you care about,
but do it in a way
that will lead others to join you.
Ruth Bader Ginsburg

*W**ait! Aunt Dot? Temporary custody? What in the world!*

Landry snapped to attention. She'd been admiring the way Davis's broad shoulders, trim waist, and muscular thighs filled out his navy blue, pinstripe suit just right. She'd admitted — only to herself — that his silly tie with the large four-leaf clover on a plaid background in various shades of blues, greens, and lilacs should've looked ridiculous but brought out the depth of his eyes and positively popped off his crisp, mint green dress shirt instead. Landry had even spent a second or two daydreaming about mussing his thick hair, more than wavy but less than curly today, and wondering how he'd combed it — or molded it — into submission.

"Elijah Davis," Judge Rogers barked at Davis's dad. "What is the meaning of this?"

"It's the first I'm hearing of it, Sis," Elijah said with a shrug. "Perhaps we should hear Danny out."

Danny was Davis. Elijah Davis was Davis's dad. And Judge Rogers was Elijah's sister, Aunt Dot. Landry's head started spinning.

Only in Green Hills.

"Start talking," Judge Rogers growled at Davis. "And don't call me Aunt Dot in my courtroom."

"I'm sorry, Aunt— your Honor." Davis corrected himself mid-apology when she shot daggers at him through eyes chilled to the temperature of icicles. "You know Eddie Cadell and I went to school together. We've stayed friends over the years. As the family court judge here in Green Hills, you're already aware of their family situation. You know that he and his boy, Zane, have been through a lot. Now Eddie's fighting for his life, and Zane's going to be handed over to the state because some corporate entity is refusing to pay anymore insurance for Zane to remain at the hospital. I've been spending a lot of time with Zane; we're friends. He's well enough to be released from the hospital, and I want him to stay with me until Eddie is home and able to take over again."

"Thank you for that update of my resume," she said with pursed lips. "I'm delighted to know it hasn't been altered without my approval." She frowned down at the lot of them before settling her displeasure on Davis again. "The last I heard, you have a job that requires you to be away from home for long hours at a time. Has *that* changed without my knowledge?"

"No, ma'am. I work twenty-four on and forty-eight off, out of Fire Station #2."

"So, every third day you're going to leave that little boy— How old did you say he is?"

"Zane turned eight yesterday. We had a birthday dinner, a cake, and a party for him right there in his hospital room. It wasn't ideal, but we still made it special," Davis hedged. Everyone in the courtroom knew exactly where Judge Rogers was heading with her argument. The social worker hadn't needed to say a word... Aunt Dot had raised the objections for her. "And of course, I will not leave him alone. Like any working parent, I'll arrange for a sitter."

"Your Honor, if I may?" Chief Everett spoke from the gallery behind Davis. Judge Rogers made a grunting, harrumphing noise that the fire chief took as a green light to proceed. "I applaud Lieutenant Davis's initiative and willing-ness to serve. I need him too much to grant an extended leave of absence, but I can guarantee the fire department will work with and support him while he's caring for the boy, as we do every firefighter and their family."

"Elijah and I will be on-hand to help whenever they need help, too," Jacqueline Davis pointed out to her sister-in-law with a challenging sparkle in her eye.

"All that is—"

Miss Sadie stood, interrupting the judge without so much as a peep.

"I seem to recall when Helen broke her hip, you were first in line to help. If I remember correctly, with her husband deployed overseas, you stayed at her house, got her kids to school in the mornings and back home in the afternoons, and cooked all their meals...*around your hectic schedule*. If I'm not mistaken, you were making quite a name as an up-and-coming family lawyer in those days," Miss Sadie commented with omniscience second only to the Lord himself.

"As I was saying..." Judge Rogers glared at her brother, her sister-in-law, and her long-time friend. "That's all well and good, but caring for a boy who's just been through a serious medical ordeal is a lot. Just because insurance says he's fine doesn't mean he's fully healed. I must also consider his emotional and mental well-being. Daniel said it himself: Eddie and Zane Cadell have had a rough road. A foster home community with medically trained staff on-site will be a better placement for him. I'm sorry, Danny—"

"Doctor Stark will do it," Davis cut her off.

"Excuse me?" Landry chirped. "Doctor Stark will do what?"

Davis turned to her, pleading. "Live with us, with me and Zane," he said. "Please?"

Vaguely aware of Davis's parents, Judge Rogers, Maree, Rhys, and Miss Sadie all speaking at once, Landry concentrated solely on Davis. With his heart in his eyes, he tilted his head in a persuasive plea.

"Please," he repeated.

Their two-year flirtation, their now daily phone calls, and their recent kisses flashed through her mind. She didn't know what they were anymore. Good friends? Something more? She wasn't sure, but she knew they didn't need to live together. Not like that.

On the other hand, Landry couldn't say no to what would be best for Zane. "No more flirting," she said, setting out ground rules.

"Done," Davis agreed, hands raised in surrender.

"No more hinting at dates or dancing or anything romantic," she decreed.

"If you say so," he agreed again, but less enthusiastically.

"And absolutely no more kissing," she demanded with strong emphasis on *no*, *more*, and *kissing*, sending Jacqueline, Maree, and Miss Sadie into atwitter.

"None at all?" Davis challenged.

"None whatsoever."

"You drive a hard bargain," Davis allowed, not quite capitulating to her last term.

"If we're doing this for Zane, he needs us to be present,

one hundred percent. We can't explore whatever might be developing between us *and* be all-in for him."

"Deal." Davis smiled triumphantly. Landry worried that perhaps he'd submitted too quickly, wondered if she'd won too easily.

Her confirmation came when he leaned over the rail, close enough to Landry that only she could hear as he said, "For the record, there *is* something between us. But I can wait to resume said exploration until the time is right."

Then Davis waggled his eyebrows and winked at her! He *winked at her,* less than three minutes after taking an oath — in a court of law, no less — that he wouldn't flirt with her anymore. What had she gotten herself into?

"Order in my court," Judge Rogers banged her gavel, much more dramatically than the situation called for. "I haven't agreed to this harebrained scheme."

"Oh, Dottie," Miss Sadie said, gathering up her purse, coat, and scarf. "Call that precious boy and ask what he wants to do. You've heard from the doctor and the foster parent's friends and family. Interview the nurses and anybody else you can find if it'll make you feel better. Meet with the social worker. Get all the questions answered. Dot the i's. Cross the t's. Then sign that request. It's temporary, for heaven's sake. Not to mention, it's the very best option Eddie and Zane have right now." She stood, meeting her friend's unwavering gaze for a long, drawn-out moment.

"We've got open sew at the library this afternoon," Miss Sadie continued. "I need to get home and pack up my machine. And Dottie, don't forget to bring your quilt blocks for the guild's community project; you know we plan to feature your appliqué work in the center medallion. Like it or not, you have the best hand stitching in southeast Oklahoma." Then Miss Sadie turned to her companions on the long wooden bench. "Come along, Maree. You and Rhys can drive me home for a quick bite of lunch before I have to get back to town."

Judge Rogers grunted an indelicate snort, then muttered something under her breath about bossy friends. "Danny, approach the bench. Y'all too," she said, making eye contact with both Landry and the social worker. She said the last part in the kindest voice the older woman had used since entering the courtroom. Her eyes had also taken on a loving softness. Miss Sadie's flattery must've softened "Dottie" a smidge.

"Caring for an eight-year-old child is no simple task, especially one who's seen so much of life's rougher terrain. If at *any* time you two feel you're in over your heads, come to me. I won't let anybody — certainly not some behemoth insurance corporation — harm that sweet boy. I respect what y'all are trying to do. Really, I do." She stopped her speech just long enough to reach her hand out to Davis, who lifted his own to rest on her bench so she could hold on to it. "Just remember, y'all are not alone. We're all here to help, all of us. Whatever you need."

Davis lifted his Aunt Dot's hand to kiss the back of it. "Thank you," he said in a voice raw with gratitude. Meanwhile, the grin he'd plastered on — from cheek to cheek — made him appear happier than a kid in a candy store.

"Is the Department of Child Services on board?" She asked the social worker.

"This is certainly a unique situation," the young woman expressed.

"Well, we're living in unique times," Judge Rogers told her.

"Yes, that's true," the social worker agreed. "Both Mr. Davis and Doctor Stark will need to fill out the required paperwork, agree to background checks, and receive training from the Department of Human Services. That training just transitioned to virtual delivery, so they can complete it online. As the presiding judge, you'll have to sign an emergency approval.

And of course, I'll need to visit the home. One visit will take place before Zane moves in. After that, I'll stop by regularly for both scheduled and unannounced inspections."

"Sounds more than reasonable to me," Judge Rogers commented. "Danny? Doctor Stark? Any objections?"

"No, ma'am," they answered together.

Judge Rogers signed the petition, handed it down to the bailiff for copies to be made and filed, and smacked her gavel once more with a gruff order for everyone to get out of her courtroom.

"All rise," the bailiff said again, signifying Judge Rogers's exit to her chambers. Davis whooped loudly the moment her door clicked closed.

Landry let out a laugh borne partly from Davis's antics and partly from nerves. The poor bailiff had rather failed at enforcing the rules of behavior in family court that morning, but Landry figured the proceedings had gone as well as anyone could've hoped for.

Then she stopped cold, eyes wide.

Had she really just agreed to move in with Davis?

Oh, my.

12

———

Celebrating good news
reminds you that there's still hope —
and that the end of the story isn't here yet.
Branden Harvey

*B*ummed to find Zane sleeping when they arrived at the hospital, Davis busied himself packing up the get-well cards, stuffed animals, candy haul, and comic books that had collected in Room 516 over the previous ten days.

"What's in the box you brought him that first day?" Landry had been reading Zane's charts and entering notes into the computer attached to the medical cart while Davis fidgeted. Looking up from the screen until he met her questioning gaze, he knew she waited for his answer. "The nurses say Zane won't let it out of reach."

"My baseball card collection. Dad and I spent years finding our favorite players, researching the antique cards, grouping them by teams, and organizing the all-stars in plastic sleeves by their career." Emotion caught in his chest.

"That's quite a gift," Landry observed. Then she pushed the medical cart aside to give Davis her undivided attention.

Davis shrugged off the importance she'd attached to his gesture.

"It is," she reiterated. "No wonder he's so protective of that box."

Her effusiveness embarrassed him; it wasn't that big of a deal. He'd just seen them in the bottom of the closet at his parents' house and thought Zane might find them pretty cool.

"When can we wake him up? I'm ready to tell Zane the good news." Davis couldn't sit still. "You think he'll be excited, don't you? I mean, I know he'd much rather go home with his dad."

"I think Zane's going to be thrilled." Landry picked up a stack of sweatshirts, t-shirts, and pajama tops to fold.

"Thrilled about what?" a small, sleepy voice asked. Both Davis and Landry turned toward the bed.

Davis dashed a quick glance to Landry, who smiled encouragingly and nodded, prompting Davis to share the big news.

"I get to live with you, Davis?!?!" Zane lit up like a Christmas tree.

"Easy," Landry warned, reaching out to settle him back in his bed.

"Can we leave now?" Zane asked, looking between Davis and Landry with hopeful eyes.

"Not until tomorrow. Doctor Bradford wants to see you in the morning, and if he gives us the all-clear, we'll be home by lunchtime," Landry promised.

Davis really liked how she said they'd be *home* together.

"We were just organizing your things," Davis offered. "How in the world did you collect so much stuff in such a short amount of time?" He'd been extra dramatic, moaning through *so much stuff*, so Zane knew he was only teasing.

"I have a lot of friends." Zane's smile brightened the hospital room.

"I know that's true, Z Man." Davis folded the flaps of the box he'd finished filling. "Looks like you've got an entire crew of good buddies."

Suzanne, Zane's nurse for the day, came in to help him with leg exercises and a shower before a nurse tech delivered lunch trays.

"How about I take these boxes home and put them in your room? Then I'll be back for supper? Maybe Landry can join us before her shift begins."

Zane's demeanor had mellowed dramatically when Suzanne had mentioned exercises. Shoulders slumped, he did little more than nod his head to affirm Davis's plan.

"Hey, you've got this," Landry said in her bubbly way, gently lifting Zane's chin to look him in the eye. "I know your leg hurts, and I know the exercises are hard. But you're doing great, and they're going to get easier and easier every day."

"But they're little baby exercises, and I can hardly do them." Zane's rebuttal carried a hint of defeat that Davis hated to hear.

"All the more reason *to* do them," Landry pointed out. "Doctor Bradford ordered four weeks of physical therapy."

"Yeah, so?" Zane questioned.

"So, Doctor Bradford is the most brilliant doctor I know."

"I don't get it." Zane sat up a bit, curious by what Landry meant.

"*Soooo*," she dramatized. "If Doctor Bradford says you only need PT for four weeks, that means you'll be as good as new in less than a month."

Somehow, Landry's loop of reasoning worked wonders. The cloud over Zane's mood lifted, and his usual smile reappeared.

"I've already been here over a week," he announced. "That means I'm almost done. I'm ready, Miss Suzanne. Let's do this!"

"That's the spirit, sweetie," Landry encouraged. "And guess what? I'm moving in with you boys — to keep y'all in line," she teased. "So I've got to go gather a few things, too. I believe I saw meatloaf, mashed potatoes, and red Jell-o on tonight's menu. It's my favorite meal from the cafeteria. I'll be back in plenty of time to eat before I clock-in."

Zane nodded again, but that time with a positive energy. Then he turned his attention to Suzanne as Davis followed Landry out of Zane's room.

"How do you do that?" Davis marveled.

"Do what?" she asked absently, greeting patients and nurses and doctors in the corridor as they walked. Preferring her undivided attention on him, Davis stepped in front of her, forcing her to stop, and to look at — to see — *him.*

"You knew exactly how to motivate Zane and how to give him the confidence he'd lost. You didn't fake enthusiasm, just told him the truth. But you knew precisely what he needed to hear. How do you do that?"

"You're giving me too much credit." Landry shook her head and stepped around Davis to walk toward the hospital entrance. "Zane needed a little reassurance."

In typical Landry style, she didn't recognize her gifts. Davis would've argued more to open her eyes to her impact on others, but when she reached for the handle on her car, his mind jumped to something else. He didn't want to spend the afternoon without her. Shuffling the box of Zane's belongings to rest on one hip, Davis reached his free hand out to stop her from opening the door.

"Let's go together," he said. "Come on. I'll drive."

"I don't need much from Miss Sadie's. I can handle it.

Besides, I'm sure you have other things you wanted to do today."

"Nope. The social worker set the initial home visit and site inspection for tomorrow morning." Davis took the keys from Landry's hand, clicked the lock on the fob, and kept walking to his truck. "I was supposed to be working today, but I traded days with a friend so I could be in court first thing," he said over his shoulder, not waiting to see if she followed. He'd pocketed her keys; she had no choice. That made Davis smile.

"About that," Landry said, jogging to catch up. "A little heads-up might've been nice. None of us had any idea what you were up to with that cryptic text this morning. And the judge is your aunt? Why did you need us?"

"I bet Miss Sadie knew what I was up to all along," Davis allowed. "And there's strength in numbers. They don't call Aunt Dot *Difficult Dorothy* for nothing. She's ruthless when it comes to protecting kids and punishing the adults who don't do right by them."

"I see nothing wrong with that. In fact, it'd be a much better world if more people — family judge or not — strove to be that way."

"I don't disagree," Davis said to defend himself. "I'm just saying that my status as her favorite nephew wasn't going to do the trick. I needed my team there to bat for me. And it worked," Davis grinned at Landry like the Cheshire Cat.

"No flirting," she instructed, opening the passenger-side door to his truck and climbing in.

"That's not flirting," he argued, stepping between her and the door she'd reached out to close. He placed her outstretched hand over his heart, covering it with his own. "That's celebrating." Then he leaned in to place a quick kiss — hardly a peck, really — on her lips and hustled to move out of her reach.

He closed the door as she grouchily ordered, "No kissing, either!"

When Landry and Davis arrived at Marshall Mansion, Miss Sadie had already left for her quilt guild meeting and open sew session at the library. She had also left an envelope with Landry's name on it next to instructions for heating two lunch plates. Beside the note was a shiny green, square-shaped metal tin. A bow around the container made from Happy Birthday ribbon indicated the goodies inside were intended for Zane.

Davis inhaled deeply.

"Mmmm, smells like chocolate chip cookies," he announced. "I sure hope Z Man shares better than you do."

Instead of rising to his bait, she grabbed the two plates of spaghetti topped with sauce and meatballs from the refrigerator. She placed a paper towel on top of one plate and put it into the microwave to heat. Then she set the other plate on the countertop to zap next.

How had Miss Sadie known to make two plates?

While the microwave hummed, Landry opened the card.

She turned her back to Davis while reading it, but he still noticed when she wiped both eyes before turning back to face him.

"Miss Sadie says she'll be at your house Friday morning by 6:30 to sit with Zane when you need to leave for the fire station. She says not to worry with breakfast; she'll bring what she needs to cook."

"Yes!" Davis pumped a fist in the air. "I hope she makes extras for plenty of leftovers."

"I'm sure she will."

"She likes me," he teased. "She wouldn't cook for me otherwise."

"She likes Zane," Landry said, evidently trying to temper his exuberance. It didn't work.

Davis was in too good of a mood. "She's also offered to

stay all morning so I can rest after my shift ends," Landry added.

The microwave beeped, and they both moved to switch out the plates.

"I've got it," Davis offered.

"What are we doing?" The sudden desolation in her voice alarmed Davis. He started the microwave and carried the first plate to the table, where Landry stood, setting out forks and napkins. "I work from 7 p.m. to 7 a.m., four or more days a week. Your twenty-four-hour shift begins at 8 a.m. every third day. What in the world are we doing bringing a vulnerable eight-year-old boy into that chaos? How will we manage?"

"The same way millions — probably *billions* — of parents do it every day."

"We're not parents," Landry contested.

"No, we're not. But for the time being — until Eddie is back on his feet — we're all Zane's got. We *will* make it work, and it's going to be great."

Davis grabbed the other plate when the timer dinged and continued detailing his plan as they sat down at the table to eat.

"We'll create a master calendar, we'll mark off our work obligations, and we'll arrange for help when shifts overlap. You saw our support network in that courtroom. That's a pretty outstanding team to have backing us up. Like Aunt Dot said, we're not alone. We've got this," he promised.

"I hope you're right," she said, but a strong thread of doubt lingered in her tone.

"I'm always right," Davis claimed with what he believed to be his most charming smile, followed by a silly wink.

"Huh," she grunted — not terribly lady-like — around a bite of pasta.

Davis dove into his spaghetti, decidedly happy that he'd made his point. He declared himself the unanimous winner of round one.

Or was it round two?

13

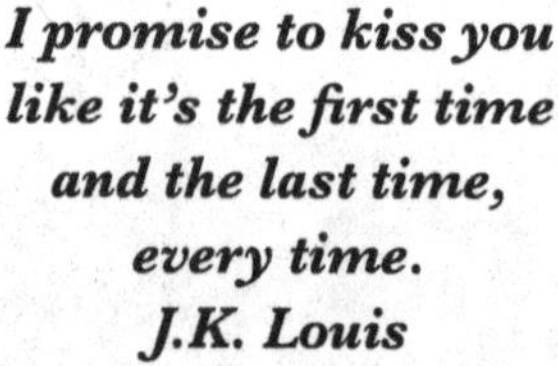

I promise to kiss you
like it's the first time
and the last time,
every time.
J.K. Louis

avis offered to clean up from lunch while Landry gathered the things she wanted to take to his house. He washed and dried their plates, forks, and glasses, and left them stacked neatly on the counter for Miss Sadie to put away in the correct cabinets and drawers. Then he went to see if he could lend Landry a hand.

When he arrived upstairs, he heard her humming along with a big-hair band ballad, which made him chuckle. He stopped in the open doorway to her room; her back was to him as she removed clothes from hangers and used the bed as a folding table. A small duffle bag lay open next to a short stack of items ready to be packed. She'd tied the long-sleeved flannel shirt she'd been wearing around her waist. The tank top she must've been wearing underneath it revealed smooth, tan skin over strong shoulders. Davis hadn't exaggerated when he'd said she was beautiful.

A lesson learned at the hands of an older sister, he knew to announce himself before entering, so he knocked on the door frame.

The sound startled Landry; she jumped around to face him.

From that direction, the fitted tank top displayed flat abs and the long, beautiful lines of her figure. The scoop-neck of the cotton also revealed a trail of puckered scars across her collarbone and the soft flesh above her chest.

Any firefighter recognized such scars. All of Davis's jovial good humor vanished.

Landry scrambled to untie her flannel, but in two strides, Davis stood in front of her and stilled her hands.

Every moment of them playing sand volleyball, taking the stand-up paddle boards out on the water, or simply swimming at the lake over the past two years whirled through his mind like a home video on fast forward. He couldn't remember a single time she hadn't had a t-shirt, a fishing shirt, or a swim top over her suit.

He lifted a hand to place his fingertips on the white dots that overlapped to create a swath of leathered skin. She tried to push his hand away. The look of embarrassment in her watery gaze broke his heart.

"Please don't hide from me," he begged. "You have nothing to hide. Whatever this is" — and he knew exactly what it was— "it wasn't your fault."

Pride washed over him at the way Landry stood her ground, valiantly. She didn't try hiding the burns, but she turned her head to look away. Again, he wouldn't let her. Lifting his fingers from the shriveled hollow V at the base of her neck to her chin, Davis made Landry look at him.

"I told you: we had very different childhoods," she said defiantly.

Temper was good. He'd take that over unwarranted shame any day.

"I'd say so," he allowed. "Wedgies and wet willies from my brother and my sister's threats of telling Mom for snooping in her diary are worlds away from cigarette burns, repeatedly administered, on a child's fragile skin." Davis tried to neutralize the outrage and unadulterated anger he felt on her behalf, but he heard it in his voice, plain as day. "Who did this to you?"

"It was a long time ago," she answered, yet not answering his question at all. "Please let go of my hand so I can put on my shirt." Davis didn't budge, but continued to look directly into her eyes, steaming at the thought of what she'd been through. "Please?" The whispered shakiness of her plea did the trick. Davis stepped back, releasing her hand and her chin at the same time.

"Who did this to you?" he repeated.

"I don't know."

"How do you not know?" Davis's urge to blow up warred with his wisdom to remain calm. Under no circumstances did he want Landry to think she disgusted or revolted *him*. He'd trained extensively in victim services and advocacy, and while Landry knew better than to blame herself for what someone had done to her, Davis needed to tread carefully, all the same.

Landry returned to her menial task of folding clothes while Davis paced the rug.

"I don't know because my mother allowed any piece of trash — no matter how heinous or despicable — into her bed. She thought sex was her only skill, her only means of caring for her darling daughter. So precious to her that when the monsters she let into our house turned their attention to me, she simply held out her palm for more money."

Landry spit each word; contempt hung heavy in the air.

Davis recalled Rhys saying that he'd vomited uncontrollably upon seeing the wreckage of Maree's car after her near-death accident. Davis hadn't been able to imagine such stomach-roiling nausea. Standing in Landry's bright and sunny bedroom in Miss Sadie's warm and welcoming home, Davis understood. He swallowed hard to prevent the bile from coming up. How could anyone inflict such harm on a child? And how could a mother allow it to happen?

"When?" He moved to stand beside her, grabbing the duffle bag and methodically placing the items she'd folded into it. He needed something to do, some way to channel the negative energy pumping through his body.

"The burns? That was a guy she let live with us for about a year while I was in grade school. When I was in junior high, she moved us in with her boyfriend-of-the-year. He decided I needed an attitude adjustment and had just the belt to do it. The morning I turned sixteen, she explained that the hideous loser she'd *fallen in love with* — yet another in a long line of them — had a special gift for me. She said if I didn't fight it when he came to my room that night, it wouldn't hurt as much."

Davis's queasiness intensified. He turned to tell her she didn't need to go on, to apologize for asking her to relive it.

"Landry—"

"Until then, she'd never stopped them from punishing me, had looked the other way when some of them pulled me onto their laps, petted my hair, or even touched me. But she'd never allowed one to rape me."

"Please—" Davis tried to stop her again.

Landry plowed forward. "That was the last time I saw my mother."

"What?" Davis asked, dumbfounded.

"I nodded after her speech so she wouldn't suspect anything. I rode the bus to school that day and acted like everything was fine. But I never went back to that house. I've been on my own ever since."

"Since you were sixteen years old?" he asked, baffled. "Where did you go? How did you manage?"

"I'd been selling research papers, biology labs, and chemistry homework at school." She looked at him with a guilty glint in her eyes and shrugged. "I felt terrible about it, but I needed money of my own. I justified that the rich kids buying my work were destined for college whether or not I did a few assignments for them. It was horribly dishonest, but I didn't know what else to do."

"I feel certain you've long since been forgiven. You have nothing — absolutely *nothing* — to feel bad about. I'm just so glad you escaped that awful home."

"Davis," Landry said, dropping the jeans in her hand and shifting to look up at him. "This is a home. What Max provided for M'Kenzee and Maree after their parents died is a home. What you grew up in is a home. That filthy, horrid house I ran away from was *not* a home."

"We'll give Zane a home — together — until his dad is healthy and they can be a family again." Davis reached out to smooth a long strand of her glossy, mahogany-brown hair, testing its softness between his fingers. He gazed into her dark brown eyes, admired her thick eyebrows, and noticed her heavy lashes. Landry's high, prominent cheekbones reflected her incredible strength. Her rich, olive skin glowed under his scrutiny.

She didn't look away, didn't turn away, which spurred Davis's confidence.

"You know," he said, and realized his voice had taken on a husky sound. "We don't have the notarized custody agreement back yet. I'm still waiting to hear from the clerk that it's ready to be picked up." Davis closed the slight distance between himself and Landry. "And we don't get to bring Zane home until tomorrow, so we're not officially guardians yet."

He ran the backs of his fingers down her cheek to enjoy the velvety softness of her skin. "So, you're thinking the No Kissing Clause isn't in effect?"

"Hmm, you said it," he dared.

"All right, Danny Boy," Landry said, full of sass and spit and vinegar. Davis loved hearing her like that; their special style of sparring delighted him. "Let's enjoy one last kiss."

14

———

When everything goes to hell,
the people who stand by you without flinching—
they are your family.
Jim Butcher

The kiss they shared convinced Landry she'd need to enforce the No Kissing Clause with the strictest of standards. It also demonstrated how incredible they could be together.

Attentive, gentle, passionate, caring, kind-hearted, giving, fun, and far too sexy for his own good, Davis embodied a figurative unicorn: a magical creature too unique and precious to be real.

In Landry's experience, men simply weren't that good. Except for Max Davenport, who'd loved and cared for his family and Janie Lyn against all odds. And Rhys Larsen, who'd overcome tremendous tragedy to love Maree. Oh, and Brennigan Stewart, who'd proven his love and devotion to M'Kenzee from the farthest regions of the globe. And Davis, who ran into burning buildings to save strangers, refused to let Miss Sadie carry even a basket of bread, and assumed care for little boys who'd been through hell.

Yes, time and time again, she'd found Davis to be way beyond good.

Landry didn't deny that as the truth.

And yet, regardless of how safe she felt in his arms or how warm and soft his lips felt on hers, no matter how much fun she had when they were talking and teasing and picking on one another, Landry also could not deny that watching a failed romance destroy their friendship would be infinitely more difficult than maintaining the No Kissing Clause. Pursuing the affection and chemistry between them could ruin what they had, not to mention tear apart the camaraderie and friendship they both shared with Maree and Rhys. Relationships like that didn't work out for people like Landry. The idyllic love stories she'd witnessed in Green Hills were just like Davis: fantasies that existed in alternate universes and accidentally found their way to earth every once in a blue moon. The fact that she knew a handful of happy couples only meant that those select few had beat the odds. It further proved that the quota had already been met on *happily ever afters.*

No Kissing Clause it was. How hard could it be?

After adding her toothbrush and toothpaste, hair products, and makeup bag to the duffle, Landry announced she had everything she needed.

"That's it? One little bag?" Davis looked around her room, essentially bare. "You'll have plenty of space at my house if you'd like to bring more."

"This is all I have," she replied.

"You've lived here for two years." He looked at her like she'd become the mystical creature. "My sister packs more than that for a matinee movie." She looked at him with a smart aleck smirk. "Seriously, a sweatshirt or sweater for each of her kids, a variety pack of candy bars, multiple baggies of popcorn, and several sodas... It's unbelievable."

Landry shook her head at his silliness and lifted the duffle bag, small as it was, to her shoulder. "Well, this is all I've got," she said. "And it's all I need."

Before she could take even a step, Davis lifted the strap from her shoulder.

"I can carry it," she fussed, digging in her heels.

"I know, but with me here, you don't have to," he stated with an innocent grin.

Landry frowned at his reasoning but decided not to argue.

Davis followed her down the stairs and into the kitchen. He stood by, not saying a word while she checked the counter for crumbs and turned off the lights. When Landry reached for the handle to open the back door, Davis beat her to it.

"You can't do everything for me. Opening all the doors, driving me around, buying breakfast every morning? It has to stop." Landry did not know why she felt the need to show her independence. In all honesty, his chivalry and attention had been a treat to enjoy.

"Okay." He sounded giddy, for goodness' sake.

"Okay?" she repeated, stepping through the doorway he obviously expected her to walk through. "What does *okay* mean?"

"Okay, you can open the doors, do the driving, and buy the breakfast. But not today," he said with a placating smile once he'd closed the door and tested the lock.

"Why not today?" She argued, not following his reasoning. Maybe that kiss had done more damage to her brain cells than she'd realized.

"Because," he explained slowly, as though speaking to a child. "Today, we've already had breakfast, we've already driven my car here, and we've already locked the door." Then he walked to his truck, set her duffle bag in the bed of it, and opened the passenger door.

"Good grief," she muttered.

"Yes?" Davis asked, patient and jovial as ever.

"You opened another door," she whined. She hated whining!

"Hmm. I guess I did," he acquiesced. Right before winking. *Winking!* Then he closed her door and practically skipped his way around the front of the truck to climb into the driver's seat.

Landry glared out the side window on their way to Davis's house in town. Overly tempted to be temperamental, she tried to think of something snarky to say. She'd never been a snarky person; what had come over her? Whatever drove her irritability needed to go away.

Sitting up tall, Landry closed her eyes, inhaled a deep breath, decided to be happy, and reopened her eyes as she expelled the negative energy she'd been holding. She turned to look at Davis, who turned to look at her, and she bestowed her widest smile upon him. What good was picking a fight when the other participant refused to engage? Might as well choose joy.

"All better?" Davis asked, a satisfied grin plastered on his own face.

"Yes, all better," Landry agreed, happy as a lark.

"Good," he said. She detected a hint of mirth in his voice. "You're adorable when you're grumpy, and I'm not supposed to notice that anymore," Davis added.

Landry shook her head with a disbelieving frown. The nerve!

But she also kind of liked that Davis didn't shy away from

her, even when she felt out of sorts, when her mood soured, or when she became downright irascible. She'd never known anyone who stuck around, particularly when the going got tough.

Davis really was a good man.

"Why does a single male, whose parents live in the same small town, own a four-bedroom, three-bath house?" Landry asked as they entered the side door into Davis's kitchen.

"It's a long story," Davis said, evading her question. "Pick a room, any room," he instructed.

"The master," she sassed.

"Perfect—"

"No! I was teasing," she exclaimed. "I'm serious about us."

"You know, oddly enough, I think I'm serious about us, too," he challenged, intentionally misconstruing her words. "So, if you want your own bedroom, pick... Blue or green?"

"You identify the bedrooms by color?"

"You'll see," he said, continuing through the kitchen, across the living room, and down the hallway, where he stopped between two open doorways. Davis turned to look at her, extending both arms in opposite directions, one toward each of the rooms.

Landry peeked into the room on her right.

Eureka! slipped out under her breath.

Blue paint, a soft dusty shade, took up the space below a darker navy blue chair rail. Above the wood trim, someone — Landry guessed it had *not* been Davis — had hung large-print floral wallpaper that coordinated with every stitch of fabric throughout the room, including the bedspread, the dust ruffle and pillow shams, the valances and drapes, the throw pillows, the lampshades, and the upholstered chair in the corner. Blue ruffled tablecloths, the exact shade of the navy accents in the floral patterns, covered small, round tables set beside each side of the bed. A thin disk of glass, ceramic lamps highlighting hand-painted flowers, and a plethora of knickknacks topped each nightstand. A phone, also blue and possibly from 1987, adorned one table; an alarm clock — digital, but an ancient model — adorned the other. An oversized basket of magazines, which turned out to be a hefty collection of *Reader's Digest*, sat on the floor, serving as a doorstop to the adjoining bathroom. Floor to ceiling, the bathroom matched the bedroom. Right down to the shade of the blue tiles covering the floor, another shade and design for the tub and shower, with a third shade and design on the countertop. *Yikes.*

"The blue room?" She ventured a guess while miraculously maintaining a straight face.

Davis merely lifted an eyebrow in confirmation. Then Landry turned toward the room on her left.

A replica of the blue room, with only two substitutions, opened before her. Everywhere the blue room had shades of sky, denim, and overcast grays, the green room had hues of hunter, sage, and fern. Instead of *Reader's Digest*, the door-holding mega basket contained an enormous stack of *National Geographic*. Otherwise, the rooms looked like identical twins.

Desperate not to laugh out loud, Landry crossed one arm across her ribs and covered her mouth with her other fist.

"The green room?" Voice strangled, a giggle escaped. Tears threatened to fall from her eyes.

"Exactly," Davis answered, the picture of butler professionalism. "And which do you prefer?"

"The better question is, which one will Zane prefer?" Landry said above her laughter. "Davis, I need to hear the story of this house."

"Nana lives next door," he began.

"Wait— Your grandmother lives next door to you?"

"Of course— Well, at least when she's in Green Hills. She loves to travel and is gone a lot," he said. "She and Mrs. Hartley lived next door to one another since the year they both married boys from Green Hills. They hit it off immediately, and that was over sixty years ago." He walked into the green room, dropped Landry's bag on the bed, and sat down in a corduroy chair that strongly resembled a conglomeration of celery stalks. Feet wide, Davis propped his elbows on his knees and leaned forward, apparently settling in to tell his story. Landry slid off her shoes and climbed to the middle of the bed, folding her legs crisscross underneath her and next to her bag.

"Anyway," Davis said, circling back to the beginning of her tale. "Four years ago, I'd just finished college and the fire academy. I planned to visit my family in Green Hills for the summer, and I intended to land a *real job* at a big fire department in a happening city. I grew up here, had already done all there was to do in Green Hills. I already knew every person there was to know and envisioned bigger and better things for my future."

"And yet, here you are. In Green Hills," Landry pointed out.

"Quite true," Davis said with a wry eye lifted. "The week I arrived home, I was at Nana's house, helping her move heavy storage tubs around her garage and bumming a home-cooked lunch. She'd just stepped inside to mix up potato salad to go with leftover pulled pork she'd heated for barbecue sandwiches—"

Landry held up a hand to make him pause mid-sentence. "You remember the precise menu?"

"I remember every meal. Food is quite important, you know." How did he always keep a straight face when he was such an adorable goofball?

"What was I thinking? Please, continue," she said, smirk and shrug notwithstanding.

"So, Nana had stepped inside, and I heard Mrs. Hartley's smoke detectors going off. I ran to her house and tried to get in, but, of course — an elderly widow living alone — she kept all the doors locked tight. I looked in the living room windows, but nothing appeared out of place. Then I hustled to the side of the house to look into another set of windows. Immediately, I noticed smoke. That door had three locks securely fastened: the handle, the deadbolt, and a slide latch. Grabbing a grape-fruit-sized rock—"

"More food?"

"Mmm-hmm," he nodded with enthusiasm. "I used the rock to break the breakfast nook window, fearing a back draft. Luckily, the flames, which consumed the cooktop and iron skillet on it, weren't too starved for oxygen. Yet! Mrs. Hartley lay unconscious in the middle of the kitchen rug. Just as I reached for a canister of sugar and a lid to put out the flames, they jumped. In a fraction of a heartbeat, the cabinet above the stove glowed with fire. It's anyone's guess how many coats of paint had been layered on those wooden cabinets throughout the years, but it didn't take them long to catch. And worse still, they'd be a perfect conduit for a quick spread.

"I lifted Mrs. Hartley, used a dishtowel to open the locks and turn the handle, and carried her to Nana's front yard. Nana called 911 and sat with Mrs. Hartley. I found a water spigot and tried to douse the flames as best I could with a garden hose, but it was a losing battle. By the time the firetruck and ambulance arrived, the kitchen, living room, front entry-way, and a chunk of the roof were gone."

"What about Mrs. Hartley?" Landry asked with concern. Davis's storytelling skills had her on the edge of her seat.

"The good news: after being treated for smoke inhalation, Mrs. Hartley made a full recovery from the trauma of that day.

The bad news: the incident revealed the severity of her memory—"

"Do *not* say Alzheimer's," Landry said, heated by where his story seemed to be headed. "I've seen entirely too many families touched by dementia."

Davis cringed. "Sorry." He spoke with kindness. "Mrs. Hartley's family is also dealing with it. And with them scattered across the country, they had no choice but to move Mrs. Hartley into a memory care facility."

"Here in town? I've never met her at Memorial."

"No, they moved her to Denver, where her son and his children live. They're best equipped to watch over her and direct her care."

"She lost her home, her independence, and her community — even her best friend — all at once." A wave of deep regret washed over Landry for the way the woman's life, at one time so full, would end foreign and lonely.

"Nana understood the why, but Mrs. Hartley leaving devastated her. I couldn't leave her, too."

"So, you bought the house next door to her?"

"Yep. I helped Mrs. Hartley by purchasing the house, and it's great. I like living next to Nana. It's a gift to see her so much, and I enjoy mowing her yard and tinkering with things that need fixing around her house. I'm especially fond of eating the food she cooks for me. It helps Mom and Dad as well, knowing someone is close by to keep an eye on Nana. We wouldn't dare tell her, but she's not as spry as she used to be."

Simple as that, it made perfect sense to Davis. "Your family is very important to you, aren't they?"

"Family is everything."

Landry hadn't experienced that in her life, but she accepted it was true for Davis.

She also saw it for the glaring example of how differently the two of them approached life.

"Of course," he continued, pinning her with a meaningful and direct look. "Family is the people we're born with, but also the people we choose along the way."

15

> *There's only one requirement of any of us,*
> *and that is to be courageous.*
> *Because courage, as you might know,*
> *defines all other human behavior.*
> **David Letterman**

"So, wait— she covered *every* room in flowery things?" Zane wiggled his hips to sit higher in the hospital bed. His wide eyes and strangled expression made it nearly impossible for Landry to keep a straight face.

"Well," she answered around suppressed giggles. "The living room and kitchen are great. They're not decorated in florals. When Davis remodeled that part of the house, he made it an open-concept common area. That means it's one vast room, so people cooking can still hang out with people sitting on the couch or watching TV. And the furniture in there is strong and manly, oversized and made of leather that shines like a saddle someone has used and loved for a long time. The appliances in the kitchen aren't fancy, but they're definitely new and of good quality. They're also shiny, but in stainless steel.

The curtains in there are definitely masculine, a heavy tweed with strands of brown, blue, and tan on a gray background. It's very nice."

"What's tweed?" Zane asked with youthful innocence.

Caught up in her mental image of Davis's house, Landry had forgotten to whom she spoke. An eight-year-old boy cared little about fabric selections or metal finishes.

"Sorry," she said with a grin. "It's like the fabric in a man's suit, but that's not important. The thing you need to know is this: how a house looks and how it compares to others — how many rooms it has, how it's decorated, or how much it costs — doesn't mean a thing. All that matters is the love inside. As long as the people inside those four walls respect and care for one another, it's a beautiful home. And I can guarantee that Davis's house is chock-full of affection, kindness, and love. We're going to be good there, Zane. For however long it lasts."

"But why didn't he put the suit fabric in those bedrooms? That might've been a good idea." Landry found his worry over her description of the blue and green bedrooms adorable and endearing. When faced with life's toughest challenges, adults could learn a lot about courage from the pure heart of a child.

"It definitely would've been," Landry agreed. "But the only areas Davis redecorated were the parts that burned in a fire."

The mention of a fire sobered Zane.

"A fire?" he whispered. "Was anyone hurt?"

"It could've been much worse," Landry began. "When situations are difficult and scary, it's always a good idea to focus on the fact that things are better than they might otherwise be. With that house fire, the previous owner, Mrs. Hartley, was very lucky. Davis was next door at his Nana's house and noticed the smoke. He knew to call 911 immediately, and he got Mrs. Hartley to safety."

"But if she didn't die, why does Davis have her house?"

"Well, the fire did not harm her, but her family decided she shouldn't live alone any longer. Davis saw how sad his Nana was to lose her friend and neighbor, so he bought Mrs. Hartley's house and made it his own."

"Kinda," Zane supplied with speculation.

"True," Landry laughed. "He *kinda* made it his own, and he's *kinda* living in Mrs. Hartley's beloved redo from the early 80s."

"You must love it," Zane pointed out.

"Why is that?"

"Because you love the 80s," he said matter-of-factly.

"You know what? You're right. I think I *am* going to love it." She shared a conspiratorial look. "Because *you* will be there."

"Our last supper in Room 516," Davis announced from the doorway of Zane's room. He carried two trays and used his foot to hold the door open for Paige Collins, the nurse tech assigned to Zane for the evening, who carried a third food tray.

"I believe this one — with *two* extra-large Rice Krispy Treats — belongs to you," she said with a smile, placing dinner in front of her patient. "Mr. Zane, I'd like to know how you arranged to have double dessert — in addition to the very best meal we serve — on your last night here. At least once a month, I beg Ms. Talia to make meatloaf on my work days, but so far, it hasn't worked even once. She never relents or goes off-schedule for me. And heaven help us all if I ask for bonus sweets on the down low."

The young nursing student worked evenings and weekends around her class schedule, and she'd quickly become a respected and relied upon member of the staff. She exuded enthusiasm and empathy in equal measure, paid incredible attention to detail, and absorbed instruction and recommendations like a sponge. Her curiosity and determination to learn made her wonderful at her job and would pay off exponentially when she finished her degree and began working full time.

With her hands on her hips in a pose of sassy interrogation, Paige continued to razz Zane about winding the hospital's Director of Food Services around his little finger. When he shrugged and giggled in response, Landry noticed a slight redness to his cheeks and the tips of his little ears.

"I think he's smitten," Landry whispered to Davis.

"I know how he feels," he replied in exaggerated agony.

His candor made her heart skip a beat. Blessedly, she recovered quickly.

"She's a little young, don't you think?" Landry teased right back.

"Oh, I think you know who's caught my eye." He didn't even whisper, just tossed the words at her with a suggestive lift of one eyebrow. He said it loud enough that Zane and Paige and likely everyone in the hallway heard.

"We have a No Kissing Clause," she reminded him under her breath.

"But we don't have a No Admiring Clause," he answered smoothly. Too smoothly.

His charm and energy filled the room. Landry felt it, warm and comforting.

Huh... How hadn't she noticed that before?

He brings peace wherever he goes.

The thought flittered through her mind of its own accord.

Before it could take root, Davis stepped behind Landry, placing both his hands on her shoulders. They, too, were warm and comforting through the fabric of her scrubs.

"Come on... Your dinner is served." He'd leaned so close that she felt the scruff of his five o'clock shadow against the side of her jaw. The moist heat of his breath sent cold chills skittering across her skin as he whispered into her ear.

He does not *bring peace wherever he goes*, she mentally corrected herself.

He brought nervous tingles and wreaked havoc on her senses. Davis evoked thoughts of wishes and dreams she didn't believe in, and he appeared downright destined to wreck her world, a world she'd purposefully and painstakingly built one tiny piece at a time over the past twelve years. She'd vowed to never — ever — give a man that kind of power over her. She'd watched helplessly as her mother made that mistake over and over again. Not Landry. No promise of love was worth—

"Don't you agree, Doctor Stark?" Paige had asked a question. Completely lost in an internal battle with herself, Landry did not know how to answer. In a knee-jerk reaction, she looked to Davis for help.

"We both do," he chimed in, taking the spotlight of everyone's attention off Landry. "Landry and I were talking about it just the other day. We can't predict how long this virus will last, but we can take all the precautions set forth by the CDC, follow the guidelines they give us, and do our best to keep it out of Green Hills. And you're absolutely right, Paige. The homemade masks can't hurt. Not to mention, they are a wonderful project for the quilters and sewing groups around town. They provide a way for everyone to take part in keeping the community safe."

"What's a CDC?" Zane asked before digging into his meatloaf.

"The Center for Disease Control," Landry told him around bites of her dinner, proud to have her wits about her again. "They, along with medical specialists, hospital administrators, local and national government leaders, and other health organizations, are laying out guidelines for people all over the world to follow, trying to stop the spread of COVID-19."

"That's a lot of people," Zane commented with enormous eyes and a mouthful of mashed potatoes.

"Reminds me of Ms. Talia claiming that too many cooks spoil the broth when she's shooing me out of the kitchen," Paige added ruefully.

"She's not wrong," Davis agreed. "But until we know more about this disease, treating it is tricky. And with the sheer numbers of those suffering with it increasing every day across the country, hospitals are going to run out of beds, and meds, and breathing machines."

"And doctors and nurses," Paige added again.

"We're all tasked with flattening the curve," Landry said. "So, we follow the recommendations."

"And when all those people telling us what to do contradict one another?" Paige made a good point with her question.

"Then we do what we always do in any situation: we use our common sense and make the best decision we know how to make with the information we have," Davis instructed.

"We're gonna be okay, aren't we?" Zane asked. "My dad's safe at the big hospital in Dallas, right? It's been ten days. I still haven't heard from him. He's okay, isn't he?"

"Eddie's in one of the best burn units in the entire country, in the very best hands," Davis promised.

"Zane, I'll call Parkland before my shift begins to ask for an update. I'm sure they have sedated your dad to help manage his discomfort during the procedures he needs. But I know hearing that from the doctors treating him means more than my speculation, so let me see what I can find out. I'll be back around to say good night in a few hours, and hopefully I'll have some news by then."

"I need to go check on my other two patients, too," Paige

told them. "But I'm just the push of a button away if you need anything. Okay, Zane?"

He gazed up at her with glowing adoration in his brown puppy dog eyes and nodded his head eagerly. Smitten, indeed.

"I'm off, too," Davis said when he'd finished eating, a while after Paige left the room. His announcement surprised Landry and Zane, who were used to him staying at the hospital to watch TV and hang out with Zane until Landry's dinner break at midnight.

"You're leaving?" Zane asked before Landry could utter the same question.

"Sorry, Z Man. I've got a few things to do before move-in day tomorrow."

"Like what?" Landry had finally found her voice.

"Well, Nosy Rosy." Davis pivoted on one heel to face her. "I'm going to the grocery store."

"That's it? You're going to the grocery store?"

"Yes, there. And a couple of other places."

Why the avoidance?

"At seven o'clock in the evening? What other places? What are you up to?" She wanted to know.

"That's for me to know and you to find out," Davis sassed like an immature kid.

Landry opened her mouth to demand more information, but swallowed her inquiry when Zane's hospital room door opened.

All three occupants turned, expecting Paige, but Sadie Jones, Dorothy Rogers, and Jacqueline Davis walked in together.

"Mom, Aunt Dot, Miss Sadie," Davis greeted, beaming with joy at their arrival, which hastened his departure. "It's great to see you, but I've got to go. Good night, all. I'll be here bright and early to drive everyone home, just as soon as we have the green light to leave." He gave each of the four women in the room a quick kiss on the cheek, adding that infuriating wink after his lips lingered on Landry's cheekbone. Then he mussed Zane's surfer-style, shaggy brown hair that perfectly matched the depth and darkness of the boy's rich brown eyes and shimmied out.

Just like that. Gone.

Once the door clicked closed from the whirlwind Davis had created, Landry set down her plastic silverware and focused on the visitors.

"What a pleasant surprise," she said, curious why they were there, but also at a loss for anything else to say.

"The ladies—" Miss Sadie began before quickly being interrupted.

"And Skipper," Aunt Dot interjected.

"Yes," Miss Sadie started again. "The ladies *and Skipper* spent the afternoon and evening sewing masks—"

"Sixty-seven total," Aunt Dot interjected. Again.

"We spent the day making *sixty-seven* cloth masks and wanted to deliver them straight away in case anyone in the hospital needed one."

"But you're not wearing them," Zane chirped from his bed. All eyes turned his way.

"No," Aunt Dot replied dryly as she walked toward him. "We're not. They're a precaution, but seeing as how none of us have any symptoms and no one in Green Hills has the virus, we're saving them for those who might need them in the future."

"Davis says we just need to use our common sense and make the best decisions we know how to make with the information we have," the boy extolled.

"Did he now?" Aunt Dot asked, with her eyes trained on Zane.

"Sure did," he answered. "Said we're all going to be just fine, even if all the chefs try to ruin the soup."

"Hmph," she grunted back.

Aunt Dot seemed to bring out Zane's precocious side, and he hers.

"Yes, well, we're actually here to discuss soup with you, Zane." Jacqueline Davis eased between her sister-in-law and the innocent child perched in the hospital bed, as though she were protecting him from a vulture.

What an odd moment. Landry, normally one of the sharpest minds in the room, struggled to keep up.

"Well, soup and other foods," Jacqueline clarified. "The three of us will help Danny and Landry take care of you, do some of the cooking while y'all are living together."

"Who's Danny?"

Zane's perfectly timed question provided just the exit strategy Landry needed. "Zane, these three women run Green Hills, and you're going to love them," Landry explained. "Miss Sadie, here, is my landlord and the grandma I never had before coming to Green Hills. And this is Judge Rogers, Davis's aunt and the person who allowed you to stay with us until your dad is better. And this is Davis's mom, Mrs. Davis—"

"The children all call me Ja-mère. It's a cross between Jacqueline and *Grand-mère*, which means grandmother in French, dear."

"Okay..." Landry's head threatened to spin again. "Ja-mère is Davis's mom, and Davis's first name is really Daniel, or Danny, for short." She let Zane sort all that out. "Y'all are wonderful to help us out," she said, turning to face all three women. "I need to go to briefing for my shift, but please stay as long as you like. You'll love getting to know Zane. He's a very special young man."

With that, Landry shared a smile and a nod with him, silently wishing him a little Saint Patrick's Day luck. Then she walked out, leaving him in three sets of very capable hands.

16

*Good company in a journey
makes the way seem shorter.*
Izaak Walton

"Are we ready to ride?" Davis bounced — loudly — into Zane's hospital room at 8 a.m. on the dot, clapping and rubbing his hands together. His eyes shone with excitement and anticipation. His smile lit up the space. Kids on Christmas morning displayed more patience and decorum.

His enthusiasm halted when he saw Zane still in bed, wearing his hospital gown, and frowning.

"Why aren't we dressed, chillin' in an exit wagon, ready to roll?"

Zane's expression transitioned to pure grumpiness in response to Davis's question. "We will be soon," Landry answered. "*Soon,*" she repeated, giving Zane a pointed look.

"Doctor Bradford's assisting with a complicated surgery. He'll be here to sign discharge orders as soon as he can. In the meantime, we're being patient. You know, since we benefited from his undivided attention and unparalleled care not that long ago, *and* since we understand how that family feels, we don't want to rush Doctor Bradford when he is doing the same for others."

She'd already been through that explanation — multiple times — with Zane, and she needed him to get on-board with the plan. Yes, it was hard when he was so keen to leave, but Doctor Bradford's skill might be the difference in someone's quality of life after surgery. For that, they could wait as long as necessary.

"Of course," Davis offered, switching gears. He seemed to comprehend Landry's unstated request for solidarity. And she appreciated it! "We have all day," he supplied. "Did y'all eat? I can run to grab some breakfast, if not." Then, turning toward Zane, he confided, "I'm starving."

"You didn't eat this morning?" Landry asked, intrigued. Davis didn't go without meals, eating being his favorite pastime and all. To her count, he consumed more calories per day than she did in three. Skipping breakfast the moment his day began would've been extremely out of character.

"Nope," he said cryptically.

Landry looked closer. Faint shadows of silvery gray glistened under his eyes. Normally a vivid sky blue, they currently carried a definite reddish tint. The product that he used to hold his wavy curls in place had worn off, leaving his hair frizzier than he liked it. The t-shirt under his plaid flannel button-down looked mysteriously like the one he'd been wearing under his favorite GHFD sweatshirt the day before.

"You stayed up all night."

The observation sounded like an accusation, but the guilty grin that blossomed on his face proved her right.

"What have you been doing?"

He pretended deafness.

"Davis, what are you up—"

A knock at the door ended the interrogation.

"I guess y'all are waiting for me," Doctor Bradford said in his matter-of-fact, mumbly way. Both Davis and Zane popped to attention with an energetic duet of "Yes, sir!"

Slow to set Davis's secretive behavior aside, Landry took her time turning to face her mentor and coworker.

He's definitely up to something!

Landry refocused on Doctor Bradford, listening as he asked Zane a series of questions, consulted charts on the computer in his room, and assessed Zane's leg. Throughout, all three males in the room did copious amounts of mmm-hmm-ing and nodding.

"When's the season start?" Doctor Bradford asked Zane.

"My baseball season?" Zane asked in wonder.

"I'm guessing in the next week or two," Doctor Bradford said with a look of consternation as he poked, prodded, and pushed on the muscle and flesh around Zane's surgical site.

"Yes, sir," Davis answered for Zane, who had turned a little green around the gills, but didn't shy away from Doctor Bradford's ministrations. "Practices begin after spring break. Games are scheduled for April, May, and June to have it all wrapped up in time for the July 4th Fun Fair. Of course, that's praying this pandemic doesn't mess up anything."

Zane looked at Davis, hope and uncertainty warring in his eyes.

Doctor Bradford mumbled a few things that sounded political and of firm opinion, so Landry figured it was just as well that no one could tell what he said. Then he gave the instructions that healed a sizable portion of Zane's bruised heart. "If physical therapy goes well — as I expect it will — you'll be able to join the team in about a month."

Zane's face lit up, as did Davis's. Worry for Eddie weighed heavily on everyone; the updates from Dallas were few and far between, and the information lacked a lot by way of reassuring Zane that his dad would be home soon. But Doctor Bradford's certainty that Zane would be with his team, on the baseball diamond he loved so much, in a matter of weeks went a very long way to putting the boy's world back in order.

"Yes!" Zane exclaimed. A jubilant smile spread across his face as he looked at Davis.

"Be sure to follow orders and do what the physical therapists tell you to," Doctor Bradford reiterated.

"Yes, sir," Zane promised.

With that, Doctor Bradford informed the nurse that Zane could go home.

Emotion welled in Landry's chest when Zane once again looked to Davis. Sadness and worry twinged the hope and thankfulness in his eyes, but the hope and thankfulness won out. Zane smiled — a small, nervous, lopsided grin — and Davis answered with an encouraging nod and that wink that seemed to be an involuntary action, as natural and reflexive as breathing. Offering comfort and cheer came naturally to him.

"I'll go get the truck," Davis offered.

"I'll go grab my bag from the locker room," Landry said as the nurse began shooing them out so Zane could get dressed. "We'll meet you downstairs, okay?"

Landry barely got the words out before the door to his room closed in her face.

"I guess he's ready to go," she said with a chuckle, walking down the hall with Davis until they reached the elevators.

"He looked a little nervous," Davis worried. "Do you think he's scared?"

"No," she answered. "Scared is too big of a word. I think Zane's making a valiant effort to go with the flow. And I know he's grateful and excited to be going home with us and not strangers."

They stepped into the elevator, and Landry pushed the button for the second floor. Davis reached to push the button for the first. Their hands bumped, and before Landry could pull hers back, Davis covered it with his. Her eyes darted to his. His expression had flipped from concern for Zane to something totally different in a fraction of a second.

When Davis stepped forward, effectively pinning Landry in the corner of the elevator, her pulse sped into overdrive.

"Da—"

"Shhh," he coaxed, placing a finger gently over her lips. "I just want to say thank you." His eyes never left hers as he spoke. "I couldn't do this without you. And I really want to do this for Zane. So, thank you."

Then he ran the back of his knuckles down her cheek, studying the path of his fingers, before stepping away from her until his hips leaned casually against the handrail on the far side of the elevator.

Good. A safe distance is just what I need.

It took longer to get Zane loaded in the truck's backseat than it took to drive to Davis's house.

Regardless of how many times Landry told Davis that Zane didn't need a pillow under his leg, or an ice pack for the road, or a blanket to keep him warm, Davis fussed over him like a momma hen. And no matter how ardently Zane reassured Davis that he was comfortable and completely pain-free, Davis refused to relent on the TLC.

Finally, Davis put the truck in gear and pulled out of the hospital parking lot.

Exactly two miles and five minutes later, he parked in his driveway, shut off the engine, and hustled to help Zane back out of the backseat of the truck.

Poor kid. With Davis hovering to this extent, his recovery might be harder than we originally thought.

"Landry, I left your stuff in the green room. Hope that's

okay," Davis informed her as he unlocked and opened the front door.

"That means I get the blue room?" Zane asked.

"How'd you know there's a blue room?" Davis asked, looking at Landry with an air of accusation.

She feigned innocence and headed down the hall toward her room, exhausted after her night shift and ready to sleep a few hours. Both bedroom doors were closed, so she paid no attention to Zane's room as she entered hers and immediately kicked off her shoes.

She'd just set her bag on the celery chair when Zane exclaimed loudly, "This. Is. Awesome!"

Wait — What?

Landry did a double-take and dashed for the room across the hall.

Where yesterday there'd been floral wallpaper above the chair rail, beautiful wood paneling the color of aged honey gleamed. Metal lockers stood on either side of the bed where the flowery drop-cloth tables had been. Atop one of the short lockers laid a stack of baseball card magazines, and atop the other was a baseball glove. By the way Zane slid his hand in it like a second skin, Landry guessed Davis had retrieved it from Zane and Eddie's home. Across from the headboard of the bed — not the fabric-covered one that matched hers, but a plain wooden one, stained a dark chocolate brown that picked up the depth and rich hues in the paneling — a chest of drawers painted white with red trim lines to mimic a baseball stood centered on the wall. A small television on a stand had a DVD player resting beside it. A quilt lay tossed in the blue corduroy chair, one made of baseball t-shirts and baseball fabrics. Someone had replaced the floral linens with gray sheets made from knit that looked as soft as the old t-shirts in that quilt. A deep red blanket and a pinstriped comforter completed the bedding. Davis's box of baseball cards held center court right smack in the middle of the bed. And where yesterday there'd been about a hundred *Reader's Digest* magazines sat an oversized basket full of movies, most with baseball players on the covers, but a few with football and basketball players mixed in for good measure.

Zane was in heaven.

Landry was in shock.

So, this is why he didn't go to bed last night. Always full of surprises...and charm.

"I put your clothes in the closet and dresser, but you should move things around," Davis told Zane before she could comment. "Take your time settling in. Maybe rest that leg for a bit, and I'll holler when I have lunch ready, okay?"

"Okay," Zane agreed, already opening the lid to the baseball card box. He didn't even notice them leave the room as Davis ushered her out to the hallway.

Landry grabbed his arm, pulling him into her room, the green room that still resembled a 1980s funeral parlor.

"Davis, *what in the world?* How did you get all that done last night?"

"It's not that big of a deal," he said, dismissing her with a shrug and looking down at his feet.

"Yes, it is," she insisted, sitting on the edge of the bed and tugging his hand until he sat down beside her. "It's incredible, and it's a wonderful gesture to welcome Zane here. You did good," she said, bumping her shoulder against his.

"I had a lot of help. The sheets and blankets were mine when I was a kid. I couldn't believe Mom still had them."

"Is that t-shirt quilt yours, too?" Landry scooted back to sit against the headboard. Davis followed her lead as he answered.

"Yeah, Mom used the Little League jerseys, junior high travel team t-shirts, and high school spirit tees from every team I've ever been on."

"That's impressive," Landry marveled after a moment. She couldn't imagine it, really.

"She is that," he agreed, his fatigue clear in the slowing of his speech. "Rhys and Maree painted that dresser, an old one Miss Sadie had in the storage shed behind her barn. Chief Everett put out a call for kid-friendly sports movies and ended up with donations from his men's group at church and every fire station in town." Davis slid his hips toward the center of the mattress and slumped until he could rest his head on the pillows.

"What about the wood walls?" Landry tried to get her question in before he dozed off, but all she got in return was an incoherent mumble that somewhat resembled, "That was the easy part."

Within two breaths, he snored softly.

Unable to resist, Landry touched a wave of his hair that framed his temple. Then she smoothed the back of her hand over his cheek and down his jawline as he'd done to her in the elevator.

What would it be like to know the love Davis took for granted in his life? The love of a mom who couldn't let go of your sports gear from twenty years ago? The love of a dad who helped you find and collect baseball cards, just to have another hobby to share? The love of friends who stayed up all night redecorating a bedroom because a special little boy had worked his way into your heart?

What would it be like to receive that kind of love from Davis?

Letting her thoughts run in that direction was a fool's errand, and she knew it.

To corral their wayward drifting, she plumped her own pillow, rolled away from Davis, pulled an afghan over her shoulder, and closed her eyes. She decided a little cat nap couldn't hurt and resolved to kick him out of her room in just a few minutes.

When Davis pulled her blanket his way and stirred her from sleep, Landry simply held on tighter. When he shifted close enough for Landry to feel the warmth of his chest against her back, a fissure of danger made its way through her nerves, but she couldn't muster the energy to be concerned. When Davis's muscular and heavy arm draped over her, Landry awoke with a start.

What kind of parents are we? Napping — together — while Zane might need us!

Landry tried extricating herself from the cage of Davis's arm and torso. It didn't work. His steely strength resembled a life-size vise grip. She tried wedging a pillow in her place and crawling away. Davis tightened his hold. Landry sighed in defeat and strained to listen for noise from Zane's room. Silence lulled her back to sleep.

"*H*ey, Z Man," Davis said. Gravelly from sleep, his voice sounded distant, but the way she had curled into his chest — absorbing his body heat — left no doubt that Davis was *very* close.

"I'm hungry," Zane said.

"Me, too, buddy. Let's go get that lunch I promised you. We'll let Landry rest a little longer, okay?"

Zane must've nodded because Landry — eyes squeezed shut in hopes both boys assumed she hadn't woken up — felt Davis reposition her like a sack of potatoes, tuck the afghan around her, and roll to the edge of the bed to stand up. Landry didn't release the breath she held until her door clicked shut and their footsteps shuffled down the hallway toward the kitchen.

Whew.

When had she rolled to face Davis? How had she ended up nestled in his arms? Worst of all, why had it felt so right?

17

———————

Every mistake I've ever made
started with
"It's too good to be true."
Jonah Hill as Owen Milgrim
in Maniac (2018)

*D*avis wondered — *hoped* — their nap together replayed in Landry's mind as often as it did in his. He couldn't be in trouble for flirting. They'd simply fallen asleep talking. He hadn't been angling for a kiss, or even a hug, but how nice that she'd naturally ended up in his arms. Davis considered himself an expert when it came to sleeping, yet he was hard pressed to think of a better nap in his entire life.

Leaving her to find food for Zane had been tough. He would've been perfectly happy to remain cocooned with Landry for a few more hours, but he'd been rewarded when she joined them in the kitchen not ten minutes later, her hair rumpled and tangled, her cheeks rosy, and her eyes droopy from rest. The sight of Landry, so naturally *her* — a remarkable blend of stunning beauty and down-to-earth, hard-working independence — caused a flutter through his chest. Indeed, he could get used to this.

The rest of their afternoon was equally wonderful.

Together, they'd assembled lunch. Davis made peanut butter and jelly sandwiches. Zane added a handful of potato chips to each plate. Landry sliced fruit and divided it amongst the three of them. They watched a spring training baseball scrimmage while they ate using TV trays in the living room.

True to form, Davis had insisted that Zane prop his leg across the couch to keep it elevated. Both Zane and Landry had argued with him that a pillow under the wound wasn't necessary, but Davis would have none of it. Zane would be on that pitching mound, healed and stronger than ever. Davis was determined, and despite his typically easygoing, amiable demeanor, he could be quite bull-headed when he wanted to be.

Just as the scrimmage ended, Rhys and Maree stopped by with a little something for Zane. Davis had been mighty curious about the whispers between Landry and Maree across the room, but Zane's jubilance over the goodies in his gift box drowned out their soft voices.

"An autographed jersey!" Zane had exclaimed. "And a football, and pajama pants, and three Kansas City t-shirts, and a sweatshirt, and a bunch of trading cards!" His face lit up with joy.

"Read the card," Maree had nudged with a smile.

The adults watched as Zane's eyes scanned the paper. His expression turned thoughtful, then a tad sad, then he giggled, and finally he looked up to them with a strong smile back in place.

"Max Davenport," Zane marveled. "*Max Davenport* sent me these. He said he's thinking about me while I go through rehab, just like the pros do after an injury. He said he's praying for me. And that no matter how hard it is to be without Dad, I'm never alone. He said life is full of ups and downs, and to remember that I'm strong enough to climb out of this portion of downs. He said—"

"A lot, apparently," Davis had interrupted.

"He has a way with words," Maree had laughed. "Max is my big brother, Zane, and when they're allowed to leave their 'bubble' that the NFL is mandating because of COVID-19, he'll be here to meet you in person. He told me he can't wait to shake your hand, that it's not every day he gets to meet someone so courageous."

Zane spent the rest of the afternoon exploring and sorting his new football cards. The girls did whatever girls do when they vanish into another room. And Davis and Rhys discussed what they'd learned from the gym explosion.

The crime scene investigators swore that someone had tried to defuse the bomb, a homemade contraption placed strategically in the boiler room under the stage on one end of the building. It made no sense. Had someone set the fuse and then changed their mind? Who would light such a thing in the first place, put a plan like that in motion, with families and kids filling the gym?

The answers were out there, and just like his determination to see Zane happy and whole and playing with his friends, Davis *would* make sure his community had the answers they deserved to feel safe in Green Hills again.

Landry finally had to leave for work. Rhys and Maree had left after supper, which Maree kindly offered to make. The boys had managed showers and established a bedtime routine new to both of them. Davis especially enjoyed reading the first chapter of a Matt Christopher book about a boy who hit only home runs. To help set up Zane's room, Jacqueline had brought over two shelves-worth of chapter books and sports biographies that Davis fondly remembered reading when he was a young, sports-infatuated boy. She never ceased to amaze, knowing exactly what they needed well before Davis did.

Moms.

Thinking of his brought an invisible cloak of peace over him, but it also made him think of the horrible relationship Landry had known with her mom. That brought a series of shivers down his spine.

Gathering his stuff to head home after Friday's blissfully boring shift at the firehouse, Davis's mind continued meandering through the past couple of days. Just as Zane's expression had run the gamut when reading the get well note from Max Davenport, Davis's emotions volleyed between contentment from his time with Landry and a strong urge of plain ol' desire to jump off the deep end with her, between happiness at having Zane live with him and stomach-churning worry for Eddie, between hope for the weeks to come and a cold dread that the happiness he felt might be too good to be true.

"You good?" Rhys asked as he closed his locker. Rhys's voice and the sharp clank of the metal latch shook Davis from his daydream.

"I don't know," Davis answered truthfully. "How can things — life — seem so great and so difficult at the same time?"

"How do you mean?" Rhys set his backpack down on the bench between their lockers, leaning a shoulder against the one he'd just closed to give Davis his full attention.

Davis organized his thoughts. "The night of Maree's accident, you said that you craved being around her. I didn't get it. Now, I'm starting to."

"Landry's pretty amazing," Rhys said with a sympathetic nod.

"The world feels right when she's around. But that's not love — at least not the kind you and Maree have, the kind my mom and dad have. Those are big, powerful thunderbolts of chemistry and devotion that alter the universe. I've never felt that, and I'm pretty sure Landry would run the opposite way if she ever got remotely close to it."

"You've never felt that because you weren't open to it, or maybe because you were looking for it with the wrong people."

"Lord knows I've tried. I think I've taken every girl in Green Hills and the counties within a two-hour radius to the movies or dinner at least once. At the end of the date, I've never *needed* to see them again. I need to see Landry, to check on her, make sure she's okay. But that's the definition of friendship, isn't it? Platonic friendship. Brotherly love."

"Do you feel brotherly when she's around?" Rhys asked with an incredulous lift of one eyebrow.

"No, not so much," Davis confessed. "But I don't feel like a thunderbolt has struck me, either. Except when I'm kissing her. Then..." he trailed off.

"Has this kissing happened often?" No response from Davis. "Davis, you still here? Has this kissing happened often?" he repeated.

"Not often enough," Davis finally responded. "And it won't be happening again after her ridiculous No Kissing Clause I agreed to at the courthouse. She seemed to enjoy our kisses just as much as I did, but as soon as she found a way to stop them, she eagerly tapped the brakes."

"Maybe that's self-preservation more than a lack of desire," Rhys offered. "I've seen the way she flirts with you, the way she gazes up at you when y'all are picking on each other. I'd be willing to bet you're not alone in your craving."

"I don't know," Davis said again. They'd gone full-circle in their conversation, and Davis had landed back at square one, uncertain of his feelings, his hopes, his dreams, and his place in Landry's life.

*H*e pulled onto his street a little before 9 a.m. to find a hive of activity buzzing around his house.

His dad pushed his lawnmower across the front yard while his mom kneeled in his flowerbed, pulling winter weeds and dead growth from the dirt. Miss Sadie had stayed over Friday night to sit with Zane, and her car still sat in the driveway. Landry had parked on the street, leaving room for Davis to pull his truck into the garage. Before he'd made it to the back door, Rhys pulled in behind him.

A cacophony of sewing machine motors, a movie turned up extra loud on the television, Maree singing in the kitchen, Miss Sadie *tsk*ing at Landry who sat in front of one sewing machine, Landry grumbling under her breath, and Zane giggling at them both stopped Davis in his tracks. So suddenly, in fact, that Rhys ran right into him.

So much for a slow, relaxing Saturday.

"Sorry," Rhys apologized with mirth in his eyes, clearly not meaning it.

"Why are you here?" Davis asked.

"Got a text," Rhys answered, waving his cell phone at Davis before stepping around him.

He walked directly to Maree, took the rolling pin from her hands, wrapped her arms around his neck, and proceeded to kiss her socks off, right there in Davis's kitchen.

"We have a No Kissing Clause!" Davis hollered from where he stood across the room.

"What's all this?" he asked, approaching the dining room table where not one, not two, but three sewing machines sat on one end and a large, green mat with rulers and rotary blades took up all the space at the other end.

"Miss Sadie's teaching us how to sew," Zane shared with a tone of excited adventure.

"Yes," Landry added with much less fervor. "We're learning to sew." She might've been undergoing torture.

Davis had to laugh. "Being a doctor, who stitches people up for a living, don't you already know how?" he asked.

"It's not the same, and the whole *for a living* concept is a bit of an overstatement at this point in my career." He found her cantankerous grumpiness adorable.

"I bet you'll figure it out," he teased.

"I already have," Zane announced. Landry tossed him a belligerent glare, which made Davis laugh even louder.

"Let's see," Davis said. Pulling a chair next to Zane's, he plopped a decorative throw pillow from the couch on it and gestured for Zane to place his leg on top. With a playfully dramatic eye-roll, Zane followed orders. Then Davis hovered over Zane's shoulder to check out his work. "What are we making?"

"I'm making masks. Maree cuts the pieces for us, Miss Sadie pins the parts for me to sew, and I stitch right along the edge like this." With professional pride, Zane pushed a button lit up green to stitch. Set to a slow speed, Zane guided the layers under the pressure foot like a seasoned master. When the needle reached the end of the fabric, he tapped the now-red button which stopped the motor, pressed another button to back it up one stitch, and finally clicked one last button to cut the thread.

Davis reached out, and Zane handed his project over for inspection.

"Wow! Z Man, this is good work. Nice job," he effused. Zane glowed under the praise. "This really is fabulous. If you have an extra, I'd be honored to keep one with my gear. That way I'll always have one with me while this virus is going on."

"And that way you won't forget me while you're at work," Zane added.

Davis laid the mask on the table and kneeled down to Zane's side, prompting the boy to look directly into his eyes. "Z Man, I'll never forget you. Even when you've moved home with Eddie, and these few weeks are a distant memory in your busy world, we'll be fast friends. I'll always be here for you; that'll never end."

Without a word, Zane launched his arms around Davis's neck. Davis absorbed the impact without budging and held the boy tight. He had no doubt this time with Zane, and with Landry, would change his life. Infinitely for the better, but altered all the same.

Davis patted Zane's back a few times before Zane released his death grip and wiped his eyes. When he turned back to the sewing machine in front of him, the tide of emotion had run its course. Zane picked up another set of pinned fabric pieces and returned to work.

"And what are you sewing, Doctor Stark?" Davis stood and walked around the end of the table to where Landry sat across from Zane at a machine that looked much older than the one Zane used.

"Not masks," she groused.

"Her curves aren't any good," Zane explained with the earnest wisdom of an expert. That earned him another petulant glare.

"I think her curves are just fine," Davis said with a wink at her, earning him his own menacing look.

"Turns out that — like cooking — Landry's talents lie in the basics," Miss Sadie said. Landry didn't dare scowl at Miss Sadie. "She's putting the selvedge pieces left over from the masks to good use."

"Show me," Davis said, pulling another chair beside Landry and settling into it.

"What Miss Sadie calls basic, I call fool-proof. I take one of these pre-cut eight-inch squares of white fabric, and all I do is sew strips of selvedge to it. I add one next to another until they completely cover the white fabric. Then I stack it over here to trim later."

Davis picked up a finished block, made a big show of studying it, and then nodded with approval.

"I love them," he announced. The blush that tinted her cheeks did not escape his notice. "Will you put sashing between them to finish the floppy?"

"Come again?" Landry looked at Davis like he'd sprouted wings.

"You really keep that gorgeous head tucked in medical books, don't you? How have you managed to *not* absorb *any* quilting knowledge with the company you keep? It's incredible," he joked. "After you finish stitching the selvedge strips onto your squares, I'll help you turn them into a stunning quilt. We'll trim and square your blocks, frame them with sashing, add a few borders, and then maybe Maree will let us borrow her fancy long arm machine to quilt the batting between the topper — aka: flimsy — and the backing fabric. Once that's done, I'll show you how to sew on the binding. That's the part you'll like. It's exactly like stitching cuts in the emergency room. Our last step is to wash and dry it, so you can see how the fabric puckers around the quilt stitches, how the layers provide warmth for the body while the colors and prints and patterns you created provide beauty for the soul. It'll be a quilt you'll treasure."

Landry sat perfectly still, studying Davis's face, looking into his eyes, assessing him with scrutiny as though seeing him through an entirely new lens. Moments later she asked quietly, "You quilt?"

"Of course Danny knows how to put a quilt together," Jacqueline Davis chimed from the open front door, where she stomped her feet on the porch before entering the house. Landry's eyes never left Davis's face. "He's been sewing since he was Zane's age, probably even younger. There's no telling how many times I fell behind on a project and needed his help to get it done for a wedding reception, baby shower, or charity auction. He's a whiz with binding, that's for sure."

"She's biased," he said.

Then, in a quiet voice, for Landry's ears only, he asked, "Hey, is everything okay?"

"I'm not sure I can keep up. With your family, the way everyone just *does* for one another. I don't know how to be part of that."

The doubt in her soft words and the forlorn wrinkle of her brow worried Davis.

"You belong here, Landry. Trust me, you're an integral part of this community. You love Green Hills, right? And it loves you." He lifted a hand to gently grip her chin so she had to look at him and hear his words. "You're family. *My* family."

Hope shone in her eyes. At the same time, she licked her lips, then worried with them. Afraid to believe she'd found home? Wishing he could seal his message with a kiss on her glistening lips, he resigned himself to feeling the velvet softness of her skin under his fingers and a light peck to her forehead.

The sliding glass door to the backyard opened, but Davis didn't pay attention. Jacqueline carried a large plastic cup of ice water in that direction. Davis didn't notice.

Maree continued to bustle around the kitchen; Rhys continued to chat with her. Zane continued to sew, and Miss Sadie continued to pin. Davis ignored the activity.

He and Landry continued to gaze at one another.

Something's happening here, Lord. Please give me the words and the guidance to handle it well. Show me what I'm looking for.

"Son, I brought my weed eater over, so we have two to work with. We need to do your yard and Nana's. No telling how long she'll stay in California visiting with her sisters, but when she gets back here, I don't want her yard to be a mess. Grab a weed eater and let's knock this out before lunch." Elijah Davis had apparently finished mowing both lawns and wanted help with the trimming.

"He's busy quilting, Mr. Davis," Rhys teased from the kitchen when Davis hesitated. Maree had him using a pastry brush to coat egg wash over homemade rolls before she placed them in the oven to bake. "I'll help you."

"You're one to be talking, Betty Crocker." Davis didn't take his eyes off Landry, didn't release the tender hold on her jaw. But he acknowledged the other men as he pushed his chair back. With a wink and one small swipe of his thumb over the soft skin just under her bottom lip, Davis stood and walked toward his bedroom. "Give me two minutes to change, and I'll meet y'all out there."

In those one hundred twenty seconds, Davis accepted two undeniable facts:

1. He'd lost all control of his world.
2. He loved every bit of the chaos.

18

____

Our doubts are traitors,
and make us lose the good we oft might win,
by fearing to attempt.
William Shakespeare,
Measure for Measure, Act I, Scene IV

After considerable nagging and begging from the boys on Saturday afternoon, Landry relented to an early dinner at the Fish & Spoon before she went to work.

Not uncommon when Davis devised a plan, Zane's first outing since the explosion escalated. Their dinner out transformed into an impromptu preseason party for his baseball team.

"How did this happen? I agreed to a quiet supper that *wouldn't* tax Zane or his energy."

She and Davis stood at the counter, waiting for trays — not just one tray, but *trays,* plural — of brookies: Fish & Spoon's famous chocolate chip cookie sandwiched between two layers of brownie and topped with toasted almonds, caramel, and crunchy granules of coarse sea salt. They needed multiple trays of dessert because all fourteen of Zane's teammates, their parents and siblings, and even a grandparent or two had somehow heard that Zane would be there, and they *all* decided the day called for an early dinner of fish and chips.

Landry and Davis both looked at Zane, who held court from his throne at the head of the table, which comprised four, four-tops pushed together in a long line so the boys could be together. Davis had insisted on pulling an extra chair to the side to prop Zane's leg upon, and after the first hour of the "party," Landry procured an ice bag from the kitchen and a clean towel for him. Zane and his buddies were having a great time. They talked — loudly. They teased one another and one-upped one another; they ooh'ed over this and ahh'ed over that. And they never ran out of steam, or giggles, or tales to share.

"His energy doesn't look too taxed to me," Davis laughed.

No, Zane looked like a happy, healthy eight-year-old boy loving life.

"I'm glad he has this moment. I know he's worried sick about Eddie, even though he works so hard to be optimistic and grown-up about the situation. Thankfully, Zane has an incredibly high pain tolerance for a child. His leg is still healing and must be uncomfortable, but he never complains. You were right to pull this together. It's exactly—"

"Wait," Davis interrupted. "Let's go back to the *you were right* bit. Say that part again." He raised both eyebrows in anticipation of hearing her admit his brilliance again.

Landry refused. "Never."

Her adamant snub awoke a beast. Davis mocked outrage. Then he basically attacked her, pulling her under one arm, and tickling — *tickling!* — her ribs until she begged for mercy.

"Say it," he commanded. "Say it, or you're going down."

Her legs crumpled under her attempts to get free. Davis's arms around her didn't budge, preventing her from dropping to the floor. He kept tickling her until she laughed so hard she cried. Even if she'd been willing to say the magic words, "Davis, you were right," she couldn't voice them. She couldn't even breathe.

But she could fight back.

Twisting her arm just right, she returned the tickles. Just as she suspected, Davis squirmed. That did the trick. He released the arm around her, and she took the offensive. He tried blocking her hands, but she fought on and gained the upper hand.

Pretty confident that he merely allowed that, she took full advantage. She pursued, dishing out all the torture he'd bestowed upon her just seconds earlier. They both laughed and giggled with every step until she'd backed him into a corner.

The wall stopped his body; his body stopped hers.

Chests heaving and eyes alight with silliness, they froze.

Davis took Landry's hands, entwining their fingers and clutching them to his heart. "You were right," she whispered.

His eyes darted to her mouth. Because she spoke so softly, he needed to read her lips? Or because he intended to settle his lips on hers? And which reason did she prefer?

"Order up!" someone shouted.

"That's us," Davis said, finally peeling his gaze up to her eyes.

"Yes, this is us," Landry agreed, pulling her hands from his grasp and stepping away from the heat and shelter of his strength.

Carrying two trays each, they delivered brookies to the boys and set a couple of platters at parents' tables. Landry said her goodbyes, reminded Zane to do his exercises, and headed toward the door to leave for work.

As she walked out, Jinx Malone and Scotty Philips walked in.

"Oh, hey guys," she greeted with a smile and a hug for each of them.

Jinx had been instrumental in helping Maree's sister, M'Kenzee, refurbish a home her husband had secretly purchased for them. The remodel had taken place the previous couple of months, during which time M'Kenzee's husband, Brennigan Stewart, had been missing-in-action from an operation with the FBI. A wild and emotional time, Landry had pitched in as much as her schedule allowed to see the project completed. She'd gotten to know Jinx a bit during those weeks and considered him a friend. It was great to see him.

Scotty, the head football coach for the Green Hills High School Wolf Pack, was one of Max Davenport's best friends in town. Maree had mentioned once that the two met when Max sought Scotty in need of a weight room to use when visiting her in Green Hills. Landry didn't know the whole story, but she'd heard that Scotty struggled through school, made some poor choices that put him on tough paths. Supposedly, his athletic abilities had been the only thing that kept him in college and out of real trouble. Miss Sadie had commented more than once that Scotty's friendship with Max, and Max's repeated invitations for Scotty to join him at church, had been God's work. Landry didn't know him all that well yet, but he seemed like a good guy.

It didn't surprise Landry to see the two together and would've enjoyed catching up with them for a few minutes, but hospital shifts waited for no one, so she had to run.

*D*avis watched Landry with Zane, watched her interact with the baseball families on her way to the door, and watched her visit briefly with Jinx and Scotty. Even if she couldn't see it, Green Hills had become her home. He'd been sincere when he'd told her she belonged. He didn't know what that meant for them — didn't even know what he wanted *them* to be — but he knew the community needed and adored her.

"Pull up a seat," he told Jinx and Scotty when they approached his table.

"Thanks," Jinx said, taking in the throng of second grade boys and their families surrounding Davis. "You get invited to a birthday party?"

"Nah, not exactly," Davis answered, half-shaking his head with a grin. "See the boy at the end? That's Eddie Cadell's son, Zane. It's his first time out since getting released from the hospital a couple of days ago. I sent a few texts to see if any friends from his baseball team might want to join us, and this just happened."

"I heard you'd twisted the judge's arm so she'd let Zane live with you for a while," Scotty said. "An email went out for everyone to put y'all on their prayer list. How's it going?"

"Well, no one manipulates Aunt Dot, but after some hard bargaining and a bit of begging, she granted me temporary custody. So far, it's been great. Between my rotation at the station and Landry working nights, we'll have to depend on family and friends sitting with Zane here and there. We've had plenty of volunteers, though. I think with some intentional planning, we can make it work just fine. I have faith Eddie's going to pull through and be back soon enough."

"How's he doing?" Jinx asked. Also growing up in Green Hills, he'd known Eddie his whole life.

"I think it's pretty rough," Davis answered. "To be honest, I don't think he's out of the woods just yet. Landry's explained the surgeries and procedures necessary to treat major burns. The process she described makes me queasy, and I have a strong stomach. On top of the burns, he sustained additional injuries when the building started collapsing. Eddie has a lot to live for. He won't stop until he's healed and home with Zane."

"And Landry? She's helping with Zane when you're at

work?" Jinx asked. The way he asked caused a nerve to prickle in the back of Davis's neck.

"Yeah, living with us, actually." Why did he feel the need to include that up front? "A stipulation of my custody agreement with the court requires medical oversight while Zane's recuperating and going through physical therapy. Landry agreed to help out."

"I'm not surprised," Jinx said. "She's really something — has a way with people."

"I've noticed the same thing at church," Scotty added. "She's a healer through and through. Although, it seems you've gotten to know her better than I've managed," he teased Jinx. "I've asked her out a few times, but the timing never seemed to fit with our work schedules."

Scotty had asked Landry out on a date? She'd never mentioned it. Rhys and Maree hadn't said a word. Did she enact the No Kissing Clause to push Davis away gently, because she had an interest in Scotty Philips? Until two weeks ago, Davis and Landry had been nothing more than friends. What did it matter if she'd been asked out — and wanted to go — on dates with other guys?

"I've shared a few meals with Landry," Jinx added. "Mostly over at M'Kenzee and Bren's. We've spent a bit of time talking. You know, Grandad is in the final stages of Alzheimer's disease. It's really hard to watch, hard to go through with him. Landry's talked me through some of the most difficult days. She's put a lot into perspective, taught me about dementia and how to be Grandad's caregiver." Jinx grew quiet for a minute.

"Beauty, brains, and a big heart for others," Scotty said with a whistle. "Doctor Landry Stark is the total package. Maybe I'll invite her and Zane out to football practices this spring, take them for ice cream afterward. I'd like to get to know her better, spend more time with her. Maybe I can entertain Zane a little along the way."

After a nod toward Scotty's brilliant idea, Jinx added, "Davis, I want to help, too. My schedule is flexible. I can sit with Zane, teach him a few basketball tricks, take him to the hardware store with me. I grew up at Malone's, shooting baskets in the back of the shop, following Grandad around like a shadow, straightening up the inventory, learning about tools and construction and woodworking. It's a great way to spend the day. Do you think Zane would enjoy that?"

Attend high school football practices? As a special guest of the head coach? Ice cream dates? Hanging out with a local basketball star? Playing with tools and listening to the locals for hours on end?

Yeah, I think Zane would enjoy that.

Before Davis could voice that thought out loud, Jinx added the bit that raised the hackles on Davis's neck...

"And all the better if Landry decides I'm the irresistible man of her dreams. There aren't that many available women around Green Hills, and none as remarkable — or as drop-dead gorgeous — as Landry. Who knows, after we've spent time together, we might just fall hopelessly in love."

Davis couldn't tell if Jinx truly hoped that would happen or if he'd only been joking. Either way, Davis didn't like it.

But what if Landry did?

What if Jinx, or Scotty, or some other unknown fellow was her soulmate? What if the Lord intended for Landry to be with one of them?

The consideration quickly soured Davis's good mood and put doubts in his head — doubts determined to fester.

With a forced but amicable smile at Jinx's plan, Davis stacked the plates and gathered the napkins on his table. He made polite excuses to check on Zane, claiming the boy had partied enough for the day and needed to get some rest at home. In reality, Davis just wanted to leave.

Between well-wishers, promises to drop by, and chatty boys,

it took a full thirty minutes to leave. Zane begged to go to the movies next; Davis promised they would another day. Zane asked to drive by the baseball fields; Davis claimed they were headed in the opposite direction. Zane said he'd like to see the Rec Hall; Davis said, "Not today."

In as close to a pout as Davis had ever witnessed on Zane's face, the precious boy leaned his head against the seat and looked out his window. By the end of the block, his eyes had closed.

Davis carried Zane into the house, set him on the couch, propped up his leg, added an ice bag, and then covered him with a quilt. Walking down the hall to his room, Davis paused outside the green bedroom and glanced in. Landry had so few things, no trinkets or knickknacks, not a single photo framed by the bed. But he could smell her — the warm, floral scent of her perfume. Davis could sense her, even when she wasn't there.

She'd taken up residence in his home. Had she also done so in Davis's heart?

He went on to his room, changed into comfortable sweatpants and a t-shirt, and made his way back to the living room. Zane hadn't moved.

Davis settled into his recliner and turned on the TV. The noise didn't bother Zane in the least.

In fact, the day had worn Zane out completely. When he still hadn't woken up at 10 p.m., Davis carried Zane to his bed, tucked him in, and spent the rest of the night flipping channels, not paying any attention to what he watched, only thinking of Landry.

At midnight, he brushed his teeth, climbed into bed, and grabbed his phone.

She should've been on her dinner break. He decided to send a quick text, just to check on her.

A text didn't require any commitment. In case she was

busy. Or had other people to call. He and Landry shared a fun friendship. They liked to flirt. And kiss on rare occasions. That didn't mean she wanted anything more. And neither did he. He enjoyed being friends. He enjoyed flirting — with lots of stunningly exquisite girls.

So, what if other guys vied for Landry's affection?

He reminded himself once more as he hit send on his text message... *We're just friends.*

19

———

There's no place like home.
Judy Garland as Dorothy in
The Wizard of Oz (1939)

"*I* thought you'd be asleep by now," Landry commented when Davis answered her phone call, not thirty seconds after sending her the text.

"Just climbed into bed," he admitted. "But I wanted to see how your night was going."

"Boring, which is more than welcome around here. Like Eddie and Zane, most of our patients from the explosion have either gone home to finish healing, or we have transported them to specialty hospitals and in-patient rehab facilities." She paused a split-second before adding, "How is he?"

"Wiped out," Davis chuckled. "He fell asleep before we made it halfway home from the Fish & Spoon and hasn't woken up yet."

"It might take a day or two for him to catch up after the outing. His body naturally commandeers his strength for healing; Zane will be surprised how quickly his energy feels zapped. But it's been two weeks now... He's young and healthy. He'll be a hundred percent in no time."

"Without a doubt," Davis agreed. "I'm not settling for anything less."

"If he's up to it in the morning, should we take him to church? Miss Sadie invited us to lunch afterward."

Not a church-goer growing up, Landry had come to enjoy Miss Sadie's Sunday morning routine.

They'd have a quick cup of coffee or tea with a bowl of oatmeal before getting dressed for church. When she'd arrived in Green Hills, Landry hadn't owned a single "church dress" to wear. Miss Sadie had assured her it didn't matter what one wore to worship; it only mattered they were there to add their voice to the singing and to soak up the promise and hope that being in the building provided. Landry hadn't understood what she meant, but over time, it made sense.

Even though she didn't know all the stories and parables, and despite the fact she couldn't recite the books of the Bible or specific scriptures, Landry experienced a sense of balance from attending Sunday services. No matter what their pulpit minister spoke about, Mr. Mitchell's words always addressed exactly what she needed to hear that day. She found it incredible that his lesson seemed created specifically for her every single Sunday.

Little by little, Landry had added a few dressier outfits to her wardrobe, and while she agreed with Miss Sadie on her policy that everyone was welcome in church — *period* — Landry discovered that wearing a skirt and blouse, or a dress, or nicer slacks with a sweater, taking a little extra care with her makeup, helped her to feel her best. Doing so made her feel "put together" so she could focus on the sermon and the singing. Somehow, she imagined herself showing up for the Lord, as Miss Sadie and Mr. Mitchell assured her that God would always do the same.

Miss Sadie never spoke much on their way to church, but she hummed hymns from door to door. Landry loved when the music leader started a tune she'd heard Miss Sadie practice in the car. She'd look at Miss Sadie with a raised eyebrow, impressed and wondering how Miss Sadie always knew what songs they'd be singing that day. Miss Sadie would simply dismiss Landry's teasing with a slight wave of her hand, a tiny shrug, or a gesture for Landry to join in. That slight gesture — Miss Sadie extending her hymnal for them to read from together — went further to making Landry feel welcome in church than any other invitation she'd received. And she'd received a lot!

Something special floated in the air in Green Hills, Oklahoma. Choosing joy came naturally to the residents there; people around town were genuinely happy, most all the time. Their open arms and kind gestures had surprised and touched Landry simultaneously. At times, their easy acceptance had overwhelmed her.

Those moments tempted Landry to put up walls. But each time she tried stepping back from the community, Miss Sadie had pulled her through.

Landry would've made it through residency — she wouldn't have allowed anything to stop her — but she wouldn't have enjoyed the two years nearly as much as she had in Green Hills, living with Miss Sadie and building friendships with the Davenport girls. And spending time with Davis. Quick to admit the gifts and blessings, Landry thanked the Lord daily that He'd sent her to Green Hills.

After church services ended, Landry typically loitered in the parking lot, laughing with the kids running around, hanging out with the teenagers, and visiting with the adults. When Miss Sadie called her name to leave, she never knew who'd be joining them for lunch. She did, however, know exactly what they'd be eating: pot roast with carrots, potatoes, and onions; corn pudding; creamed spinach; and homemade biscuits topped with whipped butter and Maree's strawberry jam. The menu never changed; its consistency didn't get old. Instead, the predictability reinforced stalwart strength.

"Lunch at Miss Sadie's is *always* a good plan," Davis replied. Landry chuckled at his ever-present, deep and abiding love for food. "Church is a good idea, too. I think Zane will enjoy it. You know, I've urged Eddie to meet me at church over the years, but he's been resistant. He's worried people might blame him for Raven leaving, assume he'd been a bad husband and that's why she took off. I suspect the exact opposite will happen. I can easily see the entire congregation racing to take care of Eddie and Zane...cooking, cleaning, and probably setting him up on dates with every single woman in town."

"Oh yes. I can imagine," she said, easily commiserating with the hypothetical situation Eddie would absolutely find himself in when he got home from the hospital in Dallas. "Of course, well-intentioned meddling is still meddling."

"I guess you've been a target of their match-making?" His light, playful tone turned a degree more serious.

"They mean well," she replied before drawing their conversation back to the present. "Would Eddie be all right with Zane attending church? I don't want to overstep our bounds."

"I think he'd be good with it. I'll ask Zane if he'd like to go, make sure he's not too tired after this evening's outing."

"If he's game, it won't take me long to shower and change when I get ho— to your house, I mean." She'd stumbled over the word *home* and had to remind herself that Davis's place was *not* her place. Landry didn't have one.

"Don't rush; I'm sure you'll have reports and charts to do after your shift," Davis reassured. She appreciated his not mentioning her slip up. "We'll be here waiting for you."

"Knock on wood, it's actually been a slow night. We're inching our way back to normal operations, and not a moment too soon, I'm afraid. According to news reports, COVID-19 is continuing to get worse. Hospitals and treatment centers are preparing plans to function at full capacity, possibly even with over-flow numbers, for the long-term. It'll be a tremendous challenge, caring for so many at once."

"I'm definitely praying this pandemic ends before it gets any worse," Davis empathized. Neither spoke for a moment, but the silence remained companionable and comfortable.

Finally, Landry gathered the courage to ask Davis for something that had begun as a random thought but grew into a tangible wish...

"Davis?"

"Hmm?" He sounded distant over the phone, like the length of the day had taken over and sleep would soon prevail.

"After lunch, do you think we could have a quiet afternoon at the house? Just the three of us?"

20

———

You have not been this way before.
Joshua 3:4

Davis's eyes popped open.

Had he heard her correctly?

He'd been on the precipice of sleep... Perhaps he'd dreamed her words? Surely he'd heard her correctly.

Landry wanted to spend the afternoon with Davis. That's what she said. *Right?* Not Jinx Malone? Not Scotty Philips? Not anyone but Davis? And Zane, of course. The three of them. A quiet afternoon together.

Davis's pulse sped up. He wanted that, too. Time with Landry — and Zane — felt very important.

"An afternoon at home, relaxing with you and Zane, sounds perfect," he told her, attempting to balance his desperation to make that happen with a semblance of nonchalance.

Play it cool. It's just Landry. Y'all have spent dozens of afternoons hanging out. Why all the nerves this time?

Because there was nothing *just Landry* about her these days.

"Yeah, it sounds perfect, doesn't it?" Her voice soothed and energized in a special way, one wholly unique to Landry. Around Green Hills, Davis had overheard multiple people comment on Doctor Stark's natural talent for saying the right thing, always at the right time, to gently guide a conversation or situation past a pitfall and onto stable ground. His mental list of Landry's gifts continued to grow with each passing week of their friendship. As he'd told his mom, Landry impressed and amazed him daily. "They're paging my team; looks like our dinner break is over. Get some sleep, and I'll see you in the morning."

"I hope it continues to be a boring shift," he said, meaning every word. "Good night."

An unwanted, unexpected, unfamiliar place...
Mr. Mitchell used those words in his lesson that morning. During the sermon, the parallel of God's people in the book of Joshua to the world's current state registered with Davis. In Biblical times and now in present day, the people found themselves in unprecedented times, where everyone lived in an anxious state with no frame of reference of what could come, how they'd navigate, and what they would do to keep it all together.

The message stuck with Davis long after the service ended. It remained on his mind throughout lunch at Marshall Mansion. Devouring Miss Sadie's cooking, surrounded by his family — who was the day's special invitation to lunch — Davis reveled in the comfort of being there while simultaneously fighting off a tingle of apprehension.

The beef pot roast melted in his mouth, as tender and juicy and delicious as always. The vegetables fell apart on his fork, seasoned to perfection with broth and spices. A warm, gooey peach cobbler, topped with cold vanilla ice cream, completed the heavenly meal exactly as it had every other Sunday he'd been a guest at Miss Sadie's table.

But because of the pandemic, their chairs had sat at tables on the back patio of Marshall Mansion instead of at the magnificent dining room table Miss Sadie's dad had made by hand. Each family sat at a different table: Davis, Landry, and Zane together at an outdoor glass-top table, his mom and dad at another one, Rhys and Maree at a small desk moved from the entryway, Miss Sadie by herself at a round accent table that usually held remote controls and drink coasters in the family room. At least ten feet separated the tables from one another. Miss Sadie wore a fabric mask when she went inside, and she plated the food for everyone from the kitchen. They held hands only with those sitting next to them when Davis's dad blessed the meal.

Right and wrong all at once, coexisting.

"Lunch was amazing," Jacqueline offered, smiling at Miss Sadie, whose eyes appeared to take in all Davis's mom meant in her words, yet hadn't spoken aloud. "Thank you. It was exactly what we needed. With so much uncertainty, it's important to stay close, to be here for one another."

"I appreciated Mr. Mitchell's prayer for the frontline workers, the medical personnel, and the scientists working on treatments and vaccines," Landry added. "I expect this pandemic to get considerably worse before it gets better."

Davis heard the worry in her voice. He laid his hand over hers, hoping she felt his presence and support.

"I appreciated seeing my friends. Even though we couldn't sit next to each other, it was fun to be there," Zane exclaimed from behind the dessert bowl from which he scooped and slurped every last drop of cobbler filling and melted ice cream. When his face reappeared with a dairy mustache firmly in place over an ear-to-ear grin, Davis handed him an extra napkin. "And I liked the singing," Zane added with an authoritative and approving nod.

"I like how Mr. Mitchell uses history to connect the here and now with the past," Rhys shared. "His explanation of how President Roosevelt contracted polio made me think of him stopping in Green Hills, about Davis being a member of the Fifty-Three Club. It's amazing how a moment can affect so much for lifetimes to come."

"Chaos theory and the butterfly effect," Maree said. "Of course I knew President Roosevelt had polio, but I'd never heard that a virus caused it. That description of FDR in the video presentation was so impactful; the imagery of steel entering his soul as the iron braces snapped onto his legs really hit home. It's all such a powerful reminder of what the human spirit can endure and overcome."

"*So, first of all, let me assert my firm belief that the only thing we have to fear is fear itself.* That's from FDR's inaugural speech on March 4, 1933. It's still true today," Davis said.

"Just as Mr. Mitchell said this morning, the months ahead will be trying, filled with difficulty and even death for some families. We will choose faith over fear," Miss Sadie affirmed, her mask in place as she gathered the bread baskets from each table.

"Amen to that," Davis said, pulling a mask from his pocket. He tied the ribbons behind his head and neck before she got to their table. When she did, he took the baskets. "I'll take those, if you'll keep an eye on these two." He tilted his head toward Landry and Zane. "I'll warn you, though... They're a handful." He lifted an eye in dramatic fashion to lighten the tension and worry growing heavy in the air.

"I'll help you in the kitchen," Rhys added, also putting on a mask and piling plates and silverware to carry inside. "We're together at the fire station every few days, so working side-by-side here isn't much different."

"Our routines are shrinking into bubbles," Maree said. "That's what they're calling it. Max called Friday afternoon to say that Janie Lyn's obstetrician asked them to stay in Kansas City, to have their groceries delivered and not to go out in public. Max and Janie Lyn expect her to deliver the baby there since she's due during football season, so they'd already chosen a doctor there. But we all figured they'd be back and forth during the spring and summer months while Max is in the offseason. I can't imagine them being homebound for that entire time."

"And what about M'Kenzee and Bren?" Landry asked. "Are they staying in Scotland?"

"Yes, for the foreseeable future. When the United States announced the thirty-day ban for travelers from the Schengen area, Ireland and the UK were exempt. Since then, they've added those countries to the list. Even with Bren's FBI connections, I'm not sure he and M'Kenzee could get a flight home. In an emergency, they might be able to fly into Canada and drive from there."

"We'll be praying there aren't any emergencies," Jacqueline promised. "That way they can enjoy their time with Bren's parents."

"I just hope they can get back for our wedding." A dark shadow deepened the blue of Maree's eyes as her gaze locked with Rhys's. A meaningful look passed between them.

So wrapped up in his own bubble with Landry and Zane, Davis hadn't considered what the COVID-19 restrictions, mandates, and cancellations might do to Rhys and Maree's wedding plans. What a mess. They'd already delayed setting a date once when Janie Lyn's family troubles and her safety had rightly taken precedence for the Davenports. Davis felt for them. Rhys had mentioned on more than one occasion he hoped to be Mr. and Mrs. by fall. And while Davis doubted that Maree wanted or needed a huge wedding, she would certainly want her brother and sister in attendance.

"Have you started planning the ceremony?" Jacqueline asked as Davis carried an armload of bread baskets, silverware, and glasses into the house. Bless his mom for the chipper and encouraging curiosity in her voice. "Don't forget, I want to help with the bridal shower."

"I've only heard bits and pieces, but I can tell you it's going to be stunning," Landry said.

Her grace, along with Jacqueline's interest, did the trick.

While washing dishes, Davis and Rhys listened through the open patio doors as the women chatted about flowers, cakes, colors, and decor. Maree told the group about a dressmaker M'Kenzee had met in Scotland that just had to design something special for Maree. Landry added her ideas for a bachelorette weekend away at a fancy spa. Miss Sadie shared plans for a new wedding quilt.

When the guys walked back out to the patio, Davis laughed at his dad, snoozing on a chaise lounge.

"I wondered why he hadn't offered a single helpful suggestion in all those wedding plans."

"Be nice, Danny," Jacqueline scolded in jest. "You just wait. You'll be old and content, and enjoying Sunday afternoon naps one day, too."

Her words hit Davis like a slap in the face.

Could he have what his dad had? Could a wonderful life with a beautiful, bewitching wife and successful, grown kids be in the cards? Could that really happen for a guy like Daniel Davis?

A life like that had always seemed so unattainable, so farfetched. He imagined his older siblings finding it, but he'd never been able to see that for himself. He'd been more comfortable taking life as it came. Since he couldn't match the perfect marriage and soul-connecting love he'd watched his parents exemplify, it made sense to keep things light and fun.

Looking around that patio, though, Davis saw it. He saw *everything*...all he could ever wish or hope or pray for. And he wanted it: a partner to build a life with, friends to socialize with, and family to grow old with.

The yearning felt new, but it felt right.

But was *it* — the gorgeous, independent, strong, smart, and sassy doctor at his side; the love and support of family and friends surrounding them; and perhaps a few adorable kids running in the yard — too good to be true?

21

Too good to be true.
English idiom used to say that
something cannot be as good as it seems.

"What's with you?" Harleigh Steele, a firefighter on Davis and Rhys's crew, asked as they walked into the Get'n'Go Monday morning to gather the groceries needed at the fire station.

Leave it to Harleigh. Can't a person be grumpy for a few hours?

A tug of something — not sadness and not regret, but *something* — pulled at Davis's mood. He felt it, had been working hard to hide it, but had fallen short. Harleigh didn't mind barging into someone else's business, and she wouldn't quit asking until she had a full explanation...classic know-it-all.

Davis — and everyone on their crew — adored her. Harleigh stood tall, not that her five feet, seven inches towered over any of them, but her confident demeanor — shoulders back, head held high — made her *seem* like she watched over the world. The short, practical cut of her sable brown hair belied the ethereal, almost colorless, tint of her green eyes. Their delicate appearance masked discernment.

Harleigh didn't miss a thing.

A strong leader and skilled firefighter, Harleigh never hesitated to take charge. Fiercely loyal, she always had the backs of those on a call with her. Quick wit and a fierce tongue accompanied her no-nonsense attitude. Harleigh Steele was a force to be reckoned with.

Davis only wished her force focused on someone else.

He didn't have an answer. Davis couldn't pinpoint what made him uncomfortable; he only knew something festered under the surface.

Running into Maree at the Get'n'Go that morning didn't help his irritation.

"Good grief! Not in the canned food aisle," he bristled when he and Harleigh turned to find Rhys and Maree snuggling in a hug and gazing devotedly into one another's eyes, as if they hadn't seen each other mere hours ago.

"Good morning to you, too, Daniel Davis," Maree said with teasing friendship. She made it difficult to stay crabby. "Hey, Harleigh. How was your weekend?"

The two women started talking, providing the cover that allowed Davis to keep walking. He'd effectively escaped when he overheard Maree say, "Landry claims they're just friends, but I think he's hoping for more."

Davis froze, pretending avid interest in the wide variety of canned corn options.

"He talks about her all the time. It's obvious to everyone," Harleigh commented.

"They'd be adorable together," Maree crooned. "And Landry needs a great guy in her life."

"I don't know," Harleigh countered. "He doesn't really seem her type to me. I saw her with someone less... Hmmm... What's the right word?"

"Tall? Dark? Handsome? Hot!" Maree giggled through her list of adjectives.

Just a hair over six feet, Davis didn't consider himself all that tall. And he wouldn't have used the term dark to describe his dirty blond hair nor his light blue eyes. Handsome? Nah, he stayed in shape and enjoyed working out, but Davis didn't see himself as handsome. Definitely not hot.

"They're talking about someone else," he marveled.

"What?" Rhys asked, unable to make out the words Davis uttered under his breath.

"Oh, nothing." Davis unwrinkled his brow. "Maree and Harleigh are awful chummy. When did that happen?"

"Yoga friends," Rhys supplied. "Maree's at Lakeside Yoga almost daily. She's mentioned seeing Harleigh there a bunch. Over time, they struck up conversations, then met for lunch dates, and now they're friends."

"Does Landry go with them?"

"Not that I know of," Rhys answered. "I can't imagine Landry's work schedule allows for much yoga, but I think she's met them a few times for lunch after their Saturday morning class. Why do you ask?"

"No reason. Just heard her name while they were talking."

"Want me to see wha—"

"No!" Davis screeched, which attracted the girls' attention. "No." He controlled his tone of voice the second time. "None of my business," he added, turning his back to the girls, tossing a few cans of corn in the basket, and pushing it on to another — *any* other — aisle in the store.

avis's mood continued to plummet throughout his shift.

They worked a car accident on the interstate highway just

outside of Green Hills. Davis couldn't understand why people were in such a hurry to get where they were going. Cutting off cars, weaving in and out of lanes to get in front of other vehicles, and driving well over the speed limit never ended well.

A grassfire erupted a few miles down from the collision. Thankfully, the afternoon sun had weakened the morning's windy conditions. They'd suppressed the fire by smothering the smoldering earth with fire retardant. By the time they'd completed the dirty and laborious work, ash and grime covered the crew head to toe.

Desperate for a dousing of hot water, Davis headed directly for the shower when they arrived at the station. He found out when he reemerged not ten minutes later that he'd missed Landry and Zane, who'd been in the break room when he'd walked through earlier. They'd delivered a batch of cloth masks to the station, along with an enormous tray of raspberry cheesecake brownies sent by Miss Sadie. And he'd missed them.

The three of them — he and Landry and Zane — had enjoyed their Sunday afternoon the day before very much.

Just as Landry had requested, they'd cocooned themselves in the house, snacked on popcorn, and watched movies in the living room until she'd needed to leave for work around six o'clock. They'd taken turns napping, Zane in a recliner with pillows and a quilt taking up more space in the chair than the boy himself and Davis sitting against the corner of the couch with one leg on the ground and one foot propped on the coffee table. Landry had fallen asleep with her head resting against his shoulder, her legs stretched beside her on the sofa cushions. He'd stayed stock-still, afraid to jostle her in any way. Barely breathing, he resisted the urge to move his arm, shoulder, or leg when they cramped. Davis didn't dare do anything that might prompt Landry to move away from him.

Contentment.

He'd felt it the day they'd brought Zane home. He'd felt it Sunday morning, surrounded by the people most important in his life. He'd felt it in the burning cramps of his joints later that afternoon while Landry nestled next to him.

Maybe true love grew from a foundation of contentment, not from a burst of fireworks.

Then he remembered their kisses in the hospital parking lot. The one at Miss Sadie's house. He wouldn't count out fireworks.

Maybe true love—

"You're blushing," Harleigh accused from where she sat across the table.

"What? No," Davis barked back at her. "I'm not. I just stood under scalding hot water to rinse off fifty pounds of sweat and soot."

"Looks like a blush to me," Harleigh murmured with the contrite hastiness of a preteen.

"Well, it's not," Davis rebutted, equally childish. Harleigh tempted Davis to stick his tongue out at her, but he held back. Until she did it first. Tit for tat and all.

"Now, now, children," Rhys refereed, halting their antics before their sibling jabs turned to wrestling and noogies. "Let's enjoy this slice of heaven in peace." Rhys poured three glasses of ice-cold milk, then handed one to Davis and one to Harleigh. He used a metal spatula to slide a five-inch square of chocolate goodness — swirled with sweetened cream cheese and topped with fresh raspberries — onto a paper towel. Rhys repeated the motion two more times. Finally, with an indulgent nod, he granted Davis and Harleigh permission to devour their brownies and milk.

"Wow," Harleigh groaned.

"Yep," Rhys sighed after finishing his milk with a loud gulp.

"Between Miss Sadie and Maree, he eats this way all the time," Davis said, basically tattling on his best friend.

"I need a fiancé who cooks like Maree and an adopted grandmother who bakes like Miss Sadie," Harleigh bemused around a bite of brownie.

"It's not like you're a dunce in the kitchen," Rhys pointed out to Harleigh.

"Knowing how to cook and creating bliss like this? Those are two different things," she argued. "Besides, there's something special about someone *wanting* to go to the trouble to treat you with such goodness. No one had to take the time or go to the effort of sewing those masks, baking the world's largest sheet of brownies, or hand delivering them to the station. I want to live like that."

"You want to *love* like that," Rhys corrected.

Before either Davis or Harleigh could respond, Chief Everett joined them in the break room.

"I knew these wouldn't last long." He scooped not one, but two massive brownies on a paper plate. "Here you go, Davis. Doctor Stark left this for you," he added, extending a folded sheet of paper his way. "She's quite a lady. Did I tell y'all about my mother falling a few months ago? Just awful. She tripped or stumbled there at Memorial Care... Mom can barely shuffle her feet anymore. She must've been carrying something, or perhaps the dementia has already destroyed her reflexes, but she didn't put her hands out to break her fall. Didn't even try. She looked frightful: cheeks scuffed, forehead scraped raw, chipped tooth, black eye, and a nasty bruise on her hip. Doctor Stark and Janie Lyn Davenport were both there and by Mom's side in seconds..."

Chief Everett continued his story; Davis tuned it out. He'd heard it before. In fact, folks around Green Hills shared similar stories touting Landry everywhere he went. They went on and on about her. Like his own mom had said: she was special.

Daniel walked into the apparatus bay where the trucks and engines sat gleaming and ready. He welcomed the quiet space.

Get a grip. It's not like she's declaring her undying love in an unsealed letter left with the chief.

Scolding himself didn't work. Heightened nerves sent a chilled, tingling sensation up his arms and across his chest as he unfolded the sheet of copy paper.

D2 (bet you've never heard that one before - ha, ha!

Sorry we missed you — sounds like you've had quite a day. I'm sure a hot shower did more good than sweets and a visit, even from your two favorite roomies :)

Your parents are staying at the house tonight to sit with Zane when I go to work. Jacqueline said something about breakfast pizza waiting when we each arrive home in the morning. She seemed to think you'd understand what she was talking about and look forward to it... You and your food obsession!

I will confess, though: it was difficult driving that tray of warm brownies the five miles into town from Miss Sadie's place and all the way to the fire station without stealing a bite. I hope you enjoyed them.

Have a great night, and I'll meet you over breakfast pizza,

Landry

P.S: Zane says "Hi!" (He's enamored with the fire station 🖤)

Davis reread it, folded it in half, then opened it to read once more. Nothing romantic, no passionate professions of devotion.

Lately, the phrase *too good to be true* had popped into Davis's mind with alarming regularity. Well, Landry avowing feelings of true love would've been the epitome of it. That was not to be, but her words did come across heartfelt and touching, none the less. Just like Landry.

"All units: minor vehicle accident at the intersection of Interstate 75 and Main. No injuries reported. Request for hazardous material assistance and fuel clean up," the dispatcher announced in a perfectly calm, clear, and precise voice. Davis jogged to his locker, shoved Landry's note inside, grabbed his gear, and was waiting on engine #33 with the bay opened when his crew hopped on.

Thoughts of possible-love letters, delectable treats, and smart, sassy women evaporated in an instant. The rest of his shift involved one call after another...the gasoline retrieval, a grease fire at the turnpike truck stop, even a proverbial cat stuck in a tree after chasing a squirrel too far out on a limb. When 8 a.m. rolled around Tuesday morning, Davis and the crew scuffled out looking considerably worse for wear and flat out exhausted.

Sleep monopolized his mind as he drove toward home. He eagerly awaited the cool, crisp cotton of his sheets. Davis let out a deep breath as he imagined his head sinking into his fluffy pillow with its welcoming fresh scent of laundry detergent and fabric softener. His mouth watered when he remembered Landry saying that his mom would have one of his favorite breakfast casseroles hot in the oven when he arrived.

Landry.

She flooded back into his consciousness.

Landry took center stage in his head. Above all else, he most wanted to see *her*.

Landry. When had she become the best part of coming home?

22

It is astonishing how,
in a few years,
the sewing machine has made
such strides in popular favor,
and become, from being a mechanical wonder,
a household necessity,
and extensive object of manufacture.

"WILLCOX & GIBBS' SEWING MACHINE."
Page 165 of Scientific American,
January 29, 1859

"Something smells good," Davis called out from his room, seconds before Landry and Zane watched him emerge down the hall.

Earlier that morning, he'd lumbered home from work, inhaled half a pan of his mom's breakfast pizza, and gone straight to bed. Four hours later, his voice, warm with lingering sleepiness, caused a flush of heat Landry tried to disregard. The sight of him tugging a soft t-shirt over his head to cover a washboard set of hard abs caused a flutter in her pulse that she couldn't ignore.

"You're awake," Zane exclaimed. Unbeknownst, he'd provided Landry a moment to recover.

"Imagine that. You're just in time for lunch," she teased, proud that her voice didn't give away the erratic beat of her heart. "Grab a plate, a fork, and a napkin. I'll get you something to drink. Water, tea, or milk?"

"What are we having?"

"Chicken spaghetti mixed with sautéed onions and celery, pimentos, and cheese; green bean bundles wrapped in bacon and drizzled with a glaze of brown sugar, butter, garlic, and Worcestershire sauce; French baguette crostini, with—"

"Wait," Davis interrupted. "Did you make all this?"

Zane burst out laughing. She indulged the sweet child. Until tears leaked from his eyes.

"Okay, *compadre*," she said with sarcasm. "We get it. Funniest thing he's ever said. Ha ha." She ruffled the boy's hair with a wink. "Of course not," she granted Zane another admonishing glance. "Maree brought it by while you were sleeping."

"Ahhh," Davis delighted, rubbing his hands together and flashing a wicked grin in Zane's direction. "I've heard about this chicken spaghetti. Rhys goes on and on about it, but he's never once invited me to dinner or even brought leftovers to share at work. We're in for a treat, Z Man!"

"To drink?" Landry asked, unimpressed with Zane's belly laughing outrage at the notion that Landry could've made the incredible meal and Davis's unabashed joy at the opportunity to indulge in anyone's cooking, as long as it wasn't hers.

"I'll take a glass of milk, please," he said, flashing a smile and a wink at her as he slid past her, purposely walking too close when he had an entire kitchen at his disposal. Funny how different a wink at Zane felt from a wink from Davis. Funny how a tiny gesture could pack such a punch, have so many unique messages hidden inside. "Might as well bring the whole jug. I could be here a while." Again, he shared a conspiratorial smile with Zane, who mimicked Davis's enthusiastic hand rubbing and mirrored his gleeful expression.

Landry had to admit that Maree had outdone herself. Lunch *was* incredible. Luckily, a girl didn't need to cook when she had friends who loved to do it for her.

Between Landry's heaping portion, Zane going back for seconds, and Davis making quick work of the rest of the casserole, cleaning up the kitchen took no time at all. Traise Mitchell, their pastor's son and Zane's physical therapist, rang the doorbell just as they finished.

*L*ike Eddie Cadell, Traise had been behind Davis growing up in Green Hills. A freshman during Davis's senior year of high school, they played baseball together and had been friends ever since. Davis liked the guy a lot, respected Traise for the way he took his job seriously without getting too dramatic. Traise had a gift for keeping his patients positive and upbeat throughout their PT sessions and a knack for understanding the body and how it worked. Maree vowed he'd been a miracle worker after her knee replacement. While Davis attributed most of her success to her own valiant efforts and determination, he didn't discredit the influence, expertise, and assistance Traise provided. Davis had been thrilled when Doctor Bradford assigned Traise to Zane's rehab.

Opening the door for him, Davis tilted his head back to look up at Traise, who'd grown to be an inch or two taller than Davis remembered. Definitely what one would describe as tall.

Check.

Girls had fawned over Traise's fathomless, almost black

eyes and close-cropped, short black hair since long before Traise had cared what they thought. That put checkmarks next to *dark* and *handsome,* too.

Would Landry care that Traise was a few years younger than she was? Nah, she'd never get hung up on that, not for so little an age gap.

Could Traise Mitchell be the one Maree and Harleigh spoke about in the Get'n'Go?

Traise had been at the house each afternoon since Zane got out of the hospital, except for Saturday, when they'd gone to the Fish & Spoon. At that time, Jinx Malone and Scotty Philips had irritated Davis by wanting to spend more time with Landry. Had it been Traise all along? Did Landry—

"Will you help me for a minute? While they're busy?"

He jumped.

She'd snuck up behind him — well, not precisely *snuck*. But Landry had startled him. Because he'd been falling down a rabbit hole of doubt and hypotheticals and irrational what ifs.

I'm an idiot.

Luckily, he'd only thought it. Aloud he told her, "Sure." Then he turned to find her holding the stack of quilt squares she'd sewn selvedge strips onto a few days earlier. "You've been busy, too."

"Yeah, I try to stay out of their way so Zane can focus on his exercises, so I moved a sewing machine to my bedroom. I stay back there while Traise is here. I have all these ready to trim. Will you teach me how to do it?"

Davis's heart buoyed. Literally bounced with merriment. Traise wasn't tall, dark, and handsome. Well, he *was,* but not Landry's Tall, Dark, and Handsome. She didn't even spend time with Traise when he visited to work with Zane. And she wanted his — Davis's — help on her quilt. Things were looking up.

"I'd be happy to," he said with genuine excitement.

Davis hadn't been in her room in days. Seeing that she'd set up the sewing machine on the desk, stacked a pile of medical books on the bedside table, and propped a photo of their foursome — Landry, Maree, Rhys, and himself — against the mirror brought Davis immense pleasure. For Landry, those small steps constituted setting down roots.

He picked up the photo and couldn't help but smile as he looked at it. The four friends had hustled and bustled — with M'Kenzee's guidance and the community's help — to throw a secret wedding reception for Max and Janie Lyn Davenport. Somehow, they'd pulled off the surprise, and the party had been a superb balance of casual comfort and enchanting romance. M'Kenzee had snapped their picture moments before the sun set, so the camera flash lit up their expressions of elated accomplishment while the background exhibited the profound beauty of God's paintbrush. Brilliant streaks of gold, peach, and orange fused into bands of red, purple, and blue until they disappeared into the depths of a dark navy horizon. The way M'Kenzee captured the scene depicted a miracle in light and displayed the bond of their friendship.

"There's nothing as picturesque as an Oklahoma sunset," Landry commented over his shoulder. "Did Maree send you the link to all the photos after the reception? If not, I have it. There are so many great shots! But this is my very favorite." Happiness permeated her voice.

"M'Kenzee is incredibly talented," Davis agreed. He struggled to take his eyes off Landry's image in the snapshot. They'd danced that night, partaken in their typical banter and flirtatious teasing. But had he noticed how stunningly, flat-out gorgeous she'd looked?

A blue, white, and yellow floral design on an ivory background covered her floor-length dress. The fitted bodice accentuated her slender waist while poufy, off-the-shoulder sleeves showed off lean, muscular shoulders. The full, flowy skirt high-lighted Landry's playful elegance.

"Did I tell you how beautiful you looked?" His voice dropped of its own volition.

"Wha— What?" Landry stammered.

"That night," he said, finally setting the picture down and turning his attention to the living, breathing version of her standing not three feet away. "I hope I told you then how utterly amazing you looked."

Landry gulped, drawing Davis's eyes to the hollow of her throat. The pulsating rhythm pulled him to her like a magnet. She swallowed again, and Davis stepped forward, closing the gap between them. Once that close, he couldn't stop his finger-tips from trailing down her neck.

"What are you doing?" Landry sounded skittish, delicate. Neither were adjectives he'd ever used to describe such a strong and vivacious woman. Her tongue darted out to lick the dryness from her lips; his eyes followed her subconscious move-ment. "Davis?" She asked again when he made an indistinct sound, half groan and half growl.

"This..." He paused, searching for the right word, "*thing* between us? It's starting to drive me crazy." The admission shocked Davis as much as it likely surprised Landry. His hand curled around the back of her neck until his thumb caressed the line of her jaw and the velvety lobe of her ear, until his fingers tangled with her hair. "The silly games aren't enough anymore. The flirting and teasing only make me want more."

Her eyes, clearly stricken with panic, asked — no, *begged* — a thousand questions, but she didn't utter a word.

"I promised no kissing, and as much as I'd like to break that pledge right now, a man is only as true as his word. But, Landry, you need to know this: I don't want to go back to how things were. Zane comes first, for now. When he's home with Eddie, when we know what Eddie needs as far as help with

Zane in the months to come, you and I have a few things of our own to sort through. And we're starting with a kiss."

With his hand still entwined in her hair, Davis guided her forehead to his lips. Then he wrapped her in his arms, giving her time to absorb his admission and giving himself time to steady his breathing. When she returned his hug, everything clicked back onto its axis.

"Friends?" Davis asked, leaning back to look into her face, but not relinquishing his hold.

"Always," she promised with a small smile.

"Good," he said, adding a playful wink to reassure her they'd found even footing again. "Now, let's look at those quilt blocks."

*L*andry had a tough time switching gears so quickly. More than a little, she wanted to go back to the moment when she'd been a thousand percent sure Davis would kiss her again.

He'd wanted to. She was sure of that.

And she'd wanted him to. Very much.

If he had lowered his lips to hers, she'd have welcomed them. In fact, Landry would've returned that kiss. She would've tossed her stupid No Kissing Clause out the window. She would've admitted that she thought of him all throughout the day, that every night she dreamed of a lifetime with him... that she'd fallen in love with him.

And in doing so, she'd have ruined their friendship, alienated Maree and Rhys, and disappointed Miss Sadie for messing up Davis's life.

Landry had no idea how to build a life with someone. She'd never seen how a mom and a dad raise kids together, how families function successfully. Landry accepted that as a quick study she could figure it out, in time, through trial and error. But Davis's happiness meant too much to use him as a guinea pig for her experiments and imminent mistakes. He deserved someone he could rely on immediately, not at some unknown point in the future when she got it all figured out. Davis deserved it all: the perfect wife, the happy homemaker, and a nurturing mother for his kids. She couldn't be that...certainly not then, and maybe not ever.

He'll come to his senses.

By the time Zane left to go back home with Eddie, Davis would realize that Landry wasn't worth the effort. He'd find someone else to love, and while watching it happen, witnessing their storybook life unfold, would be torture on Landry, at least the man she loved would have the life he dreamed of.

Until then, she'd soak up every moment God gifted her to spend with Davis. She'd be his friend — until it killed her.

23

When the cares of my heart are many,
your consolations cheer my soul.
Psalm 94:19

Tossing and turning in bed the next morning — when she should've been sleeping after a hectic shift at the hospital — Landry decreed that one should watch what one wishes for...

Remaining friends with Davis is definitely going to be the death of me, and my demise might not take long.

"Let's look at those quilt blocks," he'd said to her, standing in her bedroom with all sorts of chemistry zapping back and forth between them, filling the air, making it hard to breathe after their near kiss. He'd said it as though they hadn't — just seconds before — narrowly escaped a landmine.

Landry had tried to match his easy-breezy attitude, but

focusing on a quilt lesson right then had been a challenge. Using a seven-inch square, acrylic ruler, Davis had shown her how to line up the edges and measurement markings on top of a pieced quilt block. He'd made it look quite simple.

But when, on her first attempt to trim a block, the rotary blade hopped the ruler and came within millimeters of her left hand, Davis had jumped in to stop her.

"I'd rather you not slice off a finger. I'm pretty sure that would be detrimental to your budding medical career."

Then he'd moved to stand behind her. "Okay, line up the ruler," he instructed into her ear. "Set it how you like the design. Good. Now..." He placed his left hand on top of hers, which was on top of the ruler. He leaned weight onto their hands to secure the ruler, the fabric, and the cutting mat. "Pressing on that side will keep everything in place where you want it. Use your thumb to retract the blade guard on the rotary cutter."

She did as directed. "Always close the blade," he told her. "Between every single cut, so you don't accidentally drop it or grab it with the edge exposed." When she didn't answer, he shifted to look directly into her eyes. "Promise?"

She just nodded. She couldn't string words together with his left hand pressing into hers, the warmth of his body behind her, and his right hand lightly gripping hers, which held the cutter.

Together, they'd run the rotary blade along the edge of the ruler, stepped to the side of the desk as one, and cut along what had been the top edge of the quilt square. Then Davis had helped her realign the fabric and ruler so they could go through the same steps on the other two sides. One square done.

Heaven help me.

By the time they'd trimmed all of three blocks, she'd reached her wit's end.

"Okay," she announced, setting down the rotary cutter, removing her left hand from under his, and ducking beneath his arm to move to a safer distance. "I think I've got it now."

He looked at her with an odd, questioning expression.

"Thank you," she'd added, wishing for her normal voice to reappear.

"Davis? Doctor Stark?" Traise Mitchell had called out at the absolute perfect time.

"Yes?" Landry had rushed for the living room, adamantly *not* looking back to see if Davis followed.

She'd avoided close contact the rest of the afternoon and had conveniently left for work an hour early that evening. She'd not minded a successful yet active night shift at the hospital, and Landry had every intention of spending all day in her room sleeping, soaking in a hot bath, perhaps even attempting to trim quilt blocks — anything to stay out of range of one Daniel Aaron Davis. Not forever, of course...just until she could be near him without temptation overpowering good sense.

*S*leep proved evasive. Even the blissful escape of a bubble bath left too much headspace for thinking. In the end, Landry found herself back at the cutting mat.

Thankfully, her hands wobbled considerably less than they had the day before.

Surely quilting doesn't usually feel like that. Like the most romantic moment of one's life, engulfed in spicy yet subtle cologne, standing in the frame of—

Stop it, Landry Stark! Focus on what you're doing. And quit thinking.

The lecture — along with a riveting edition of a new audiobook she'd rented from the Green Hills Public Library's digital app — did the trick. When her stomach growled loud enough to be heard over the narrator's voice, the clock said 5:30…just enough time to heat a plate of leftovers for a quick bite. Then she'd be out the door for work.

In the kitchen, Zane and Davis perused papers which they'd organized on stacks of folders and textbooks.

"What's all this?"

"The governor issued a *safer at home* order today and asked schools to go digital for a few weeks. The Green Hills School District must've expected it because the teachers have been putting together these class packets for the kids to work on while they wait to go back in person," Davis explained.

"Really?" Landry commented in awe.

Landry had her doubts about how well it would work. She'd had online courses here and there throughout college; she'd attended virtual workshops and test prep sessions. Being a state-of-the-art, Level I trauma unit, Green Country Medical Center stayed on top of innovations and improvements in health care, so Landry often had videoconferences with patients and medical staff.

None of that compared to one teacher managing, instructing, and engaging a classroom of elementary school students, over software none of them knew how to use, during a time of immense stress and uncertainty.

When sitting through online lectures, she often fought the urge to check emails, doodle on her notes, or daydream. She considered herself a very focused, eager learner. How in the world were teachers expected to prevent that happening in young children?

And what about their parents and guardians? How would they go to work if their kids had to stay home? Would they be expected to fulfill their job duties virtually as well, assuming that was even possible? What if the family only had one computer? Who would use it during the day?

Green Hills was a small town off the beaten path in southeast Oklahoma. On a good day, internet service came and went, spotty and unreliable in rural areas. A few houses still didn't have home computers at all. The community believed in kids riding their bikes to school, playing sandlot ballgames in the afternoons, and walking their dogs throughout their quaint, friendly neighborhoods in the evenings. Putting it mildly, Landry feared that forcing school from home on families not prepared to homeschool might be a total and horrendous flop.

"What else did the governor say?" Landry asked.

"The order lasts until April 30. He's also mandated a four-teen-day delay on all elective surgeries."

"Oh my," Landry said with a sigh. "That's going to have major implications on scheduling, surgeon availability, follow-up care, and rehab — not to mention decreased quality of life for those waiting to have their procedures. Just because it's classified as elective doesn't mean it isn't needed. This isn't good."

Landry's appetite lessened. The worried look in Zane's eyes made it disappear completely.

"This looks fun," she said, pumping encouragement into her tone as she looked at Zane's school supplies. "Will you show me what everything is?"

"My teachers sent a different folder and spiral for each subject, see? Red is History, blue is English, purple is Reading, green is Science, and yellow is Math. The folders have hand-outs that go with the books they sent. Then, I'm supposed to do my homework in the spirals. We do a week's worth of work at a time, so each Monday, someone has to go to the school to deliver this folder and pick up the next one. I have two back-packs; one is black, and one is gray. When I have one, my homeroom teacher has the other one. When I have the gray backpack, I get to use a laptop to do online school with her. Those are the days I'll get to see my friends in our computer classroom; it's called a Zoom Room. The note from Ms. Newton said we can call her anytime, but with only one of her and twenty-four of us, we should ask our parents for help first." Zane paused. His eyes dropped to the edge of the table in front of him, and his voice fell to a whisper. "Since I don't have any parents right now, would y'all mind helping me if I need it?"

Landry's heart ached for Zane, for all the children trudging through a quagmire of learning systems yet to be defined and navigating stormy waters that adults weren't sure how to survive. Again, she thought of the teachers and couldn't imagine what they were going through. How in the world could administrators expect them to keep up with this amount of prep work, teach two weeks' worth of content in five short days, grade papers, and provide feedback? All the while juggling the layers of their personal lives. During a pandemic. It was insane.

"Of course, Z Man," Davis reassured. "I'm quite an expert in history and not too bad in math. Ja-mère is an obsessive reader. I know she'll be completely fired up to help with reading and language arts. I'm guessing Doctor Stark here isn't too shabby in science, if we get desperate."

Davis's comical understatement helped. Zane relaxed and even giggled at the joke.

"I'll have you know, Danny Boy," Landry touted, feigning an air of snobby pretension, "I left high school with a 5.0 grade point average on a four-point scale. I aced not only my own homework — in every subject — but scored an A+ or above on every assignment I ever completed for others. I finished medical school at the top—"

"Landry?" Zane interjected. "Why did you do homework for *other* people?"

Davis sealed his lips to prevent an obvious burst of laughter.

"Well, sweetie," she hedged, hunting for an acceptable answer. "When I was in high school, I worked as a special type of tutor."

"Doing assignments for other people?"

"I helped…in a rather big way," she tried to explain, determined not to lie, but equally desperate not to make it seem like doing someone else's work was okay.

Zane nodded his understanding before turning to Davis with kind empathy shining in his eyes.

"Davis, I appreciate your offer," the too-smart-for-his-own-good eight-year-old boy declared. "But I think I might go with Landry on the homework help. It sounds like she's got a lot of good experience."

Zane's gentle letdown had Davis doubling over in laughter. "Z Man, I don't blame you one bit," he hooted. "And when Miss Smarty Pants can't figure something out, you just let me know. I'm always here for you, kiddo."

Davis wiped away tears of laughter as he walked to check whatever he'd placed in the oven to heat. Landry wanted to be offended, but she couldn't stave off their good humor and joined them instead.

"What's in the oven?" she asked, glancing at the clock on the microwave in hopes she still had time to eat with the boys before she needed to leave.

"Lasagna," both boys answered with gusto.

"Frozen?"

"Of course not," Davis rebuked.

"Ja-mère made it before she left," Zane provided.

"Ah, now that sounds more like it," Landry said, shooting a coy look at Davis.

If you play with fire — with a fireman — are you bound to get burned?

She gathered plates, silverware, and napkins while Davis used potholders to take the pan to the table while Zane moved his school stacks off to one side. Landry had more questions, particularly about how the school expected the next few weeks to go, but she didn't want to ask them in front of Zane.

They had a strong support network, and they'd find a way to keep Zane on track academically. Together, they'd ensure he stayed connected socially with his friends. It wouldn't be easy, but they'd figure it out. The kids in Green Hills would get through this hiccup in history.

But what about the kids in the bigger towns and large cities? What about the kids growing up the way Landry had, for whom going to school was a survival tactic? What about the kids who weren't *safer at home* anytime, much less amidst a global crisis? What about them?

"Hey, gorgeous." Davis answered the phone on the second ring.

"Did I wake you?" Landry asked, although Davis's sleep-induced greeting had already provided the answer.

"I don't mind. You okay?"

"I'm worried."

"Okay. What about?" Davis's voice sounded much more alert and awake.

"Everything. With the delayed surgery order, the hospital had to put some staff on furlough."

"Did it affect your schedule? Will it alter your residency program?"

"Not right now, but they're not making any promises. This virus is way out of hand. You should've heard the OR and post-op nurses before they went home tonight. They were in tears. Furloughs mean no paychecks; it's called *force majeure*. Because they consider the pandemic a force of nature, neither the hospital nor the employees are to blame for the terminations. Therefore, by law, the hospital isn't responsible for paying those nurses, orderlies, and support personnel."

"You'd think medical workers would be safe from those measures," Davis said, shock clear in his tone.

"I don't think anyone is safe," Landry professed. "How on earth are kids and parents and families supposed to keep up with careers, education, households, bills, obligations, and activities with all these changes, mandates, policies, virtual schooling, layoffs, and furloughs? No one has even mentioned what this will do to the mental health and well-being of our population. It's like the world is falling apart."

Landry's voice broke on a panicked sob.

"I wish I had an answer, or the right words to say. But I do have faith. Like Mr. Mitchell said Sunday morning: faith over fear. We'll get through this. There have been pandemics, mask mandates, world-wide concerns throughout history. Humans are resilient, strong, and capable. We might not like change, but we've proven we can adapt. The future won't look like the past, and our new normal — when we get back to a state of normalcy — will be different.

"I'd imagine it'll be worse in some ways, but better in others," he continued. "Determining which things improved and which ones declined will be in the beholder's eye. For every unique situation, you'll get a unique perspective. But we *will* find balance again. And in the meantime, we have each other. We have Zane; we have my family and our friends. Whatever comes, we'll face it."

They remained quiet for a moment. Landry absorbed all he had said. She didn't feel rushed to say something back; their silence worked like a salve, peaceful and comforting as usual.

"You had them," Landry said when she had stopped crying. She even tried to inject a thread of hope in her voice.

"Had what?" he asked.

"The right words. Sweet dreams, Davis. And thank you," she added before hanging up.

24

———

It is not our differences that divide us.
It is our inability to recognize, accept,
and celebrate those differences.
Audre Lorde

Between his shift at the fire station, her night shifts at the hospital, and their dual habit of sleeping a few hours when they finished working, Davis didn't see Landry again until Friday afternoon.

She and Zane huddled over a diagram of the moon's phases.

"Are we waxing, or are we waning?" Davis asked from where he stood behind their chairs.

They both jumped a mile high, as if he'd caught them up to no good instead of dutifully studying earth science.

"The better question is, what are you doing frightening us half to death? Can't you make a little noise before you walk up on someone?" Landry accused.

"I'm not waxing or waning. I'm full, maybe about to pop," Zane whined. The unusual despondency in his voice put Davis on high alert. "My brain is full, stuffed with words I can't remember and pictures that don't make sense. Can I quit?"

Landry flashed Davis a worried look. He wasn't alone in his concern. School from home didn't officially begin until Monday, and Zane had already hit his threshold for self-paced learning. Yikes.

"Quit is a pretty strong word, Z Man. I've known you a very long time — eight full years — and I've known your dad even longer than that. I've never known the Cadell men to believe in quitting. What if we pause instead?"

"How long does a pause last?" Zane asked, at least a little interested in Davis's idea.

"I'd say at least long enough to throw on some sweats, load up in the truck, swing through the drive-through at Fish & Spoon to pick up dinner and a few brookies with ice cream on top, and drive out to Daisy Lake to watch the sun set over the water while we eat our dinner."

"Can Landry go? She's been helping me all day, so I think she needs a pause, too."

"Doctor Stark?" Davis asked.

"I'd love to join you for the drive-through portion, but I have to be at the hospital for work by 6:30 this evening."

"A good plan must be flexible on the fly," Davis told Zane. "Let's eat our dinner in the park. We'll have a picnic in the back of my truck. Then we can drop Landry at the medical center on our way to the lake. We might even send her a few photos of the moon to see if she can identify what phase it's in tonight. What do you think?"

"I like it," Zane declared. "And I can take my science folder to compare the real moon with my handout, just in case Landry gets it wrong."

"Doctor Stark?" Davis asked again.

"I like this new plan, too. Except the part about me getting my science homework wrong."

Davis couldn't help but grin at her as he corrected her statement, "*Zane's* homework, you mean."

"Yes, exactly," she said, lips pursed and nose high in the air. Miss prim and proper had Davis giggling as she peacocked down the hall to her room.

He was sitting on his bed, tying his tennis shoes, when Landry knocked lightly on his door frame.

"Hey," he greeted, aware of a pleasant warmth emanating through his chest at the sight of her. "Everything okay?"

"If y'all drop me, someone will have to pick me up in the morning. I'll just drive and follow you—"

"I don't mind coming to get you from work."

"What about Zane? It'll be early."

"We're *both* happy to come pick you up." Davis refused to relent.

"At 7 a.m.?"

"Will you be ready at 7 a.m.?"

"Probably more like 7:30, but I—"

"Then Zane and I will be waiting in the parking lot at 7:30 tomorrow morning."

He stood from the bed, grabbed the sweatshirt he'd set beside him. Before it registered what he was doing, Davis handed the navy hoodie to Landry.

"What's this?" she asked.

"It's chilly out. You might need it for our picnic," he said with a shrug.

Technically, he'd have to replace the sweatshirt since the fire department issued it to him, but Landry didn't need to know that. Also, he'd need to find another jacket for himself, since he'd just given his away. And why had he felt such a keen urge to do that? Better yet, why had a vision of Landry wearing his GHFD sweatshirt flashed through his mind?

Whatever the reasons, seeing her snuggled in his go-to hoodie had been all the reward he could've asked for. The extra-large size basically swallowed her. She had to roll the wristbands several times to find her hands. Landry should've looked like a little girl in grown-up clothing — adorable and childlike. Somehow, though, she still projected class and grace.

Davis watched Landry interact with Zane. She possessed the natural instincts of a mother, listening to Zane's litany of ideas and knowledge as if in the boy's words, she'd find the answers to all life's questions. And no matter how many questions Zane asked her, Landry answered with thoughtful patience. When Zane winced with a slight twinge of pain in his leg, she soothed without hesitation. And when he shivered from the cool evening breeze, Landry pulled Zane close to her body, sheltering him from the wind.

Her capacity to love didn't seem to register in her mind. She didn't see its rare beauty.

Davis did. And right there, in that precise moment, he vowed to open Landry's eyes to the wonder.

"*D*avis, what's your middle name?" Zane's curiosity about the moon led to a fascination with the stars, which started a discussion on constellations and their names, thus his interest in *their* names. "Landry is Landry Elaine Stark. I'm Edward Zane Cadell the third. My dad is Edward Zane Cadell, Junior, so we're exactly the same. Who are you, Davis?"

"Daniel Aaron Davis the first," he answered, extending his hand in introduction. "Nice to meet you."

Zane laughed as he shook Davis's hand.

"You're a DAD," Zane said. Caught up in his giggles, Zane didn't notice the look that passed over Davis's face. Landry saw it. Fear, panic, yearning, hope...all in the flash of a second.

"Your initials," Zane explained with cheerful exuberance. "D-A-D. You spell dad."

Davis expelled a deep breath. Although he'd assumed a casual, relaxed posture, his nerves continued to electrify the air around them. "Indeed, I do," Davis indulged as he laughed along with Zane.

An image of Davis with his children popped into Landry's mind. Tickling and entertaining an infant, when he was supposed to be changing a diaper. Wrestling and wallowing around on the floor, when he'd been asked to tuck in a toddler. Swinging a preschooler onto his shoulders, when little legs became tired. She saw in that imaginary highlight reel what an amazing father Davis would be.

With so much love to give, Davis's children would never wonder if he treasured them, would never doubt their importance or place in the world. Those kids had hit the jackpot, and they didn't even exist. Yet.

They would, though. God created Davis to love, honor, protect, guide, and give. That much was plain to see.

With a heavy heart, Landry consulted her watch.

Just as she'd suspected, it was time for her to go.

"Is there a new boy in my room?" Zane asked as they turned into the hospital parking lot.

"A girl, actually," Landry answered. She'd been unusually quiet on the drive from the park. Thinking back, Davis realized she'd helped gather their trash and fold their picnic blankets, but she had said little since they'd finished eating. "She came into the ER yesterday with appendicitis and moved into 516 after an emergency appendectomy. When I left this morning, she seemed to be feeling better already."

"How long will she be there?"

"If she continues to heal with no complications, she'll probably go home either tomorrow afternoon or Sunday morning."

"How old is she?"

"Six."

"What grade is she in?"

"Kindergarten, I believe." Landry grinned at Zane's twenty questions, but her smile held a hint of sadness, too. Davis sifted through his memory of the drive from home to the restaurant and tried remembering exactly what they said during their tailgate picnic. Something along the way weighed heavily on Landry. For the life of him, Davis didn't know what he'd missed.

"Does she know me?" Zane asked. Between his interrogation and Landry's gloom, Davis felt like a spectator at a tennis match, head on a swivel, thoughts bouncing back and forth.

"I doubt it," Landry answered. "She's not from Green Hills. Her family rented a cabin at Daisy Lake for Spring Break. That's where she was when her side started hurting, which brought her to the emergency room."

"It's a good thing they were close," Zane commented. "So you could be her doctor." Finally, Landry's smile reached her eyes.

"You, my sweet boy, might be a little biased. But thank you. I'm glad I could be her doctor, too. Now, I better get in there and check on her. I'll see you two in the morning?"

"T-minus thirteen hours," Davis confirmed after glancing at his watch. "Have a good night, Doctor Stark. And call if you get bored."

Landry smiled, nodded, and opened the door to hop out of the truck. She'd only taken two steps when Zane hollered her name.

"Landry." Zane waited until she tucked her head into the cab to see him in the backseat. "What's her name?"

"Doctor-patient confidentiality means I can't tell you that."

Zane's face fell. "But I'll ask her permission. And if she doesn't mind, I'll text you her name in just a bit, okay?" The light in his eyes returned. The boy had such a huge heart.

"Thanks! I'll keep Davis's phone by my side until you text."

"And I'll keep my phone by *my* side after that," Davis said with a chuckle. Landry smiled at each of the boys, then turned back to the hospital.

They'd barely made the fifteen-minute drive to Davis's cabin at Daisy Lake when his phone lit up with Landry's message.

- Zane, meet Mollie. Full name: Molinda Renee Graves. She is indeed in kindergarten, and I'd wager she's ahead of her class. She likes to fish and hike with her older brother (full name: Landon James Graves) who is about to turn eight and is in the second grade, just like you. They live in Dallas, Texas, but Mollie says she likes the country better than the city and hopes they will move someday. She also wishes she could meet you, wanted me to thank you for asking about her, and is wondering if you'd like to see her picture.

"Can you text her back *yes*, please?" Zane asked, handing the phone back to Davis after reading Landry's text.

"Of course," Davis answered, humored by Zane's serious tone.

They sat on the dock, waiting for the sun to set, but Zane didn't speak, or throw rocks and sticks into the lake, or share what he was thinking. Davis respected his solitude and remained silent beside the boy.

When the phone pinged to announce a new text message, Zane scrambled to see it.

"Don't drop my phone in the lake in all your haste," Davis teased. He'd laid back against the warm wooden planks, tempted to close his eyes but resisting since Zane was with him.

"She's pretty," Zane whispered.

Davis managed not to giggle as he rolled toward Zane and propped his weight on an elbow to look at the phone screen.

Zane continued to stare at the little girl.

Davis gave a low whistle.

"I'd say so, Z Man. That adorable little girl is going to be a knock-out when she grows up."

"Her eyes are different."

"Unique," Davis corrected. "Most people would describe them as almond-shaped, but that doesn't do them justice."

"Do you think her hair's too big?"

"Nope," Davis answered without hesitation. "It's amazing. Natural curls, picked to show off her personality and creativity. I've always believed that an afro — that's what Mollie's hairstyle is called — represents confidence. That she fixes her hair that way tells me Mollie is strong and sure. She knows who she is, and she's proud to be the individual, beautiful *her* that God made her to be." Davis let that sink in for a moment. He admired the way Zane absorbed and sorted information. Like a sponge, he actively soaked up the people and places and things around him. "Buddy, you might want to keep in touch with this one... She's going places in the world."

"Will you take my picture? To send back to Mollie?"

"Of course." Davis sat up and took his phone from Zane. "Switch sides of the dock with me, so the sun's in front of you instead of behind. That's it. Do you want to smile?"

"No, I'm good," Zane said, with an introspective look of a teenager or young man much older. Sweet kid had lived through a lot in his eight years.

Davis snapped the photo, then checked to see that it wasn't fuzzy or off-center.

"You know, Z Man... I'd say you're going places, too."

Zane only sighed with a slight nod in response.

"Ready for me to send it?"

"Yes, please." Zane looked back over the water. The sun had begun its descent. Truly, nothing compared to an Oklahoma sunset. They watched the orange ball drop into the water, looked up to see the stars take their place, twinkling in the dark navy sky. When the cicadas began their nightly concert of high-pitched crescendos, Zane said he wanted to go home.

Once there, Zane settled at the kitchen table with one of his school spirals.

"You good, buddy?" Davis looked over Zane's shoulder to glance at the paper in front of him.

Dear Mollie,

"Yes, sir."

"I'm going to hop through the shower, if that's okay," Davis offered, happy to give Zane some space.

"Yes, sir," he repeated, fully focused on the near-blank page in front of him.

Davis put a hand on the boy's shoulder as he walked by, impressed by his kind, friendly nature and laughing just a tad at Zane's keen eye for beauty. First, he'd been a little smitten with Paige Collins, the cute nurse tech at the hospital. Then, he'd noticed the underlying features which would turn the adorable Mollie Graves into a stunner. He'd have to warn Eddie; once hormones and adolescence set in, Edward Zane — the third — might be a little girl crazy.

Davis couldn't blame the kid. He, too, had been feeling more than a little crazy over a certain girl lately.

25

———

> *Love is the master key*
> *that opens the gates of happiness.*
> *Oliver Wendell Holmes, Sr.*

Saturday turned out to be nice and lazy.

The boys picked up Landry precisely at 7:30 a.m., at which time Zane asked Landry to run his letter up to Mollie, in case she got to go home before Landry returned that evening. From there, they circled to the donut shop to get breakfast, which they took to the youth baseball fields for another impromptu picnic. Traise met them there, and after splurging on a couple of the leftover donuts and an extra bottle of orange juice, he guided Zane through his physical therapy exercises.

For the rest of the day, they simply hung around the house... Landry slept, read a medical journal on the couch, and then napped some more before showering and leaving for work. Zane worked on building a pirate ship he'd received for his birthday from Davis's parents, practiced navigating the online conferencing platform he'd be using for school by having a "meeting" with his baseball team, and watched a new movie about two brothers in a fantasy land who were on a quest to find their dad. Davis did laundry, cleaned off the back patio, wiped down the outdoor furniture and set out the cushions he'd stored over the winter, put together sandwiches for lunch, and cooked corn dogs for dinner. He fell into bed that night with a keen sense of accomplishment and a hunch he'd just lived a day in his dad's shoes.

Davis didn't mind it; he discovered that working around the house while his family puttered between this and that brought with it a satisfaction he'd never known. For years, Davis had bounced from date to date, ensuring relationships never grew serious, trying his best to avoid entanglements, because being with someone else had always felt like a noose tightening around his neck.

In the ten days since they'd moved in, Davis had settled into routines with Landry and Zane. It happened easily — organically — without many changes or too much effort.

Perhaps he'd been trying too hard before. Had he fought God's plan all along? Maybe that's why it had felt as though *his* person didn't exist, making him believe that he'd never have a love, a partnership, and a forever like his parents.

Or possibly, he'd been attempting to find those things with the wrong person.

Son, you're trying to fit a square peg into a round hole.

His dad had said those words a thousand times.

With Landry — and with Zane, for as long as he needed to stay — Davis's world fit just right.

Thank you, Lord.

"Hello," Davis said, opening the front door for Landry to enter. "And goodbye." With the duffle bag he carried back and forth to the fire station on his shoulder, he scooted to one side of the doorway to allow Landry space to walk under his arm, which still held the door open.

"Oh, well. Hi," she answered, twirling to face him as she moved under his arm. "You're off?"

"I thought about trying to trade shifts so I could go to church with you and Zane this morning, but I figured I might need to ask for that favor down the road, so I'm saving it for later. I'll be back in the morning."

Then he gave her a quick kiss and walked away.

The reality of what he'd just done hit Davis like a ton of bricks.

He turned back to face Landry, who stood frozen in place.

"I am so sorry," Davis said in genuine apology. "I don't know what happened. I didn't mean to kiss you. Really, I didn't plan that. I'm so—"

"It's okay," she insisted. The stricken terror on Landry's suddenly pale face said otherwise. She gazed at him for a long moment before attempting — yet failing — to smile. "Have a great shift," she told the floor as she shut the door.

You're an idiot. A fool. A complete imbecile.

Kissing Landry goodbye had happened as naturally as inhaling oxygen. But she'd declared a No Kissing Clause, and he'd agreed to it. Given his word. Then he'd gone back on it.

What a heel.

Davis continued to beat himself up over the slip-up all morning. He could barely eat when his crew sat down to lunch, and he'd declared himself the world's worst human by midafternoon.

Lost in self-loathing, Davis didn't see Landry step onto the basketball court behind the firehouse, where he'd been dribbling, shooting, and muttering reprimands for almost half an hour.

He missed an easy post shot from the paint — bricked it, at that. The rebound ricocheted off the rim at the speed of light, just outside Davis's reach. When it didn't bounce on the concrete behind him, Davis pivoted to see why.

He stopped dead in his tracks.

"Competing with ghosts?" she questioned.

Landry should've looked out of place, holding the scuffed and aged basketball while standing in gold high heels, adorned with fake gemstones and pearls from the tip of the skinny heel to the arch of her foot, as though she'd stepped in rhinestones, and magic or magnetism made them stick.

She'd not yet changed after church and embodied an exquisite, modern-day interpretation of an angel. The calf-length, layered skirt of flowing, ballerina-pink material — tulle, he'd heard it called — and the long-sleeved, crisp, white button-down Oxford shirt that she'd tied at her waist matched her personality: smart, tidy, and sharp without sacrificing elegance, grace, and a touch of playfulness. Tendrils of her hair, too heavy to be held back for long, had escaped the bun she'd tied on top of her head. Fighting the urge to test their silky texture brought sweat to Davis's forehead.

Maybe she wouldn't notice his desire, since sweat from his basketball exertion already drenched his clothes.

Landry dribbled once and shot the ball from behind the arc. Swish.

Davis recovered from his stupor to shag the ball, toss it back to her, and answer her question in one smooth motion.

"Yeah, I think I might be," he admitted with a wry chortle.

"Did you need me? Don't get me wrong; I'm thrilled you're here," he scurried to explain. "But, Landry," Davis paused. "Why are you here?"

"They canceled church. Well, not canceled— The service took place virtually."

"Y'all didn't go?"

"No, not to the building. But Zane and I went over to Miss Sadie's and watched with her. She was fretting about how to make the internet work, where to log on to watch the live stream, and what to do if the computer didn't work. Serving as the audio/visual tech was easy for me, but stressful for Miss Sadie."

"You look awful nice for church in Miss Sadie's family room."

"I guess it's a habit now to dress up on Sunday mornings. Give me a few weeks; if online church lasts long, I'll likely be singing on the couch in my pajamas."

"That's a sight I'd pay to see."

She shot the ball. Another swoosh. Davis passed it back, and Landry caught it without taking her eyes from his.

The wheels in her head turned; machinations of thoughts reflected in her eyes. Davis stood patiently, giving her time to string together what she needed to say.

Looking down, she dribbled the ball, picked it up in hesitation, and then dribbled again. She walked along the scraped and faded court lines painted long ago behind the engine bays, the bouncing ball a comfortable extension of her movements. On her second pass around the free throw line and arc at the top of the key, she started talking again.

"Mr. Mitchell's sermon hit home today," she told him. "It's funny how they always do. First, he said that prayers are with the medical community. I felt like he prayed specifically for me. I cried. Silly, huh? But I couldn't help it. The tears just started falling.

"Then he taught from Matthew chapter eight," Landry went on. "Building on last week's message of focusing on faith instead of fear, today's lesson questioned how we respond in times of great storms. It was fantastic. I guess the silver lining of online church is that we can rewatch the videos anytime we want."

Mr. Mitchell's words touched her heart. Davis put value in whatever affected Landry; she needed to know that what mattered to her also mattered to him.

"Mr. Mitchell said we're called to kneel down in prayer and rise up in our response," Landry continued.

"Sounds like a great lesson. I'll watch it tomorrow morning as soon as I get home," Davis told her.

"Lots of ladies from church have been sewing masks for frontline workers." Landry switched gears quickly. But he'd been paying close attention and had no trouble keeping up with her train of thought. "Maree volunteered to deliver them around town this afternoon. Zane and I are helping. He's with Rhys, enjoying another VIP tour of the station."

Landry halted her steps, stopped dribbling, and faced Davis. "I wanted to talk to you."

Her stoic voice sounded much too serious for Davis's liking. She looked at the backboard and tossed up the ball. Three shots, three baskets. Not bad.

When the basketball fell from the net and into Davis's hands, he didn't pass it. Instead, he tucked it on one hip and walked to stand less than a foot in front of her.

"Landry, I'm so sorry for this morn—"

She placed a finger to his mouth to silence him. Then she replaced it with her lips.

Davis held himself in check, resisting a clawing need to take Landry in his arms and deepen the kiss. More sweat beads popped along his hairline.

"I stink," he announced in a low, scratchy voice when she broke their contact but didn't move away from him.

"It's okay," Landry said softly, reassuring him with a sweet smile. "I'm not going to ravish you; the No Kissing Clause is still in effect."

Davis dropped the basketball and took hold of her arm, slid his hand down the satiny skin until his hand grasped hers.

"Why?" He'd meant for his question to be light and casual. It wasn't.

The rapid pulse in her neck proved she felt it, too, that insane yearning to be in the same room, close enough to touch...to talk and encourage and support each other...to share their lives.

"Don't say Zane," Davis half begged, half warned. "We're doing a great job with Zane. He's happy. Understandably, he's worried about Eddie. But getting to talk to him on the phone a few times has been huge. Zane's unsure about starting school tomorrow, but that's to be expected, too. For all that's going on in his world, I'd say Zane is doing amazingly well. And in part, that's because *we're* doing amazingly well with him. He loves us, individually *and* as a unit. Zane knows he's loved in return and taken care of. That doesn't change whether I kiss you goodbye in the morning or not."

"No, it doesn't," Landry agreed, far too easily.

When she looked up at him with a tragically sad smile, a pit of dread fell to the bottom of his stomach. Davis searched her eyes, which grew glossy with moisture.

"I'm leaving," she said.

The beads of perspiration on Davis's brow transformed into a cold sweat all over his body.

"What?" he gasped.

"There's going to be a national press conference tomorrow. The governor of New York is going to issue a nationwide plea for medical workers to help them with the staggering influx of

COVID-19 cases." She spoke calmly. Meanwhile, a maelstrom erupted in Davis's heart. Somehow, he managed to be still and listen.

"I received a pre-press release email through the medical school, encouraging my cohort to accept that call if we're able. They assured us that the rotations will count toward residency requirements. They didn't say it directly, but reading between the lines, it's clear that stepping up to assist during this medical crisis will be favorably looked upon in the future.

"I didn't give it much thought last night... I'm not terribly worried about pumping up my resume," Landry admitted. "Maybe it's arrogance, but I like to think my work speaks for itself. But then, that sermon happened. Mr. Mitchell spelled it out for me. Yes, kneeling in prayer is important — a necessity. But we must also rise up. He listed ways the congregation, the community, even the world, can be there for one another during the storm and throughout the extraordinary, uncertain days to come.

"Davis, I can't make meals for the neighbors or bake pies and cobblers for the workers— by the way, Miss Sadie sent a peach cobbler and two apple pies, which are in the kitchen. I set the whipped cream in the fridge and the ice cream in the freezer."

Davis couldn't help but smile at her inclusion of that aside. Her adorable rambling tangents might seem inconsequential, but in reality, they acted as windows into her soul, again pinpointing the things most important to her. Knowing how he loved food, and especially desserts, she'd wanted to be sure Davis didn't miss out. Landry loved him; she just hadn't accepted it yet.

"I can't sew masks or decorate get-well cards for the sick," she said. "But I *can* treat the sick. Thankfully, those people aren't here in Green Hills. You said it the other day: a tiny town that's off the beaten path of a flyover state isn't likely to be inundated with the virus. That's a wonderful, fabulous thing. But half the positive tests in the country — the *entire* United States — are in the state of New York. And half of those are in New York City. The email I received said around thirty-six *thousand* people have already tested positive with the virus. Those are just the cases they know about, those with official confirmation. I'm needed there."

Davis wanted to argue that he needed her in Green Hills, too. He wanted to beg and plead for her to stay. But he couldn't. Landry's compulsion to help others made her *Landry*; that essential need defined who she was and made her tick. He loved her exactly that way.

The truth settled into place with a click of finality, like a key in a lock, made only for one another. They could function correctly *only* in tandem.

"It's hard to fathom those numbers, hard to imagine what the doctors, nurses, and hospitals are facing there. You'll be a tremendous blessing to them, for sure."

A smile, less sad and more determined, bloomed on her beautiful face. Had she been afraid to tell him? Had she thought he could do anything *other* than support her decisions?

He needed to make his feelings clear before she left for New York.

"And here I thought Jinx, and Scotty, and Traise were my competition," he teased, tugging her hand playfully, drawing her back to where he stood. "Now I learn there are tens of thousands of people vying for your attention." Again, his voice turned husky when he'd been going for flirtatious.

"Jinx? And Scotty? And Traise? Your competition?" Landry considered the clouds above them. "Maybe they are," she bantered back. "All three are very sweet, always offering to help me, or feed me, or entertain me. Aaand..." Landry over-emphasized her words. She lifted an eyebrow at Davis in a challenge. "They are *pretty nice* to look at."

"Tall, dark, and handsome?" Davis wrapped her in his sweaty embrace, no longer caring that she looked and smelled like heaven, whereas he did not.

"Mmm— Without a doubt," his vixen agreed in a sassy, saucy voice of pretend longing. Then Landry pulled her arms from under the pin of his hug and wrapped them around his neck. She lifted even higher onto her tip toes — which wasn't easy in those sexy stilettos — to look directly into Davis's eyes. The way Landry leaned into him did crazy things to Davis's heart rate. "Too bad I've developed a thing for sandy blond, ridiculously goofy, and completely incorrigible."

---

26

*Lying to ourselves
is more deeply ingrained
than lying to others.*
Fyodor Dostoyevsky

The days between Landry dropping the bomb that she was going to New York and her actual leaving flew by.

Saying the words out loud to Davis on Sunday afternoon had solidified her decision to go. She *had* to go.

Monday through Friday, Landry and Zane worked side by side at the kitchen table. Landry spent the days filling out online forms, submitting applications and credentials, reviewing schedules and responsibilities, reading policies, and researching housing options in New York City. Zane wiggled and flounced endlessly, but still completed his spelling and math assignments for the week and got halfway through a social studies packet, which included diagramming and coloring a series of maps. He also managed to sculpt a collection of pipe cleaner constellations and compare them to the night sky to find each set of stars. Last but not least, they started a family book project, together...

When Davis had emerged from his room for lunch on Monday, he admired their set up. Then he disappeared into the garage. Landry and Zane wondered about the sounds of rummaging and tools clanking Davis created, until he returned with a pencil tucked behind one ear, a decent-sized whiteboard tucked under one arm, and carrying a tape measure, a hammer, and two nails. He measured, made pencil marks on the wall, pounded nails, and hung the whiteboard. Finally, using dry-erase markers in an array of colors, Davis made a restaurant sign on the whiteboard that read *Classe de Cuisine*...The Kitchen Classroom.

"This way you can hop out of your chair when you feel restless." Davis modeled his vision for the hop and pretended to be writing and solving a thought-provoking, life-altering equation on the board. "And see all these dry erase markers you get to use?" He held out a basket Jacqueline sent for Zane, which accompanied several others that held crayons, colored pencils, regular markers, snacks, paper, rulers, and then some. "You name it, it's here. Mom might've gone a little overboard on gathering school supplies for you, buddy. But, hey, math problems will look much cooler in color!"

By Friday, Davis had "borrowed" a wooden bookcase from Jinx, whose legendary woodworking skills could only be topped by the mystery barn, set out in the middle of nowhere. Only Jinx could locate the treasure trove, which housed hundreds of jaw-dropping pieces of furniture that he or his grandad had made.

Sturdy and made of strong cedar, the bookcase weighed a lot. It took both Davis and Jinx to carry in the tall shelving unit. They placed it on a windowless wall at the end of the eat-in kitchen, and oddly enough, the grain pattern, knotting, and stain matched the china cabinet left by Mrs. Hartley's family.

"It's magnificent," Landry said in awe once the guys stepped back from adjusting it to the center of the wall. Saved from a saw, the raw front edge of each shelf — at least an inch and a half thick — followed a natural wave. Void of delicate trims, the unique shelves drew the eye and provided all the decoration needed to make the bookcase a real showpiece.

"It's heavy!" Davis added, hands on knees, doubled over in theatrics.

"I'm pretty sure you two were up to the task," Landry replied, dismissing his dramatic appeal for sympathy.

"It's big," Zane commented. "I only have a couple of books from school."

"No worries, there, Z Man. Ja-mère will have those shelves filled in no time — trust me," Davis laughed.

"Did you make it?" Zane asked Jinx.

"I did," Jinx answered.

"How?" Filled with wonder and grandeur, Zane's eyes opened to the size of saucers.

"My grandad, Duke, taught me."

"How'd you make the edges look like that?" Zane's voice filled with equal amounts of interest and awe.

"It's called a live edge, and I can't take any credit for it. The tree did that all by itself. Machines and hand tools are used to plane the boards, cut them to length, and sand them before finishing. For a live edge, I use the tools on only five edges of each shelf: the top and bottom of the wood plank to make it smooth for your books, then the back and the two sides to make it fit in the frame, which is called casing. But the sixth edge — the front — keeps its original shape and all the natural characteristics the wood took on as it grew."

"In the wild," Zane marveled with even bigger eyes.

"Yes," Jinx chuckled. "Exactly how it grew in the wild."

"Nice geometry lesson. I like how you slipped that in," Landry commended.

"You've heard the old adage measure twice, cut once? Well, Grandad might've been the one who started it. He could've been an architect or an engineer, the way his mind worked." A light glowed in Jinx when he talked about his granddad.

"Did something happen to your grandad? Did he die?" They barely heard Zane's quiet questions.

"No, Grandad's okay. It's just that his brain has developed a sickness; it makes his mind give out sooner than his body. Too soon," Jinx's light dimmed.

"So, he's not the same now?"

"That's a good way to put it, Zane. I love him just as much as I would if he was healthy, and I know he still loves me. He just can't display his feelings, or accomplish many tasks, or function the same now. Dementia stole those abilities from Grandad, but he'll always be Grandad. Always."

"Do you get to see him?" Zane had an endless list of questions. Luckily, Jinx seemed willing and happy to field them.

"Before COVID, I saw him every single day. I'd go by after closing up the hardware store — Grandad's shop. I'd tell him about the customers that stopped in that day, share the projects they'd told me about, and describe new tools and gadgets that companies send for us to try out, in hopes we'll want to sell their products in the store. Grandad doesn't speak, but I'm certain he understands elements of what I'm telling him. That old business is in his heart and in his bones. I'm sure he can still feel it there. The only things Grandad loved more than the hardware store and all his customers were God and Gran. And possibly me," Jinx said with a humorous shrug. His joke light-ened the tension and soothed the sadness evoked by Alzheimer's discussions. Such was the roller coaster ride fami-lies living with the disease experienced...ups, downs, smiles, tears, good days, bad days...until there were no days left.

"Does he have the virus? Is that why you don't see him every day anymore?"

"Oh, no. I don't think anyone in Green Hills has it. Have we had any positive cases, Landry?"

"No," she answered, intent on reassuring Zane. "No one here, but we've seen how outbreaks have spread elsewhere, particularly in the larger cities. Medical facilities are struggling. That's why I'm going to New York to help. The Green Country Medical Center and all the local doctors' offices are adopting the same protocols being used across the world to reduce the risk that patients could get sick from someone who didn't realize they carried it. Unfortunately, that means visitors can't enter the medical facilities, including the care center where Duke lives."

"At all?" Zane's sweet, childlike tone turned to angry accusation.

"There are a few special instances where they'll allow someone in the hospital with a patient, but mostly, guests are denied entry right now. It's for the patients' protection. And it's the best way we know to keep the medical staff and workers safe, so they can keep helping those who are sick." Landry tried to explain, to help Zane understand *why*, but even as an adult and a medical professional, it broke Landry's heart to imagine families going through emergencies, milestones, surgeries, treatments, and end-of-life care without their loved ones.

"That's not fair," Zane burst out. "Patients need their family. They need to see them and talk to them and be with them!" Tears filled his eyes. Color flushed his cheeks. "That's wrong. They can't just take someone's family away from them. They can't!" he yelled.

Zane had never raised his voice or thrown a tantrum around Landry and Davis before. Landry figured he was due.

"I'll check on him," Davis offered when Zane stormed from the room.

"Sorry. I didn't mean to upset Zane."

"You didn't. Going through a medical ordeal these days is a

lousy experience for anyone. Zane's a bright kid; he can't help but see similarities to his own situation with Eddie. It's a scary time."

"And you're walking into the worst of it. How long will you be gone?" Jinx asked Landry.

"I've signed on for a five-week rotation beginning April 12. I leave on the ninth."

"That's next Thursday," Jinx pointed out. "So soon? I've heard it's a madhouse there."

Landry forced a brave face. She'd heard the same and didn't know what to expect or what she'd find when she arrived.

"They've assigned me to the Jacob K. Javits Convention Center in Manhattan, temporarily being called the Javits New York Medical Station, or JNYMS. They transformed it into a makeshift COVID-only hospital. It's just one of the field hospitals needed," Landry admitted. "The numbers are staggering."

"You'll be a gift," Jinx said with a kind smile. "But those two are going to miss you. A lot." Jinx tilted his head in the direction where the boys had disappeared.

Landry followed his gesture and looked down the hall. She watched particles dance in the light filtering into the hallway from the blue bedroom where Davis had trailed Zane. No additional fireworks came from the room, so Landry guessed Zane's temper had been short-lived. She trusted Davis to have just the right words; he had broad shoulders, perfect for leaning or even crying on when needed.

Perhaps *too* comfortable.

A few weeks of distance might be just the thing Landry needed to regain her perspective. She'd enjoyed sharing life's load a little too much. Counting on Davis came too naturally. Being with him — kissing those soft lips of his — felt too right.

Landry needed to take a step back, re-establish the boundaries of self-preservation she had constructed, shore up the walls she lived safely within.

And lived within quite successfully, she might add. Testing for her GED, getting into college, graduating from medical school, and fulfilling her residency requirements were big accomplishments, and she'd made them happen on her own.

She couldn't relinquish her independence. Landry watched her mom do it repeatedly, and she would never permit herself to live that way. She didn't need Davis or his strong shoulders. Or his kisses. She didn't need anyone. She'd been called to serve others as a healer, not as a wife or a mother. Being a doctor meant more than anything else.

It's who I am. It's all I'm supposed to be.

The mental pep talk sounded good in theory, but it did little to diminish the invisible yet tangible pull she felt to go to the boys. To be where they were.

"Yeah," she replied, hoping Jinx didn't notice the twinge of sadness and regret in her voice. "I'm going to miss them, too."

27

*The most dangerous adversary
is the one you underestimate.
The Fountains of Silence
by Ruta Sepetys*

"Why can we eat lunch with Davis at the fire station, but I can't play with my friends?" Zane had asked the same question forty different ways throughout Saturday morning. A week into school, church, and life, all "at home," and the poor boy was done.

"We're in his bubble. Since we're around each other at home, then it's okay for him to sit outside with us at the fire-house," she explained as she drove to the station. They'd made a plan to share lunch with Davis outside on the basketball court while he was on his shift.

"Then why did Mr. Malone get to come over yesterday?" Zane's tone bordered on whiny. He missed his friends.

"With his store closed as a non-essential business, Jinx hasn't been around anyone. He's only been in there in the hardware store, his woodworking shop, and his house, where he lives alone. Since he hasn't come into contact with anyone, it was safe for him to help Davis with your new bookcase."

"Why did he have to close his store? And if it's closed, why does he go there every day?" Ah, the curious minds of babes.

"The hardware store is closed to the public. If someone needs something, they call in their order, or send Jinx an email. Then he leaves it on the bench in front of the store for the customer to pick up, or Jinx delivers the order to his customer and leaves it on their front porch. It's the only way shop owners can continue to provide the goods and services that people depend on."

"So, now Jinx is in our bubble because he was in our house yesterday?"

"Yes, I guess that's true."

"And Ja-mère is in our bubble because she stays with me when you and Davis are both at work at the same time."

"Also true."

"And since Pop Davis lives with Ja-mère, then he's in our bubble, too."

"Okay."

"We had lunch with Miss Sadie just a few days ago..." Zane's momentum gained speed. "Maree and Rhys were there, too. Also, Rhys and Davis are firefighters together, so they're all in our bubble."

"Hmmm," Landry murmured, careful to avoid saying anything that Zane could construe as an agreement until he revealed his endgame. She parked the car, and Zane scrambled out to continue his speech.

"You know who else must be in our bubble?"

"Who?"

"Mr. Sampson."

Zane's strategy came into focus, clear as a bell.

Roddy Sampson worked on Davis's crew out of Station #2. Roddy and his wife, Juliet, had a son named Ryder. Landry first met the family at Max and Janie Lyn's surprise reception the previous fall. Roddy had helped set up the barbecue smokers, yard games, and kids' play area. Juliet played in Miss Sadie and Maree's Mah Jongg group, who provided all the desserts for the reception. She'd met them a second time at Zane's belated and impromptu birthday dinner at the Fish & Spoon, where Ryder and Zane had stayed side-by-side the entire afternoon.

Landry had heard so much about Ryder in the past few days, she could've written his biography. Like Zane, Ryder had lived in Green Hills for all of his eight years, had Ms. Newton for homeroom, and thought the world both began and ended with baseball. The two boys even played on the same kid-pitch team. In terms of BFFs, Ryder and Zane were best buddies.

"And if Mr. Sampson is in our bubble," Zane continued on, full steam ahead, "then Ryder is in our bubble because he lives with his dad, just like I live with Davis."

The exuberance in Zane's expression yelled, *Voila!*

"Let me guess," Landry said, trying to smother her smile and congratulating herself for being one step ahead in planning their afternoon. "If you and Ryder are in the same bubble, then you figure that you and Ryder should be able to quarantine together?"

"We don't want to quarantine," Zane said, looking at her as if she'd lost her mind. "We want to play."

"We'll see," Landry replied.

"*We'll see.* What's that mean?" Zane asked, still looking as though Landry was crazy.

"It's mom-speak for *my way or the highway*, Z Man. If you're getting *we'll see*'ed, I'm sorry to tell you, buddy... It ain't good." Davis contributed while walking toward them from the open garage door of the engine bay.

"You're not helping," Landry said, hands on hips.

Her air of authority proved useless when Davis winked at

her and proceeded to kiss the tip of her nose. "What are we seeing about?" he asked.

"I'm bored at home," Zane said, now in a full-fledged whine. "I want to play with—"

"Zane!" A youthful voice bellowing his name stopped Zane mid-whine.

"Ryder?"

Zane beamed at Davis and turned to meet Ryder half-way. Not yet cleared to run, but down to the final two weeks of his physical therapy, Zane moved rather efficiently across the basketball court. He made his way to his friend in a hop, a skip, and only one hobble.

"I arranged this play date, yet somehow you're the hero." Landry shook her head in disbelief while Davis grinned from ear to ear.

"*Date?* I like the sound of that," he teased. "Nice shirt— I like that, too," he said, commenting on the same navy blue GHFD sweatshirt he'd loaned her for their truck picnic.

Landry wore the hoodie with a pair of skinny jeans, faded to a light blue from years of washing, and her oldest, most beloved pair of tennis shoes. She'd piled her hair on top of her head in a very messy bun. The silky strands refused to stay put, and her ponytail holder had quickly lost its battle against the weight of her long, straight hair. She hadn't bothered with makeup, besides a little mascara to balance her big brown eyes and thick eyebrows. Casual relaxation had been her theme for the day.

The unmistakable look of appreciation in Davis's eyes, the slight lift of one of his eyebrows, and the knowing half-grin on his soft lips caused Landry to blush.

"This is the softest, most comfortable sweatshirt I've ever worn," she confessed. "I promise, I'm going to wash it and give it back before I leave for New York. I just wanted to wear it one more time."

"It looks good on you. Keep it. Take it to New York, so you don't forget me while you're gone." Davis waggled his eyebrows and gave her a playfully smug, conspiratorial smile, daring her to try.

She would never — could never — forget him.

Before she had time to respond to his joke, Davis opened the massive basket Landry had set on the edge of the concrete patio. "Mmmm, this smells great. That garlic bread has to mean Italian. My favorite! Pasta, salad, bread? It looks incredible! Who made it?"

"You'll be lucky to get a plate at the rate you're going," Landry threatened, swatting his hands away from the basket.

Davis simply snatched her around the waist and pulled her to his chest.

"I'd be happy to feast on—"

"Daniel Aaron Davis, you better stop right there before you get yourself into trouble."

Landry tried to sound stern, but his good mood proved contagious. Her arms found their way around his neck. She smiled up into his shining eyes. When the brain sent one message and the heart another, the brain didn't stand a chance.

"I think I'm already in pretty deep," he admitted. His playful tone had turned husky and raw. "You, Doctor Stark, are one hundred percent trouble." He looked at her lips; she couldn't stop herself from nibbling the lower half. Her pulse raced, waiting to see Davis's next move.

Landry wanted to appear unfazed, in control. Was hoping to look sexy and irresistible asking too much?

He moved slowly, which made Landry question where she stood. Anticipation stole the oxygen from her lungs.

"Davis?" she whispered, need and longing heavy in the air.

"I'm here," he promised with a whisper as his lips took hers.

"Ewww," Zane and Ryder gagged. "They're kissing."

"Aww, let 'em kiss," Roddy said, carrying two folding tables onto the basketball court. Juliet unfolded two chairs at each table and unfurled a quilt for the boys to sit on together. Then she walked to Landry's picnic basket to explore the contents.

"It's Luca's," Juliet exclaimed with satisfaction, taking containers and plasticware from the basket.

"Yep, y'all just keep on a-kissin', so there's more for the rest of us," Roddy informed.

Davis groaned and moved his lips from Landry's just enough to form words.

"I can't let that happen," he said, woeful but insistent. He rested his forehead against Landry's, closed his eyes, and caught his breath. Landry used the time to rein in her nerves.

What was she thinking? Kissing him with absolute abandon positively defined the *opposite* of the strict instructions she'd spelled out in her head not twenty-four hours earlier. They had a No Kissing Clause for a reason, and she'd best put it back into place.

Landry had a sneaking suspicion she'd underestimated just how difficult walking away from Davis would be.

28

Open your heart — open it wide;
someone is waiting outside.
Mary Engelbreit

nderestimated was the understatement of the year.

Driving away from Davis's house, with him and Zane waving from the front yard, nearly broke Landry. They'd been taking care of Zane for three weeks — only twenty-one days. So how could it hurt so much to say goodbye to him?

And why did leaving Davis feel like driving a jagged blade through her heart?

It took two hours to stop crying, and another two to stop obsessing, questioning, doubting, and arguing with herself.

When she stopped for lunch in Springfield, Missouri, she'd pulled herself together. Someone might've questioned her red-rimmed, puffy eyes or heard the scratchy rawness of her throat if she'd eaten inside a restaurant. But as COVID would have it, a fast-food drive-through was her only option, so she neither spoke to nor saw anyone besides a voice inside a speaker and a masked cashier behind two sheets of plexiglass.

No longer a boohooing maniac, Landry wished she could've enjoyed exploring the town's boutiques, stretching her legs in a couple of antique shops, or even browsing a quilt store to buy some pretty fabric for Miss Sadie. Sadly, they all had *Closed for COVID-19* signs. Surely, they'd be past this pandemic soon. Otherwise, what would remain when the world returned to normal?

The future won't look like the past, and our new normal — when we get back to a state of normalcy — will be different.

Davis's words rang in Landry's mind. What did her future hold?

*A*nother three and a half hours got Landry to St. Louis, where she secured a room at a reputable hotel for the night.

Upon arriving at the hotel, Landry had been told to call the front desk. Then she had to wait in her car until a clerk came to take her temperature and check her for signs of the virus. Once she'd passed those tests, they required that she answer a questionnaire, declaring her recent travel routes and promising once more that she hadn't coughed, sneezed, or hiccuped in at least five days.

The concerned citizen in her understood the hoops people had to jump through to get where they were going, but the medical professional in her couldn't help but recognize the futile silliness of timing hiccups in the fight to stop a global pandemic.

Of course, the hotel needed to follow local guidelines, which followed state mandates, which followed national policies, which followed the advice of the highest-ranking medical professionals in the world. And they were doing the best they could with what they knew. Of course, no one really knew much, and what they thought they knew seemed to change daily, if not hourly. When in doubt, they had no choice but to do anything and everything that might be helpful at flattening the curve of positive cases.

Looking at it that way helped Landry maintain a benevolent perspective throughout the hour and eight minutes it took her to check in, obtain a key for her room, and wait for her turn to ride the elevator to the second floor...because the stairwells were closed to prevent too many bodies being in the enclosed space at once. A good, law-abiding, kind, and helpful human, Landry agreed the protocols were important and necessary.

But good grief, she'd have been sleeping in her car for the night if she'd admitted to sneezing when she looked into the sunny sky at the last gas station.

Now, where was the sense in that?

Landry continued muttering to herself as she opened the door, set the room key on a nightstand, and fumbled for the light switch. Once the lamp illuminated the room, she froze.

Plastic sheeting covered most of the surfaces. The television remote lay sealed in a zippered sandwich baggie. One bath towel, one hand towel, and one washcloth sat on the bathroom counter. Signs asking guests to wear a mask at all times on hotel property hung taped to every wall, window, and mirror.

Maybe it wasn't safe to stay in public places. Was the room truly sanitized? What if she carried the coronavirus into the temporary hospital in New York? Would she harm more people than she helped?

How—

Her cell phone rang, interrupting her brief meltdown.

"Hello?"

"Landry? Are you okay?" Davis must've heard the distress in her voice when she answered the phone. He'd flipped into worry mode from the way she said one five-letter word. How had he heard so much in so little?

"Yes," Landry sighed. "Just a little freak-out moment, but I'm better now." She took a cleansing breath and released one more sigh. "Whew, yes... Much better."

"What had you spooked?"

"I was being impatient, irritated by the new normal, and then it hit me why a new set of rules exists. We've been playing at protocols in Green Hills, wearing masks when we think about it. We do school and church at home, but then when the weekend hits, we let the kids play together outside. We follow the essence of the guidelines, but we have yet to see why they are there.

"It's a real thing," she continued. "They take it seriously here; they have to. The truth of that got to me for a second. I'm fine now. How are you and Zane? How was dinner? Did the frozen casserole defrost in time? What did Traise say at Zane's PT appointment? Did Zane already take his shower for the night? Was there any swelling in his leg? He's been running around the backyard a lot the last few afternoons; I hope he didn't overdo it. And did he finish his chapter of *Flat Stanley* already? It's the last one in the first book of the series. I was trying to get checked-in and up to my room in time to read with y'all, but that process was just—"

"Hey— Gorgeous," Davis said, cutting her off. "Deep breaths. Everything's okay. We're doing great here, and you're where you need to be. Your room will be just fine for the night, and tomorrow night, you'll go through it all over again — one last night on the road. Then you'll settle into the hotel in New York, and you'll go kick COVID's— well, Z Man is here with me, and I think you know what I mean. And Landry, just like I said this morning before you left, I—"

"We!" Zane corrected in the background.

"*We* will be right here waiting when you get home. Until

then, we'll be on this end of the phone anytime you need us. Now, let's see where our friend Flat Stanley's headed tonight."

Landry kicked off her shoes, settled onto the bed, and pulled out her copy of the book Ms. Newton assigned for a family reading project. They'd found Landry a copy at the Green Hills Library, and when Zane had explained to Mr. Quinn that Landry would be late returning the book because she had to fight COVID-19 in New York City, the librarian, known for being quiet, reserved, and a strict rule follower, had said it would be an honor to send Stanley Lambchop to New York and even provided a large white envelope, padded and stamped with *Air Mail* in bold red ink for Stanley to travel in.

"No rush bringing him back when you return," Mr. Quinn had reassured. "Perhaps you'd be willing to share more about your adventures to our Bookworms reading club, when things settle down a bit?"

"I'd love to," Landry had promised.

"I want to be a Bookworm. Can I come, too?" Zane had asked.

Landry looked forward to the day when children's story hour and youth book club meetings resumed, when the Busy Bees quilt guild and weekly Mah Jongg games filled the Green Hills Public Library again.

Our new normal will be different.

Landry prayed some of the old normal would make it through to the other side.

"An air pump? That's all it took to fix Stanley? He and Arthur should've tried that in the beginning!" Zane laughed out loud at how the book finished.

"I have a feeling Stanley's flat days aren't quite over," Davis said.

Landry soaked up their rich voices over the phone. They sounded so close, but they felt so far.

You've been gone ten hours; pull it together, Stark.

"What's next in the project?" Landry asked the boys.

"I get to color and cut out my own Flat Stanley; I'm going to do that tomorrow. Want me to send you a picture of him on your phone?" Landry loved hearing Zane's joy over reading adventures. Even when her childhood had been its worst, Landry had found comfort and escape in books. They provided the best adventures and the most loyal friends.

"I would appreciate that very much, Zane. I can't wait to see how you decide to fashion Stanley. Have a wonderful day; I'll let y'all know when I'm off the road and finished driving for day two. Good night, boys." Landry blamed fatigue for the thickness of emotion, which caused a quiver in her voice.

When did I become a blubbering water pot?

Immediately, a text chimed on her cell phone:

- I mean it… Call me. Anytime. Good night, beautiful.

A tear slipped down her cheek.

That's when: when I let Daniel Davis into my heart.

29

I shall pass this way but once;
any good that I can do
or any kindness I can show
to any human being;
let me do it now.
Etienne de Grellet

"Danny, where have you been?"

"Mom, you sent me out for a run," he answered with a laugh. "Remember? When I got home from work, you literally said, *Danny, you'll sleep better if you go out for a run.* I believe you also mentioned something about breakfast waiting for me when I returned."

"You left your phone here. We've been trying to find you for almost an hour." Jacqueline's flustered tone turned Davis's blood cold. His eyes dashed around the kitchen and living room until they settled on Zane, happy as a lark, making short work of a tall stack of pancakes.

Landry.

A memory flashed through his mind. Two years earlier, their fire crew heard a dispatch over the radio and instantly Rhys knew, without a shadow of a doubt, that Maree was injured. The agony of responding to a call to find a loved one needing help had been gut-wrenching. Seeing Maree trapped in that car did a real number on Rhys. Davis had questioned many times since then if, in that same circumstance, he would be — could be — as strong as his best friend had been.

Doubts came flooding back.

Oh, please, Lord. Please let her be safe.

"Mom, is it Landry? Has something happened to her? Is she okay?"

"Oh, honey," Jacqueline rushed to amend. "I'm sure Landry's fine. She checked in last night, spoke to Zane, and said she'd had an uneventful day driving to Wheeling, West Virginia, where she was spending the night. She's bound to be on the road already this morning, driving the final leg to New York. I'm so sorry to scare you that way."

"I spoke with her last night, too. And texted with her this morning. I just panicked. You're right. Landry's fine." Speaking his prayer aloud helped calm his nerves. "Then what's wrong?" Davis asked.

"It was the fire station dispatcher. He said all crews were being called to the City Park for a full-staff meeting. And then Rhys came looking for you, too. He saw your cell phone in your room and flew back out of here like his hair was on fire."

"I'll call him and run through the shower. Can you stay here with Zane?"

"Of course! We'll have a wonderful day. You know I love helping with schoolwork and projects."

"I seem to have a vague recollection of that...beat into my head over the course of my childhood." Davis yelled his teasing taunts over his shoulder as he walked down the hall. Before entering his room, he leaned back to look at her with an adoring smile. "And Mom, *hair on fire*? Not a good idiom to use with firefighters," Davis said, shaking his head to give her a hard time.

Ten minutes later, showered and feeling much better after calling Landry to talk while she drove and he dressed, Davis returned to the kitchen.

"Did you find out what's going on?" Jacqueline asked. "It must be bad to call the entire fire department together. Particularly with an ordinance in place prohibiting group gatherings."

"Rhys didn't know anything. He said he'll see me there and that we're supposed to meet at the outdoor amphitheater, sitting every other row and at least six feet apart from one another."

"Please text with an update as soon as you can. We all know my imagination is worse than reality," Jacqueline admitted. "We'll be fine right here until you get back."

Davis grabbed two dry pancakes from what remained on the platter that had been full the first time he'd walked through.

"Thanks for saving me some, Z Man." Sarcasm dripped from his voice.

Zane missed Davis's meaning but nodded effusively while dredging a slice of bacon through the leftover syrup on his plate. Carefree delight shone in his eyes, matching the grin splitting his cute face.

Davis laughed, mussed the boy's hair, and kissed his mom's cheek on his way out.

"We received a call from Latimer County this morning," Chief Everett began, no *good morning*, no *everything's okay*, no greeting at all. "While camping in the woods, some high school boys discovered an unresponsive elderly male. Afraid of the repercussions of sneaking out and having a party when they're supposed to be quarantining independently in their homes, the kids tried treating the man with their first aid supplies. When he still didn't wake up, thankfully, the teenagers called for help. Paramedics transported the man to their local hospital around 8:30 a.m. From the flyers we've been circulating the last two years, asking for information on the spree of fires in Green Hills and mentioning persons of interest, the charge nurse at the hospital recognized the patient as Walter Armstrong."

Sitting six feet apart did not stop a buzz of comments and exclamations from erupting.

"We know very little. It might not even be Mr. Armstrong. They're transporting whoever it is to Green Country Medical Center this afternoon. Hopefully, the doctors can help him, which will help us. In the meantime, I'm asking for off-duty volunteers to search the terrain between Green Hills and the area where the boys found the man this morning."

"Chief, that's a lot of square miles," Roddy Sampson pointed out. "What are we looking for?"

"Signs of where Mr. Armstrong has been sleeping, eating, living. Indications he's had something to do with the fires we've been battling. Proof that he hasn't."

"Talk about a needle in a haystack," Harleigh Steele commented from where she stood at the back of the outdoor theater, arms crossed and one foot propped against the stone wall behind her. "If it's Walter Armstrong — and that's yet to be confirmed — he's lived in the wilderness around here for a lot of years. There's no telling what he's left behind."

"Before Mr. Armstrong went off the grid, he served as an Army Ranger. I heard he spent time in some of the world's roughest places, doing the hardest jobs. He spent time in places like Saudi Arabia, Iraq, Somalia, and Macedonia," Davis said.

He continued, borrowing Harleigh's phrase, "As a highly trained soldier in special forces, there's no telling what he's *seen.*"

"And done," Harleigh added. Davis frowned at her. "Hey, don't shoot the messenger. I'm just pointing out what everyone here is thinking. If anyone knows how to set a trap in the woods, it's an Army Ranger."

"And if anyone knows those woods, it's Walter Armstrong," Chief Everett said. "Be careful. Watch your step. Watch out for one another; use those highly trained brains you all have, too."

"Chief, Pony Creek runs along the county line between us and Latimer County. I'll start there and work my way back toward the turnpike," Davis offered. "Rhys, Harleigh, and Roddy can join me. On ATVs, we should be able to cover the northwest quadrant of the county before sundown, as long as we don't get too deep into the brush. If he holed up in there, we'll never find his camp, anyway."

"It's amazing how you remember all that history," Rhys said as they walked toward their trucks in the parking lot.

"Let's hope I remember the countryside well enough to keep from getting us lost," Davis replied.

"I'm packing a backpack for overnight," Harleigh quipped. "It's not that I don't trust you, Davis. I expect the best. It's just that I also prepare for the worst."

Following her suggestion, they all tied sleeping bags onto their four-wheelers and carried water jugs, dry tack, and first aid supplies in their backpacks. By drawing grid lines over their quadrant of the county, the four covered their search area, systematically crisscrossing back and forth and back and forth, over and over until they'd sifted the terrain with a fine-tooth comb. When the dusk set in, and they'd not found anything, all four agreed to make camp and continue searching at first light.

Davis hated he wouldn't be able to call Landry to see how her day went, but for whatever reason, he had a hunch they were close. He needed to camp out there and continue searching first thing in the morning. Davis couldn't say why he felt that way, but the sensation was tangible.

And despite their teasing, Harleigh and the guys put a lot of stock and faith into Davis's leadership. If anything existed, anything that could help explain the firebug plaguing Green Hills, they'd find it.

Under the same stars but fourteen hundred miles away, Landry collapsed face-down on a luxurious, down-filled duvet. The cool, crisp linens and plush mattress screamed at her to crawl in, but peeling off her jacket, jeans, and shoes required too much effort.

She'd split the twenty-two-hour drive from Green Hills to Manhattan into three, approximately eight-hour days. GPS indicated the final leg took six hours and thirty-three minutes. With executive orders for citizens to stay home, there'd been little traffic. She'd stopped once to get gas and stretch her legs, twice to roll through drive-through windows for food, and three times to take pictures of the views. Add another hour for the hotel check-in and parking procedures, and she'd been in the car a little over nine hours.

Green Hills to St. Louis, Missouri... St. Louis to Wheeling, West Virginia... Wheeling to New York City... NYC into Manhattan... Final destination: the Four Seasons Hotel.

Rolling onto her back, Landry surveyed her room. *At the Four Seasons.*

High-end furnishings gleamed in moonlight streaming in from the austere, oversized windows. Stately decorations added prestige and undeniable class. Decadent linens ensured comfort.

Landry sympathized with Little Orphan Annie asking for a pinch.

Mother, if only you could see me now.

Landry heaved herself to sit on the edge of the bed. She

bounced a few times to confirm all she'd ever heard about the beds at a Four Seasons...

Yes, indeed: perfectly balanced between a firm foundation and a dreamy, pillow-like mattress.

I could lie back down and be done for the day... But I need a shower... And look at that bathtub... It's just that I'm sooo tired... The hot water will feel like heaven... This bed will feel like heaven... You'll sleep better if you—

The ringing of her cell phone saved Landry from the angel-devil argument taking place in her subconscious.

Kicking off her shoes, Landry shuffled her hips to lean against the headboard and heap of pillows as she answered Maree's call.

"I made it," Landry said in lieu of a hello. "You've got to explain to me what makes these sheets pure bliss!"

"According to the internet? Three hundred fifty count, percale-woven cotton threads that provide the silky, soft feel of sateen, laundered to pristine perfection. Not too shabby, huh?"

"I'm on the thirty-third floor. My room overlooks Central Park, which is currently glowing in warm lamplight. I can't wait to see it in the sunshine. And this is *not* a normal hotel room. I entered through a private lounge and desk area. I could live in the walk-in closet, and a TV hangs in the bath-room so I can watch a movie while soaking in bubbles. Maree, lights illuminate the pedestal under my bed."

"Wow. Quite a crib," Maree remarked. "Tell me again how you ended up in a five-star hotel."

"After being closed for quarantine mandates, the owner reopened the hotel as a dorm for doctors, nurses, and other medical workers. I get to stay here for free."

"For free? All five weeks of your rotation?"

"Yes, it's unbelievable," Landry told her. "The restaurants are all closed, there's no housekeeping or front desk or concierge, and only one person can ride on an elevator at a time. But it's the Four Seasons, and it's amazing."

"Without restaurants, where will you eat?"

"The hotel staff rolled commercial refrigerators into the lobby; they contain boxed meals. The procedure for entering the hotel is exactly like a hospital: nurses on duty took my temperature and asked about symptoms. Once cleared, signs directed me to pick up food and bottled water on my way to the elevators. Everyone waiting to go to their room stands on black and yellow caution-tape X's, positioned on the floor to maintain a safe distance. Of course, everyone is fully masked."

"It sounds like they've thought of everything," Maree said.

"I have a small refrigerator in my room, as well as a coffee pot and tea bags. And I saw a bag of extra linens sitting next to a basket of cleaning supplies in the closet. I'll clean and disinfect my room daily. Each week, I'll swap my sheets and towels for a fresh bag of linens left outside my door."

"It's crazy and wonderful, all at once," Maree marveled.

"I wish you could see it. I promise to send pictures when I'm here during daylight hours."

"What time do you have to be at the makeshift hospital tomorrow?"

"My shift begins at 7 a.m. The map says it'll take twenty minutes to get there, but I have no clue where I'm going, where to park, or how long it'll take to get inside the building. I'm leaving here at five."

"I better let you go," Maree pointed out. "I'm glad you made it safely, and I'll be covering you in prayer these next five weeks."

"Thanks," Landry said, genuinely grateful for Maree's prayers, her thoughts, and her friendship. "Hey," Landry added before they hung up. "Have you seen Davis today? He usually calls before now, and he always texts to say good night."

"You probably won't hear from him tonight."

"Is everything okay? Did something happen to Davis? Or Zane?" Landry's voice rose in urgency.

Maree sighed aloud and paused before explaining. "You've got a lot on your plate, so I didn't want to add to the load."

"Maree, please... What's going on?"

"It's a long story, and yet, I have very little to share."

30

―――

...call it an exchange of mutual respect
performed with an attitude of kindness.
Isadore Sharp,
Founder and Chairman
of the Four Seasons Hotel

"I found something y'all need to see," Davis said into his walkie talkie. "Can you pull my location from your trackers?" Their handheld survival devices kept the firefighters connected for up to eight miles because cell signals barely existed that far into the woods.

A few minutes later, Rhys crouched to get a better look at footprints preserved in dried mud around a trash-riddled campfire.

"I see at least five different shoe patterns," Rhys said, confirming what Davis had counted.

"There's no way Mr. Armstrong leaves a camp looking like this...litter, cigarette butts, open cans of food," Roddy asserted. "He's a mystery, but he's an outdoorsman, soldier, and survivalist, too. No one who's lived off the land as he has, for as long as he has, treats the earth this way."

"Any idea if he's a drinker?" Harleigh asked, kicking empty bottles of tequila and whisky from the brush under a tree.

"No." Davis's tone left no room for argument.

"No, you don't have any idea, or no, he's not a drinker?"

"No, that's not his alcohol," Davis insisted.

"I don't think he drank out here in the woods," Roddy collaborated. "Growing up, I remember him being a good guy, quiet and stand-offish but also kind and polite, not how I'd expect a heavy drinker to behave. And over the years, I've seen him in town several times, buying food at the Get'n'Go, but never booze. I'm not saying he's never enjoyed a cold beer left for him or a glass of scotch at Scooter's on the rare occasion he goes out in public. But I'm with Davis; this mess doesn't look or feel like Mr. Armstrong."

"Then how do you explain this?"

All three men turned to face Harleigh, who held a weathered and faded Army green duffle. Holes in the canvas and fraying on the straps spoke to the bag's age. The insignia, rubbed bare in spots, read *Ranger Airborne, 1ˢᵗ Battalion, 75ᵗʰ Infantry*. A patch, held on by a scant few threads, spelled out *Armstrong*.

"An animal carried it off? Someone stole it? Or maybe it was here before the people arrived who apparently partied and split?" Davis spouted off reasons as though grabbing at lifelines.

"Why are you so sure he's innocent?" Harleigh asked. "I'd say the evidence — here and what they have found at random fires over the past two years — points to Walter Armstrong being an arsonist."

Davis tugged his cap off his head with one hand and ran the other through his hair. He walked in circles, studied the scene they'd found deep in the woods. After slapping the GHFD hat against his leg twice, he settled it back in place.

"The golden rule, I guess," Davis admitted. "Treat others as you wish to be treated. If I'd trained and worked to serve my country, only to get severely damaged in the process, so that I felt like such a danger to others that I gave up my family, my home, and my life, to live in the woods for nearly thirty years... Well, I hope in that case, someone would do more than assume I'd suddenly developed pyromaniac habits to wreak havoc and do harm to the ounce of comfort I'd maintained: my place in the shadows of what once was my home. I'd want someone to take the time to investigate, rather than jump to conclusions. And I'd want to be treated with kindness and respect, at least until I proved I didn't deserve such human decencies."

"Well, let's add this to the investigation," Roddy offered, ever a level head and voice of reason.

"I'll call it in," Rhys said, walking to his ATV to radio their location to Chief Everett.

"You know," Harleigh said, not unkindly as she kicked at a rock with the toe of her black leather station boot. "If it's him, he has to pay."

"I know," Davis agreed. He sighed, trying to release the weight of the world bearing down on him. "I know," Davis repeated.

"That's great news about Eddie," Landry said later that night, after Davis updated her on the day his mom had spent with Zane. They'd fried French toast for breakfast, watched church in their pajamas, and made a dozen more masks along with fun pillowcases to send with homemade get-well cards to the children's hospital in Tulsa. Zane empathized with families separated by hospital requirements during the pandemic; making goodies to send to them gave him an action-able way to help.

Just as Davis arrived home from the overnight search, Eddie had called from Dallas.

Getting stronger and relying less and less on pain medication every day, Eddie sounded a little more like himself. He asked about school, homework, and baseball. Then he listened to Zane talk. Excited to share every detail since their last conversation, Zane rambled and rolled for a good thirty or more minutes before coming up for air.

Davis suspected Eddie timed his calls around meds, trying to have as clear a head as possible when they spoke. By the time Zane ran out of stories to share, fatigue and pain colored Eddie's voice. That's when Davis made an excuse to take the phone. He updated Eddie on Zane's physical therapy and discussed parental things. Davis ensured his part of the call ended quickly, giving Eddie an out when he'd reached his threshold and needed to rest.

Before they'd hung up that night, Eddie told Davis that his medical team had upgraded his condition and moved him out of Burn ICU and into the Burn Acute Care Unit. Hesitant to get Zane's hopes up, Eddie requested Davis not mention it to anyone.

Davis didn't count Landry as anyone. Even hundreds of miles away, he relied on her as his temporary co-parent. They were a unit, regardless of their locations on a map.

"He sounded great," Davis said, encouraged by his visit with Eddie, yet trying to temper his expectations, just as they'd agreed to do with Zane. "Tell me about your day. How's the convention center turned sick-ward?"

"I'd rather hear about your weekend; I'm champing at the bit to know what's happened with Mr. Armstrong."

Davis filled Landry in on the kids stumbling upon an older man fitting Walter Armstrong's description. He explained that at that time, the authorities couldn't positively identify the John Doe, but the small hospital in Latimer County gladly transferred the patient to Green Country Medical Center, which was much better equipped to treat him.

"Was he coherent when he arrived in Green Hills?" Landry asked.

"I'm not sure. They've been tight-lipped. As a doctor there, you can probably get better information than what I have. The hospital gave a brief statement to *The Gazette*, which they posted online, but it doesn't say much. From what I read, he suffered from severe dehydration, starvation, minor cuts and bruises, and exhaustion. As you saw at the hospital that day, he has burns, still in the early stages of healing, on his hands and arms. The gossip I've heard is that he's awake now, but still unable to communicate. It doesn't make sense why he can't answer questions."

"And they're sure it's Walter Armstrong?"

"Yes, they confirmed that much."

"There are many reasons — valid medical conditions — to explain why he can't talk. And a lot of those explanations come with treatments and cures. The doctors will figure it out, Davis."

"I hope so. I really do. We better call it a night. Promise to tell me about your new digs, the hospital set up, and all the nitty-gritty details of the Big Apple tomorrow night?"

Davis forced a bit of witty playfulness into the pitch of his voice.

"I promise," Landry said. "Give Zane a hug for me?"

"Sure," Davis agreed. "But what about me? I could definitely use a hug right about now."

"You've got one coming... I promise that, too."

"In that case, I could also use—"

"Nice try," Landry said to cut him off. "A hug when I get

there will have to suffice. Now, get some sleep. I'll talk to you soon... Bye."

Davis stared up at the ceiling above his bed long after Landry disconnected their call. He'd intentionally flirted to lighten the mood before their conversation ended. He'd envisioned her smile when his flirting worked.

She'd said a hug would have to suffice when she returned home.

We'll see, Doctor Stark. We'll just have to wait and see.

------

31

*Persistence and determination alone
are omnipotent.
President Calvin Coolidge*

"The article I read online said four thousand beds. Are there really that many?" Davis asked Monday night.

"No, although I believe a plan is in place to increase to that size if necessary. There are five hundred thirty-two general medicine beds, equipped with oxygen machines, monitors, and the supplies needed for treatments. Another forty-eight intensive care beds have all of those items plus ventilators. Besides those, some groupings of rooms — called pods — serve as barracks for the military personnel on-site. Some pods designated as sick bays provide quarantine areas for healthcare workers who don't feel well, had a temperature above one hundred degrees when they arrived for work, or are awaiting COVID test results."

"Do you feel safe?" The concern in Davis's question touched Landry. He truly had a heart of gold.

"I do," Landry answered without hesitation. "They've thought of everything. We even have step-by-step instructions for how to don our mask and protective equipment. With pictures," she laughed.

"The Army Corps of Engineers transformed the convention center into a combat field hospital in the course of a few days," Landry continued. "Somehow, they remembered everything we'd need: nutrition services, a pharmacy, labs, radiology, nurses' stations, mobile showers, modular walls—"

"Security?"

"Yes, lots of security. The 1.6-million-square-foot building now utilizes one door in and one door out. You know, the city is eerily vacant. Social distancing keeps everyone separated, so we've become a large group of individuals. And no one here seems keen on conversing with others. I suppose wearing masks every minute of every day limits chitchat because no one can hear what people are saying. On top of that, talking through a mask is just generally uncomfortable.

"Despite those alienating circumstances, until I step in the elevator to come up to my room, I'm rarely alone. Or maybe it's just the opposite. I see other humans all around me, yet I'm still completely alone. It's a desolate sensation. I'm working every second that I'm on duty. Because there are so many in need, I go from patient to patient with few breaks. And the needs vary from person to person; their symptoms are all over the board. I'm insanely busy, but I'm fighting a sense of being adrift. I'm not explaining it very well, am I?" Landry exhaled a deep sigh. "I'm sorry."

"Don't be sorry. You're there; you're making a tremendous difference in the lives of those patients. And their families. Are they all terribly sick? Is it like the news footage on TV?"

"I've seen some awful videos of gurneys lined up in hallways, of bodies stacked in the morgue. It's nothing like that here. Mostly, we're treating COVID patients on the mend and a few with comorbid conditions. They're convalescing, or they have a secondary condition that requires extra attention before they're strong enough to go home. They transfer patients here to make room in the hospitals for those in much worse condition. It's all hands on-deck around the clock — there's just so much to do — but most of our patients are through the life-threatening phase of the virus."

"I'm glad it's not a frenzied crisis," Davis said. "But it's not a walk in Central Park, either. You're brilliant and resilient and capable — I'm not questioning that — but you're not invincible. This pandemic, the work you're doing, the scene you're living hour after hour, it's big. Whatever you're feeling, it's warranted. So don't apologize, and know that you can lean on me. I'm here...for anything, for everything."

"Thank you, Davis." Landry meant it, but she couldn't find adequate words to express her gratitude.

"I've been told on numerous occasions that I'm a terrific listener," he teased.

"I can imagine," she agreed with a laugh. "You're sweet to lend an ear."

"And a shoulder when you need one. Remember, Landry, sometimes being strong requires sharing the load."

*T*he next day, she called him in tears.

"We lost a patient today."

"Oh, Landry. I'm sorry," Davis said, gently consoling her.

"I'd hoped— The people transferred here are over the worst of their symptoms when they arrive— I was naive to think..." Landry's voice faded away when she couldn't find the words to express her emotions. "The man who died fought in the Vietnam War. When veterans die, proper military honors include a United States flag draped over the casket during transport of the body. We didn't have one. We couldn't find a flag."

Her voice broke, unleashing a torrent of tears.

"One week in, and I'm falling apart," she sobbed. "What if I can't do this?"

"You can do this," Davis reassured with absolute certainty in his voice. "You *are* doing this, and you're doing great. Was the patient one with comorbidities? Did he suffer from other conditions?"

"Yes, coronary issues. We'd been monitoring his heart closely, and he'd been getting stronger each day. But this virus is unpredictable and still so unknown. Once he started declining, it happened very quickly."

"What about his family?"

"On March 25, his son picked him up from the house where he and his wife lived for sixty-three years and took him to Mount Sinai Hospital. The son dropped him at the front doors because guests can't enter with patients." Of course, Davis knew that protocol, but Landry's anger at the situation made her temper swirl. "That night, the patient's breathing required a ventilator, which he tolerated for eight days. Do you have any idea how awful it must be to go through that? Can you imagine fighting the urge to panic and rip that tube out?" Hysteria at the thought of that situation raised Landry's voice at least an octave, but she didn't care.

Davis didn't respond, which was probably for the best.

"On day nine, his respiratory functions improved. One week later, the hospital notified the man's family with information about his transfer to JNYMS. One more week, and we called to tell them he died. Alone. He lived eighty-four years, fought for his country, loved the same woman his entire life, helped raise their children, impacted his neighborhood, held a leadership role at their church. This was a good man. So why did he have to die alone?"

"Without his loved ones at his side, yes. But not alone," Davis said calmly. "You were there, Landry."

She had no response.

"How did you know so much about him?" Davis asked.

"He told me," she said with a sniffle.

"When?"

"When I'd check on him...when we'd walk...when I snuck extra pudding to him."

"So, he passed away in the hands of an amazing doctor and in the presence of a friend."

"A good doctor would've saved him," she whispered. "I didn't save him."

"We both know you're an exceptional doctor. And an extraordinary friend."

"Thank you," she allowed. Landry dried her tears, determined for the crying jag to be over.

"Thank you," Davis countered. "For telling me about your friend, for letting me share in your grief. I'm glad you did. Remember, you can tell me anything."

That's exactly what she did.

From then on, Landry and Davis ended every night talking on the phone.

Davis provided a rundown on his and Zane's day, which ironically differed from the account she heard from Zane before dinner each evening. Traise Mitchell completed his physical therapy sessions, and Doctor Bradford cleared Zane to return to normal activities. School continued to stink on the computer, and Ms. Newton introduced the idea of summer course packets to keep her kids on pace with where they'd have been if the virus hadn't disrupted the world. Eddie called every day at lunch, which motivated Zane to muster through afternoon assignments.

The city council voted to approve youth sports, as long as all practices and games took place outdoors and spectators maintained six feet of social distancing, prompting the Green Hills Park and Rec Department to set game schedules for the Little League teams. *The Gazette* printed the calendar for each age group; Zane cut his out and hung it on the fridge. He circled Opening Day on Saturday, June 6 with a red marker. The boys — young and old — counted down the days; Zane and Davis played rock, paper, scissors to see which one got to place a big blue X on the calendar at the end of each day to mark out their countdown.

Landry read with Zane after she returned to her room at the Four Seasons, if she made it there before he went to sleep for the night. She helped him research destinations for Flat Stanley to visit —virtually, of course — for his assignment. When Zane's science project refused to ooze the intended goop, she walked him through the steps again and again, until he had it just right.

"Do you think this is what it feels like to be a parent?" Landry asked Davis one night, when he'd called her back after tucking in Zane and closing up the house.

"I hope so," Davis answered.

"I think Zane makes it easy," Landry commented. "If it was so easy, everyone would be good at it."

"You know how they say it's a conscious decision to be happy, to choose joy? Well, I believe we get to choose if we want to make it easy or hard, good or bad, happy or miserable."

"That might be oversimplifying things just a bit," Landry argued. "Every child is unique; every parent is different. A challenging child isn't necessarily a handful because the parents are lacking. And it's not the child's fault if a parent is an utter and complete failure at nurturing, guiding, and protecting the child."

"True," Davis agreed. Landry couldn't stay irritated with him when he agreed with such aplomb. "But it's still our choice how we respond."

"Humph," Landry grumbled.

A few days after the parenting discussion, Davis called midafternoon.

Seeing his name on her phone startled Landry — the call didn't fit the pattern she'd settled into. While driving to the hospital early in the morning, Landry often talked to Miss Sadie, who didn't mind, or even seem to notice, the time change. During her lunch break, Landry typically called to catch up with Maree, who's work as a fabric designer allowed lots of time flexibility. Landry spoke to Zane in the evening, when he was working through school assignments after dinner and had a full day of news to share. But Davis never called until the rest of the world settled for the night and they could talk uninterrupted.

"Davis? Is everything okay?" Landry answered in a rush.

"It's Alzheimer's," Davis revealed flatly. "Walter Armstrong moved into Memorial Care today."

"Did they mention a stage? Is he still in the early stages of MCI, where mild cognitive impairment affects memory skills but doesn't disrupt activities of daily living?"

"No, it's already well past that point. Chief Everett asked me to join the task force investigating the serial fires, so now I have access to Mr. Armstrong's medical record. I figure you'll read it all when you get back and are working with Mr. Armstrong at the memory care facility, so I'm not breaking any ethical codes by telling you what's in the files."

Landry didn't comment on the gray area in which Davis tiptoed. She'd be sure to keep their conversation on the safe side of the line.

"Is someone with dementia — advanced Alzheimer's disease — capable of setting intricate fires over the course of two years?" Davis asked her.

"It's hard to say," Landry answered. "That's frustrating to hear, but it's accurate. Without prior benchmarks, neurological tests, and a thorough medical history, determining when a patient began suffering from dementia is nearly impossible. We see common patterns as the disease progresses, but we can't predict the rate of cognitive decline."

"So, it's possible that Mr. Armstrong is to blame for the pain and destruction?"

"Yes, I suppose it is."

"And if he is, there's essentially no way to make it right." Disgust clouded Davis's words.

"What does that mean, Davis...*make it right?*"

"Justice," he spat. "For Eddie, who's been fighting for his life. For Zane, who's had to live without his dad. For the Jensen family, who lost their home and all their belongings last year. For Mrs. Dawsey, the sweet old lady who owns the candy store on the square and almost had a heart attack when she saw someone lighting her building on fire. For the citizens of Green Hills, who have been living in fear. For everybody who—"

"I get it," Landry interrupted. It took a lot to push Davis over the tipping point, but there he was. "Davis, I thought you didn't believe Mr. Armstrong could be the firebug. I sensed you truly didn't want it to be him."

"I didn't. *I don't,*" he corrected. "But what if the answers we need are locked up in his mind, being eaten alive by plaques and tangles and a whole host of problems I don't understand? What if we never know the truth?"

"I wish I had an answer," Landry said, lamenting that she

couldn't help Davis, when he always knew exactly what she needed to hear. "I *do* know that you're very determined. The clues are out there. Maybe in the woods, maybe where the kids found Mr. Armstrong a county over, or maybe right under our noses. The truth will surface, and when it does, all the pieces will click into place to make sense of these horrible acts. Keep looking, Davis. Persistence is your superpower."

*L*andry's advice paid off.

With Jacqueline, Miss Sadie, and Maree helping look after Zane, Davis spent his off-shift days tracking in the woods. It took him four solid days of searching for clues before he hit pay dirt.

Little more than weathered boards protruding from the ground, with a shredded tarp and broken tree branches for a roof, a dilapidated deer blind hid a campsite. A recent campsite. Two threadbare sleeping bags lay disheveled by the still-warm remnants of a small fire. A rumpled knapsack and jacket — both military issue and monogrammed with *Armstrong* on the name patches — formed pillows at the head of two of the sleeping bags. Enough candy bar wrappers, greasy fast-food bags, and beer cans littered the ground to indicate at least two people had been living there for a while.

In addition to the camping supplies, Davis found a stash of boxes and coolers covered in leaves and brush, not twenty feet from the deer blind.

He opened each container slowly, in case any held animal traps or explosives. What he discovered inside sent his blood pumping and his heart racing.

Bingo.

32

And let us not grow weary of doing good,
for in due season we will reap,
if we do not give up.
Galatians 6:9

"Oh my," Landry gasped. "What constitutes incendiary devices? The word even sounds evil!"

"When you think about how explosives detonate, incendiary devices use materials to slow the chemical reaction of ignition. Think napalm in the Korean War and propane-fueled cluster bombs in Vietnam," Davis explained that night on the phone.

"You're talking about chemical warfare. Literally in our backyard," Landry sputtered in outrage.

"Yes, but also not exactly." Davis replied. "The boxes, barrels, and cases retrieved in the camp I came upon and in two other locations deeper in the terrain and across the county line contained a combination of incendiary and explosive bomb-making materials. Obviously, those supplies are enough to do immense harm, but a few key elements required to cause large-scale catastrophe are missing from the stockpile."

"I file the gym explosion and resulting injuries under large-scale catastrophe," Landry declared with anger.

Davis loved her haughty, offended loyalty. The thought of someone storing such weapons — and using them — on Green Hills plumb ticked her off.

"I do, too, Landry," he sympathized. "Irresponsibly starting a forest fire, or even a wildfire on the side of the highway, raises my hackles. There's no justification or explanation for what we found out there. At least, nothing acceptable."

"What now? What did y'all do with everything?"

"Rhys recommended we call Brennigan Stewart. He and M'Kenzee are stuck in Scotland, but Rhys figured as an FBI agent, Bren could point us in the right direction."

"And did he? What did he suggest?" Anxious energy traveled the miles through the phone connection. She had Davis sitting on the edge of his seat, and he was the one telling the story.

"Bren agreed the sheer amount of fire-starting materials we found constitute a potential act of terrorism. That makes it a federal concern. He called Michael Vela, who should be in Green Hills first thing tomorrow morning."

"Wow— Talk about real life being stranger than fiction."

Davis nodded, which of course Landry couldn't see, but he said nothing, instead letting her absorb all he'd told her.

"I met Agent Vela several times when Bren went missing during the holidays. He and Bren go way back, and he kept M'Kenzee in the loop on a daily basis during Bren's ordeal. He's a good guy; I'm glad he's headed your way. Whether or not Mr. Armstrong had something to do with those containers and their incriminating contents, you know other people are out there...people set on doing harm. Davis, you need to be careful. No more trips to those woods alone, okay?"

Her sweet concern warmed his heart and made his day. They talked every night, but they never spoke of their relationship. He joked and poked and flirted when she'd had an exceptionally tough day, when the weight of what she faced on the frontline of a war — albeit against an invisible enemy — became too heavy. Davis happily listened to Landry go on about anything that popped into her mind. He wanted and needed her to share what took up space in her heart.

She didn't bring up their kisses, the fact they didn't go a day without relying on one another, or their future. As a result, Davis couldn't define what they were — boyfriend and girlfriend, best friends, confidants, or simply COVID bubble mates. He hoped to be all of those, and more. He contented himself with being a rock she depended upon during the storm and figured the rest would come in due time.

"Davis, are you still there? Promise me you'll not get hurt."

"I'm here. Always," he pledged. "And I'll do my best to stay out of trouble."

"Promise?" Landry emphasized.

"I promise," he reiterated.

"In that case, I have some news, too."

"And you're just now mentioning it?" Davis accused in jest. Most nights Landry guided their topics, but that night, with so much to tell, he'd monopolized the conversation.

"Well, it pales compared to bombs and ignitors and weapons and such," she retorted. "But I think it's pretty big."

"Don't make me beg," Davis teased. "I'd normally refuse, but for you, I'd give it a try."

"I'm being transferred."

"Home?" Davis leapt from his bed. Then he cringed at the unbridled hope that blossomed in his chest. Thankfully, she didn't let on if she'd detected his over-exuberance.

"No, I'm still here for the full five weeks. I'm switching to

Mount Sinai Hospital; the JNYMS is reverting to a convention center. I start my new job tomorrow."

Davis sat befuddled for a moment before asking, "Are the numbers down that much? Is the pandemic ending?"

"Our intake numbers are certainly down, but I think we'll be fighting COVID for a long time."

"That's it? They had to have spent millions creating the temporary hospital, and thirty days later, they just take it down again. It's incredible," Davis said. "How do you feel?"

"It's all been surreal. Something like sixteen or seventeen different organizations came together to build out the facility, and most stayed on to oversee day-to-day operations. It's the first time the Department of Defense responded to a disaster with a military-civilian collaboration. I'm sure they learned a lot from the experience — I know I have."

"You're a lab rat." Davis's voice turned wild and dramatic. "They experimented with you, sucked the knowledge out of your brain. You're helping establish a whole new way of doing things, and all the while, you thought you were just saving lives."

"We lost some, too."

"How many?" Davis asked, his tone immediately sober.

"Six," Landry answered without explanation.

"Out of how many?"

"Over a thousand," she supplied.

"I'd say y'all were miracle workers."

"At times it felt like we were gaining traction, even getting ahead of treatment. Other times, confusion and chaos reigned. Despite intentional and well-thought-through decision making, an overall feeling of unpreparedness hung over us like a thick, oppressive fog. The lack of information, ever-changing expectations, and a prevailing uncertainty about *everything* caused immense frustration. Communication with the hospitals transferring patients to us — each of which were horrendously overwhelmed — made handoffs inconsistent and difficult. It's been a lot."

"Yep, definitely miracle workers," he repeated. "What do you think it'll be like at Mount Sinai? Will you be doing the same work you've been doing?"

"Honestly, Davis... I have no idea."

Just checking on you. Please send proof of life. Miss you. Landry read Davis's text and slid her phone back into the pocket of her scrubs. She didn't reply, because taking off her gloves to type a message meant donning a new set of PPE, which they didn't have enough of to go around.

They hadn't talked in three days. Landry hadn't returned to her room at the Four Seasons in four. She'd seen it from her car, dreamed about it. She'd even attempted to count the floors and windows to find her room while sitting at a red light. But she couldn't go up.

Landry had landed in the war zone.

She worked twelve-hour night shifts at the tent hospital Mount Sinai set up in Central Park. With sixty-eight beds and ten intensive care units, the East Meadow housed a COVID-19 respiratory care center for hospital overflow. Landry shuddered to think of the rolling green space, surrounded by lush vegetation and a myriad of magnificent trees — a place known for its pastoral landscape — reduced to pockmarks and dead grass when the tent hospital vacated the park.

The pandemic left evidence of its power everywhere she looked. The people, the businesses, the schools, and even the parks would never be the same.

Different, but okay. Davis's words came back to her again and again.

She missed him, too.

Making a mental note to call him in the morning, she trudged on, checking on patients, charting the trajectory of their symptoms, and praying over each one in her heart.

"Good morning," Davis answered with sleep-infused hoarseness. Amidst the fog, he sounded happy to hear from her.

"Sorry to wake you," she apologized.

"I'm glad you did." Sheets rustled, his bed creaked, and the flopping of pillows created a mental image of him sitting up to lean against his headboard. The image made her blush.

"I'm sorry I've been AWOL. How's Zane? Did he finish his Flat Stanley project? Were the photos I sent of Central Park and the enormous American elm trees useful?"

"He's awesome, and so is Flat Stanley. Did you know design work and construction on Central Park began in 1853? The original seven hundred acres displaced a lot of people...most notably a very stable African-American settlement called Seneca Village, Irish pig farmers, and German gardeners. Now the park consists of eight hundred forty-three acres. Green Hills — at least the in-town parts — could almost fit *inside* Central Park."

"Only you, Daniel Davis," Landry giggled. Ah, it felt good to laugh. "Who enjoyed researching Flat Stanley's travel adventures more, Zane or you?"

"Let's just say that teamwork makes the dream work."

"You're something else," she teased.

"Mom said I broke the mold. That's why I'm the baby of the family."

"I believe it," Landry said with a smile, her first in days.

"How's the night shift? I've been reading the *New York Times* online. I saw that they've stopped admitting patients to your field hospital and plan to close and remove the facility."

"Yes, the main branch of Mount Sinai sits directly across the street from the East Meadow, and they've caught up with COVID-19 intake numbers, so they don't need the tents for overflow. I'm shutting down another temporary hospital. Unfortunately, the hospital's Queens location is still in pandemonium. That area's been hit terribly hard by the virus. That's where I'm heading now. I've been volunteering there around my shifts at the park."

"When are you sleeping?"

"I have access to a resiliency center established to provide basic needs for health care workers at the hospital."

"I'm fairly certain you just avoided my question, but you said it so eloquently, I can't be sure."

His self-effacing humor made her grin again.

"I'm sleeping. Not much, but enough. Davis, Queens is what you saw on TV when you asked me weeks ago about the hospital conditions. Beds everywhere, not enough doctors and nurses to adequately care for them all, and patients in severe distress. Degrees of shouts and wails and cries never cease. Pre-pandemic, the eight-bed ICU stayed full. Compounded by COVID-19, they're completely overwhelmed."

"I can't imagine," Davis offered.

"You know, when I'm at the hotel, I watch the sun rise over the most iconic park in the world, watch it peek over the horizon to bathe the towering trees and the expansive gardens in its glow. Next, light hits the skyscrapers, making the windows shimmer and shine like crystals suspended from the clouds. It's breathtaking."

"That sounds amazing," Davis commented. "Absolutely beautiful."

"Then I arrive in Queens," Landry continued. "It's incredible there, too. The largest of the five boroughs, Queens is home to more than a hundred and fifty different cultures, and they're on display in the most magnificent ways. You'd love it! Especially the music. Just yesterday I heard a patient call Queens the *Cradle of Jazz*. And the food! Of course, with restaurants mostly all closed for COVID, I haven't experienced much of it, but after hearing the local citizens describe their favorites, I can only imagine the cuisine around there. You know, that's one of the worst complaints I hear in the post-COVID clinic. People miss their sense of taste so very much; some even equate it to losing a limb. Their world doesn't function right without it."

"No sense of taste? I can't even imagine," Davis said, his inflection showing that he found the thought appalling.

"I'm rambling," Landry apologized. "I'm sorry."

"Stop saying that. I never tire of hearing you ramble."

She'd have bet money he winked as he said it, disheveled, half-dressed, and still warm from sleep. In that moment, she yearned for him, to burrow into his embrace, to let his strength hold her up. Just long enough to catch her breath.

"You talk while I drive," she instructed. "Tell me what's going on there. It'll either make me feel better by distracting me or make me feel worse by making me homesick. Either way, I want to think about something other than my current reality for a few minutes."

"Baseball practices are going great. Our team is loaded; this group of boys are little studs. Even Scotty Philips mentioned he can't wait to get them up to the junior high and high school. He also asked about you, wanted me to pass along that he said hello and hopes you'll call him when you're back in Green Hills."

"He texted a few days ago. I need to reply; I just haven't had time," Landry admitted. "I'll try to reach out to him today. Thanks for the reminder."

"Hmm." Davis grumbled something that sounded like *not*

my intention, but Landry couldn't make out his words. "Michael Vela is here in Green Hills, heading up the task force. He's connected the arson evidence with fires in Arkansas and as far as Mississippi and Alabama."

"That's wild," Landry commented, mystified by the implications. "Are you still helping with the investigation?"

"Minimally," Davis said on an exhale. "Chief Everett happily handed jurisdiction over to the FBI; their resources and manpower mean we can get further, faster. I'm available if they need someone local to help. Yesterday, I took them out to the southeast quadrant of the county, where the woods are almost too thick to walk through. Arial footage pointed us toward an abandoned cabin they wanted to see."

"I'm glad they're keeping you in the loop. I know it's important to you."

"Yeah, I wouldn't say the town's written off Mr. Armstrong, but they're too willing to believe the worst of him. That doesn't sit well with me. It's not our way around here."

"Everywhere people turn these days, they see doom and gloom, astronomical COVID statistics, economic distress, political hatred, slander and divisiveness. If all one focuses on is the negative, then the ugly parts take over their perspective."

"They need to see one of those sunrises you described over Central Park."

"Or take notice of those Oklahoma sunsets I've been missing," Landry confessed.

"That's not a bad idea," Davis said, sounding impressed, as though thinking through something that needed sorting or solving. "In fact, I think I'll mention that to Mr. Mitchell."

"Well, keep me posted. Now you've got me intrigued by your plan."

"I'll let you know what I come up with. But let's get back to what you're missing in Oklahoma."

"The sunsets for sure. And Zane, of course. Miss

Sadie...her Sunday dinners. Maree, M'Kenzee, and Janie Lyn...our girls' night parties."

"That's it?"

"That's all I can think of off the top of my head," Landry confirmed with a straight face and a serious voice.

"You're sure?"

"Ah, yes. One other thing..." She paused to make him wait. "I miss Scooter's!"

"You miss Scooter's?" Landry worked hard to keep from laughing at his deadpan tone.

"I do. The burgers and fries, karaoke night, the dance floor."

"Any particular dance partners that you miss?" His fishing expedition continued.

"There's one guy I especially like to see there. He's a lot of fun — decent at pool, but deadly on the dance floor."

"Really? Tell me more."

"Well, all the girls go ga-ga over him, so I feel special when he chooses me to shower with his attention."

"He'd be a fool not to," Davis insisted.

"He's got a magnificent smile," Landry added. "Maybe it's just me, but I swear the room feels warmer when he grins at me, like just being around me brings him delight."

"I'm sure it does," Davis insisted again.

"And when we dance..." Landry sighed dramatically, "I could just melt in his arms."

Their game caught up with Landry. She no longer had to fake the dreamy desire in her voice.

"Reminds me of a night I spent in Scooter's a couple of years ago," Davis reminisced. "I met this girl — this vivacious, fun, firecracker of a girl. I forced myself to play it cool, to act indifferent, like it was any other night. But man, did I want to beg for her number, a date, and maybe even a kiss before she left. In hindsight, I think that night changed my life — ruined me — for anyone else."

Landry dropped all pretense at ignorance.

"Sometimes I wish we could go back to that night," she confessed.

"What would you do different?" Davis asked.

"I'd demand your number, schedule a date, and take that kiss."

33

———

It's the family you choose that counts.
Andrew Vachss

"Someone's in an awfully good mood," Jacqueline Davis laughed, trying to keep her feet underneath her legs as her youngest child swung her around the kitchen in a frolicking jig. "Should I try to guess what — or who — is behind it?"

"Is it that obvious?" Davis asked his mom, setting her back in front of the cooktop in his kitchen from where he'd snatched her. He made sure she'd regained her balance, performed a proper bow, and kissed her cheek before sniffing out the vegetables pan-frying in a cast-iron skillet. "Squash and potato hash... Yum!"

"No sampling before dinner," Jacqueline warned while swatting his hand away, but not until he'd snatched a sizzling bite of potato, which, in turn, he had to juggle in the air so it wouldn't burn his hand. "Will Landry be here in time to eat?"

"No, she didn't leave St. Louis until close to lunchtime," he answered as he poured a glass of sweet tea. "Can I fix you a glass?"

"Yes, please," Jacqueline said over her shoulder as she stirred the skillet. "Have you talked to her?"

"In general? Or about something specific?" Davis hedged.

"Both." He tried to look at anything in the kitchen besides his mom; she saw too much.

"Yep, chatted while she drove through Springfield."

"And you told her how you feel?"

"I don't know how I feel," he countered.

"Yes." Jacqueline pointed the spatula at him. "You do."

"And how do *you* know how I feel?" Davis tried to turn the tables on the interrogation.

"Because I know you, SonShine." Daniel Aaron Davis answered to a lot of nicknames; pulling out the one that only his mom used equated to fighting dirty. She knew exactly how to tug on his heartstrings.

"How do I know she's The One? I mean, of course I love her. She's one of my best friends; maybe that's all that is meant to be between us...a fun and flirty friendship. I've tried to have more than that with other girls, and I stink at it. As soon as we *get serious*, it falls apart." Davis emphasized what he thought of relationships that *get serious* with theatrical air quotes. "What if she doesn't love me?"

"I'm going to go out on a limb here and guess that the love you feel for Maree Davenport is not the same as the way you feel drawn to Landry."

"I'm willing to concede that point," Davis allowed with a sly smile at his wise and wonderful mom.

"I'd also wager that a fun and flirty friendship, as you put it, is just pretty packaging. From what your dad and I can tell, your relationship with Landry goes well beyond such surface wrapping."

"That's two points in your favor."

"She's worth giving *get serious* another try." She copied his air quotes. "Besides, all those other girls loved you too much."

"Excuse me? The girlfriends who loved me *too much* were a bust, but Landry will be The One? Is that because she *doesn't* love me enough?"

"The girls you've dated in the past loved the thought of you, but you only liked them. That creates a mismatch. A relationship can't work if one person loves the other person *more*. Landry is The One because you love her just as she loves you; together y'all are balanced."

Jacqueline let that sink in while she took a pan of breaded and baked chicken from the oven.

"Dinner's ready; please go tell Zane and your dad to wash up so we can eat," she instructed.

Still befuddled, Davis turned toward the door to the backyard to do as ordered.

"And SonShine?"

"Yes, ma'am?" Davis looked back over his shoulder.

"That's three points in my favor." Then she winked at him before carrying the serving platters to the table.

"Game, set, match," he said under his breath. "Mom wins again."

"What's a gathering?" Zane wondered aloud.

"Where a bunch of people gather together. Please eat your dinner so we can go to one," Davis answered between bites of chicken, wild rice, sliced cantaloupe, and warm crescent rolls.

"I thought we aren't allowed to gather, 'cause of COVID," Zane mused.

"It's outdoors, and every family will keep to themselves," Jacqueline answered, when Davis didn't.

"If every family keeps to themselves, why do they need to gather?" When the boy got on a roll, he came up with many more than just twenty questions.

"I wondered that myself. *The Voice* is new tonight on TV." Elijah Davis's contribution to the conversation earned him a reprimanding eyebrow raise from his wife.

"Will Ryder be there? Can I take a baseball and my glove?" A trio of yes's answered at once.

"What's this gathering for again?" Zane questioned.

No one answered.

"What a sight to behold," Mr. Mitchell announced over a portable sound system. "It's wonderful to see so many people out here this evening... Families and neighbors together — maintaining a safe distance — but in person, to encourage one another, to surround ourselves in the beauty of God's creation, and to remind one another of the incredible blessings we've received. I've lived here my entire life, and I'll tell you, I've never seen the old City Park look better. And the sun hasn't begun to set," he joked. "Thank you all for being part of our first community-wide sunset service. At the Green Hills Church of Christ, we begin every Sunday morning with Psalm 118, verse 24. It's Monday night, but if you'll indulge me, I would love to hear it in this tremendous setting. Friends, say it with me..."

This is the day the Lord has made; let us rejoice and be glad in it.

The music director from First Baptist led the crowd in a rousing rendition of "Heaven Came Down."

Oh what a wonderful, wonderful day...

The first line rang out loud and clear, setting the tone for a stunning night.

The youth minister from the Methodist church invited the

teenagers to join him on the baseball field for more songs and a devotional. He ensured the parents they'd maintain social distancing. One dad hollered, "Good luck!" as the minister and teens walked away.

Once the ensuing laughter died down and smaller children had climbed onto parents' laps or sprawled across the blankets and quilts each family had laid on the ground, Mr. Mitchell returned to the microphone. Facing east, the crystal blue sky, dotted in puffs of clouds, created a backdrop of unrivaled glory. In his element, Mr. Mitchell started sharing a lesson from second Timothy that focused on having grit, grace, courage, and resolve, particularly when times are tough.

Davis glanced down at his watch: *7:39.* The moon crept into the sky, even as twilight began darkening the heavens above. The sun, still vibrant in the west, sent streaks of color, vivid and resplendent in shades of yellow, orange, coral, pink, red, purple, and blue.

So taken with the view, Davis didn't notice a silhouette walking across the park. His mom elbowed him in the side and pointed toward the figure.

Long hair and a flowing skirt fluttered in the breeze. Arms crossed against her body held a sweater tight around her ribs. Watching her steps as she walked around the edge of the crowd, she'd not yet noticed him.

Davis's heart paused and then skittered back into rhythm.

She's home.

He stood and walked to meet her halfway.

Without hesitation, without a word, her arms unfolded and lifted to wrap over his shoulders. She buried her face in the space between his shoulder and neck; her breath warmed his skin until it tingled.

Davis wrapped his arms around Landry, and when her body shook with the shedding of tears, he held her tighter.

Davis held Landry as long as she needed to cry.

Then, shifting to nestle her under his arm and into the hollow of his chest, Davis lifted his other hand to wipe away her tears.

"You're home," he said, smiling into her beautiful face. The shockingly exquisite sunset couldn't hold a candle to Landry Stark. In Davis's eyes, she was God's greatest creation.

"Hi," she said, returning his smile. Landry wrapped her left arm around his torso and gripped his jacket with her right hand. Davis sheltered her body with his. He couldn't get close enough. Her body language said she felt the same. "What is this?" She peeked over his shoulder to survey the scene and the crowd.

"A sunset service. You inspired it."

"Me?"

"You reminded me of the whole yin and yang thing, talking about all the pretty things and all the ugly things you saw in New York each day. They're all connected: a vibrant city missing its spark, a dreamy hotel made available by night-marish circumstances, light and dark, hopes and fears, birth and death, good and bad.

"It's not all one or all the other," Davis added. "Media, television, politicians... They're doing a fine job keeping the ugly parts prominently displayed front and center. Green Hills needed to notice the pretty parts. And like you said the other day, what's a better representation of the world's beauty than an Oklahoma sunset?"

"I love it."

Davis swallowed the words, *I love you.*

As gorgeous as ever, Landry also looked completely worn out. She'd lost weight, and her eyes had taken on a bruised and hollow hue. Already brimming with emotion, she deserved a chance to recharge before Davis barraged her with declarations of love.

Once he'd figured it out for himself, peace wafted over him

like a thick, comforting blanket. He didn't have to tell her until the time was right; his knowing sufficed.

"I'm glad you made it in time for the show," Davis said. "And I'm not the only one. Come on, there's a whole crew waiting to see you."

Taking her hand, Davis walked Landry to the quilt where his parents and Zane listened to Mr. Mitchell wrap up his sermon. Maree and Rhys lounged on another quilt close by. Miss Sadie sat in a lawn chair between the two quilts. Others in his extended family weren't present at that moment, but they were there in spirit: M'Kenzee and Bren, Janie Lyn and Max. Even Jinx Malone, Scotty Philips, and Traise Mitchell, Davis begrudgingly admitted to himself. Each of them made a difference in his life.

That's what family did, and all those people were family.

34

____

If history repeats itself,
and the unexpected always happens,
how incapable must Man be
of learning from experience.
George Bernard Shaw

"School's out!" Zane ran around the house, jumped up and down, and raised quite a ruckus.

"Excuse me?" Landry questioned. She'd barely walked into the living room Tuesday morning when Zane's celebration erupted.

"Ms. Newton quit," Zane explained, absolutely elated and not one bit concerned that COVID, kids, and a currently fractured academic system might've broken the teacher he adored. "We were reading about government, something about the country having tree branches. We were taking turns reading paragraphs, but no one was keeping up. Ms. Newton would call a name to read, and then they'd just sit there until she told them which paragraph to read. It took forever to read one page, and half of it was a picture of an old scale like the one

Jinx uses to weigh nails in the hardware store. I told her that, and then Ryder said he and his dad were going to build a tree-house this summer. Suzy Reynolds said she's going to Bora Bora this summer, but that's not true because COVID closed the airports. Ryder said Suzy was making that up, and then Suzy started crying and said that everyone's mean to her. That's when Ms. Newton said to put a fork in her. We asked what that meant, and she said to go play outside. I asked her how long we could play, and she said not to come back until summer ends."

On that note, Zane shot out the front door, baseball bat in hand to practice his swing on the hit-a-way, which Landry recently learned attached to a pole — or in their case, a portable basketball goal beside the driveway — so young, energetic kids can train without needing a grown-up to pitch to them. She guessed an overtired parent designed it for their own survival.

"When did you exchange Z Man for the Tasmanian Devil?" Davis asked from the couch, where he'd been reading a book until Whirlwind Zane blew through.

"His poor teacher," Landry said, settling on the opposite end of the couch from Davis. "Mind if I turn on the TV? I'm in the mood for mindless entertainment, but if it'll bother you, I can go outside to watch Zane practice batting."

"You won't bother me a bit. Stretch out — I've got plenty of space." Davis tossed an extra throw pillow in her direction and returned to his book.

Deciding Davis's idea held merit, Landry snuggled into the corner of the sofa. She curled up under a lightweight quilt that never seemed to get folded or put away and flipped channels in search of something boring to put her to sleep. Station after station, the same story appeared. Landry sat up to see what had garnered such news coverage.

"Davis, have you seen this?"

"Hmm?" he asked from behind his book.

"A man died while being arrested," she told him. "In Minneapolis last night."

"Are you sure?" He set his book aside and joined her in the middle of the couch to see and hear the broadcast better. "That can't be real," Davis commented. "They wouldn't show the actual footage of a man being killed on regular television."

"I think it is. A bystander recorded it on a cell phone," Landry said.

"Why wouldn't a bystander stop the police?"

"What is a citizen supposed to do in the face of police authority?" she asked.

"I don't know, but this is wrong," Davis said with disgust.

"It's atrocious. He was already in handcuffs; what threat could he have posed?"

"Landry, you don't have to watch this. It's horrific, and you've seen enough trauma lately."

"I think I do," she said, stomach churning with nausea. "This can't occur without acknowledgement. They murdered that man."

Landry reached out to hold Davis's hand, but she couldn't take her eyes from the news footage.

*H*oping to recuperate from her time in New York, Landry had taken the remainder of May off from work at the hospital. But instead of resting, she fixated on the twenty-four-hour news cycle, which focused almost entirely on the COVID pandemic and social unrest.

Within hours of George Floyd's murder video being posted on social media, protests sprang up across the country. Many remained peaceful; a few turned violent.

Close to home, protests in Oklahoma City and Tulsa escalated into vandalism, looting, and pandemonium. With protestors out of control and no way to ensure public safety, police resorted to tossing tear gas into the streets.

Tears streamed down Landry's face as she watched business and historical districts she loved to visit fall apart, right before her very eyes.

"*Y*ou still up?" Davis asked, coming down the hall from his bedroom later that night.

"This documentary about the Tulsa Race Massacre sucked me in. Did the noise wake you?" Landry paused the program.

"Nah, I just got hungry."

"At midnight?"

"Where do you think ice cream got the name Midnight Snack? Want a bowl?"

"I'll take a scoop — *one* scoop."

Landry left the TV paused; a black-and-white photo of a prosperous, dynamic area of Tulsa in 1921 filled the screen.

"Tomorrow's the ninety-ninth anniversary," she mentioned as she took two spoons from the silverware drawer and two napkins from a metal canister. "In some ways society has come so far, and in other ways it just keeps repeating the same horrible behaviors again and again."

They sat at the kitchen table together, illuminated by that image frozen in time.

"Had you heard of the Tulsa Race Massacre before you moved here?" Davis asked.

"Not at all. Nor did I know a single thing about the brutal murders of members of the Indian nations in attempts to steal their land, their wealth, and their birthrights. Schools have a set number of hours with students, and as time passes, there is more and more history to consider... I get all of that, but these are important topics to cover. They need to be part of the curriculum. Then perhaps we can break the cycles of hatred, racism, and contempt obviously still rampant in America."

She slid the bowl in front of her to Davis's side of the table.

"You need to eat," he said quietly.

"I know," she agreed. "New York took a toll; I'll do better. Tomorrow. Thinking about all of this — so much senseless pain and blatant evil, then and now — is upsetting."

"I remember watching a movie called *The Boy in the Striped Pajamas* when I was in school. We'd been studying the Holocaust in social studies, and to finish up the unit, we watched the movie version of the book. Have you read it or seen the film?" Davis asked.

"I've heard of it, but no, I don't know the story specifically," Landry answered.

"It's about two eight-year-old boys — one German and one Jewish — who live on opposite sides of a concentration camp fence. Despite circumstances you can easily imagine, including the German boy's father being an SS officer, the two boys become best friends. Through a series of events, they realize the atrocities going on around them.

"When the Jewish boy's father goes missing, the German boy sneaks into the camp to help his friend find the missing man. To fit in, the German boy dresses like a prisoner in a striped uniform, which he thought was pajamas. At the end of the book, the Nazis throw both boys into a gas chamber and murder them with toxic pesticide pellets.

"That was it. They just died. They were good. They were kind. And they were murdered." Davis paused to let that sink in. "I was too old to be crying at school," he continued, "but that day, I couldn't stop. I cried all night, straight through supper, through my shower, and through to the next morning.

"At breakfast, I asked Mom why they made us watch that

horrible movie. I wanted her to be mad at them for traumatizing me. I'd cried enough tears to float a boat. My eyes were red and almost swollen shut. I thought she should go to school and throw a fit, make sure they never mistreated me again. But she wasn't angry. Not at all. So I asked her again, why would they show that to us? And you know what she said?"

Landry couldn't speak past the tears falling from her own eyes, so she shook her head *no*.

"So you can't forget."

35

*Love is the most important thing in the world,
but baseball is pretty good, too.*
Yogi Berra

Current events, a broken world, and flawed humanity weighed heavily on Landry.

At the same time, blessings presented themselves in many ways — both big and small — each day.

It turned out Ms. Newton merely paused school. Recognizing the kids had reached the end of their rope, she convinced the principal to release them for summer a few days earlier than planned, but with the understanding that she'd provide a gap curriculum for her students to work on over the summer. Ms. Newton also agreed to stay with her class, transitioning from second to third grade. Zane professed he was "here for it." He'd said it with a big smile, so Landry took it as good news.

Agent Vela's task force made progress in their investigation. They identified a gang of criminals trying to prove their worth to a larger, more organized syndicate. Common elements and bomb markings linked a few of the assorted fires in Green Hills to other arson attacks across the country. They'd not yet exonerated Mr. Armstrong, and in fact couldn't prove he hadn't been a party to the nefarious activities.

"Once the threads begin to unravel, it's just a matter of time before we reveal the big picture," Michael Vela predicted. Landry regarded that as good news as well.

Despite a continuous rise in COVID cases and subsequent deaths from virus complications throughout the United States, Green Hills avoided an outbreak. Landry returned to the hospital, working the night shift without fanfare, as if she'd never been gone. While she'd been in New York, the Green Hills Medical Center approved a new provider position for a pediatric fellow, which was the area of specialization Landry liked best. A not-so-secret rumor around the nurses' station on her floor purported that she had the job if she wanted it, which she did.

"It's as though they created it just for you," Miss Sadie told her with sage wisdom. "God provides. Didn't I tell you?"

He did, and she had.

Landry relished the flood of good news, yet the best of the good news happened on Opening Day.

"I hope I strike out every batter," Zane said, for the ten-thousandth time since he'd opened his eyes that morning.

"You won't," Davis assured him.

"I might." Zane reiterated.

"Sorry, Z Man. Nobody bats a thousand, and nobody escapes a walk. You play long enough, and you'll win some and lose some. It's the world order, buddy. Good and bad, ball and strike, happy and sad. Gotta learn to love the yo-yo."

"*Learn to love the yo-yo?* That's your best advice, Coach?" Landry gawked at Davis. He grinned back.

"Yeah, you know... The facts of life and all," he said with a shrug.

"Learn to love the yo-yo," she repeated as she pulled a wheeled cooler full of water and sports drinks toward the dugout.

Davis organized the bench just so...bats hanging on the fence, helmets on the hooks, and the lineup pinned to a clipboard. "You good?" he asked Landry before they began pregame warm up. He'd kept a close eye on her since her return from New York. She'd been physically, mentally, emotionally, and even spiritually depleted when she got home.

He nagged her to rest, but noticed she still hadn't been sleeping well. Miss Sadie baked and cooked for them — enough to feed a small army. Davis and Zane had put on a few pounds from the continuous feast at their door, but Landry still looked too thin.

On the down low, Davis arranged for Chief Everett to talk to Landry, under the guise of an interest in how the biggest city in America dealt with the worst numbers of illnesses and deaths from the pandemic. The fire chief hadn't needed to fake his interest. He'd been genuinely curious.

All the firefighters at Station #2 swore Chief Everett had been a counselor in a previous life; the man possessed an innate gift for filtering out the heart of a matter. Then he would always hand back what he'd learned about a person or a situation in a way that made life's answers appear easy and obvious.

Mr. Mitchell had also been by the house twice to check on Landry. The first time, he'd been on a mission to compile feedback from the sunset service. The second time, he'd been recruiting volunteers to organize another community-wide event. On both occasions, he'd listened to and prayed over Landry.

Answering the call to assist on the frontline during the worst weeks of the pandemic resulted in experiences she'd never forget. Those days became part of her as she lived them. And while recent events around the world challenged every-one's perspectives in different ways, with the support she'd been receiving since returning to Green Hills from New York, the light in Landry's eyes had begun to reemerge. Davis wanted to help her find her stride again. He wanted her faith in the world to be renewed.

"I'm good," she replied to his concern with a big smile, which went a long way to reassuring Davis that her fractured spirit was on the mend. That smile did funny things to his senses. He gazed at her for an extended moment. "Seriously," she laughed. "Go do some coach-y stuff, wrangle kids or something."

Grinning, he nodded and jogged out to hit baseballs to the outfielders.

Zane, the starting pitcher, and Ryder, the starting catcher, began warming up together in the bullpen just beyond the dugout.

Busy as ants scurrying in tandem, players, coaches, and parents prepared for the game. No one noticed the two figures watching from beyond the outfield fence.

The umpires called the teams in, the official scorer played "The Star-Spangled Banner" on a portable speaker, and the players took the field.

"Play ball!"

*A*s the visiting team, Zane didn't pitch until the bottom of the inning. By the time he walked to the pitching mound, Landry's nerves had tangled into a knot of excited anxiety.

It's kid-pitch Little League. Get a grip!

The self-talk didn't work. How did mothers do this game after game, sport after sport, year after year? Without a doubt, it aged them. Also without a doubt, they loved it.

Glancing over at the line of mommas sitting in lawn chairs along the fence — cheering and clapping and chatting — Landry could tell those ladies didn't want to be anywhere else. How might her life have been different if she'd had a mom like that? How would it feel to *be* a mom like that? They made it look so easy, so natural. But it wasn't...not for everyone. Some people just weren't meant to live that life.

Davis returned to the dugout from where he'd been standing in foul territory just behind the first-base bag, coaching and signaling their baserunners.

"Still okay?" he asked with concern in both his tone and the tilt of his jaw.

Landry pushed aside thoughts of being a mom and fears of failing a child. She plastered on her best cheerleading smile and said, "Of course! Who's up first?"

As the game progressed, both teams knocked off some rust, settled into the game, and showed they'd been working hard at practice. After five innings, the score remained tied at 0–0.

In the top of the sixth and final inning, Ryder drew a walk.

Runner on base.

The next two batters popped out on a high fly balls, one that went right to the first baseman and one that the left fielder snagged in foul territory. Ryder couldn't leave the bag to advance during either at-bat.

Zane stepped up to the plate. He watched the first pitch…
Strike one.

He swung at the second pitch but fouled it off. The third pitch came in high for a ball. The fourth did the same. With the count at two balls and two strikes, Landry checked her pulse and found it to be ridiculously fast.

The fifth pitch went wild! The catcher scrambled to locate it underneath him, but it had rolled to the fence. He hustled to grab it and assess where to throw. The boy reacted quickly, but Ryder ran faster. He stole second!

Runner in scoring position.

Landry stood up from where she'd been sitting on the bench seat in the dugout. She wanted to pace, but forced her feet to stay still. A downed power line zipping with electricity couldn't hold a candle to her nerves.

Meanwhile, no one saw the two men working their way closer to the crowd.

"Full count," the home plate umpire called.

As if we didn't know.

"You've got this, Zane," Landry called out from where she stood, gripping the fence that separated the dugout from the field.

The other coach signaled to the catcher. The catcher signaled to the pitcher. The pitcher nodded, gripped the ball inside his glove while staring down the plate, and stepped into his windup. As if in slow motion, his knee lifted to pivot. His hands mimicked the motion to stop by his shoulder.

Landry gripped the fence tighter.

Striding forward, the pitcher released the ball — a fastball right down the pipe.

Zane let it ride a split second before starting his swing.

The bat cracked against the ball with a zing on the sweet spot.

He tossed the bat as he sprinted to first base.

A line drive, right over the shortstop's extended glove. The centerfielder caught it off the bounce at the same time Ryder rounded third base. The ball and the boy raced to see who could get to home plate first.

"Run!"

"Go, Ryder!"

"Faster!"

Just as the ball approached the catcher's glove, Ryder dropped into a figure-four slide.

Landry heard her heart beating during a pregnant pause of silence before the umpire yelled...

"Safe!"

The stands erupted in cheers.

Oh my.

Landry wiped her eyes, clapped as hard as her hands could tolerate the sting, and looked toward Davis. He stood with Zane at first base. Both her boys wore fantastic smiles.

Her boys. If only it were that easy.

Davis caught her looking and winked at her. She raised her hands above her head, hopping up and down in silent cheers. He pumped a fist in the air, and they both laughed. The next batter struck out.

At the middle of the sixth, Zane's team led 1–0. Half an inning remained.

The men crept closer.

Zane walked to the mound; Ryder crouched behind the plate.

"Just play catch, boys. You do this every day," Roddy told the boys from his seat on a five-gallon tub of sunflower seeds.

Zane shrugged his shoulders, stretched his neck, and stepped up to pitch. An image flashed in Landry's mind... She saw Zane as a young man, strong and broad shouldered, ready to take on the world. In her vision, Zane still wore his sable hair a little shaggy, and his deep brown eyes still sparkled with a joyful gleam. The soft roundness of his cheeks had matured into a chiseled jaw, set with confidence and determination. His youthful exuberance had developed and been channeled into a smoldering energy, harnessed but bristling just beneath the surface.

What a heartbreaker you'll be.

She prayed to be around to witness it, hoped she'd still be part of Zane's life down the road.

"Rock and fire," Davis reminded him as he stared down the pipe, ready to pitch to the third batter after the first two popped out on fly balls.

Zane wound up, released the pitch.

"Ball," the ump called.

"What?" one parent yelled in outrage.

"No, that's a strike!" a mom screamed.

"Right over the plate," another spectator argued.

"Keep working," Landry cheered, determined to drown out the negative vibes. "You're ahead, Zane. That's just one pitch."

He wound up again and slung the ball to Ryder's glove.

"Strike."

"Looked exactly like the first one," a dad grumbled for all to hear.

"There it is," Landry said even louder.

Zane delivered his third pitch.

"Ball."

That time, Landry proactively cheered positive encouragement *before* any other fans could do otherwise. How such loving, kind, wonderful parents could transform into absurdly competitive lunatics so quickly boggled her mind.

Next pitch...

"Foul ball." It disappeared over the stands and counted as a strike.

Learn to love the yo-yo.

The umpire announced, "Full count."

Landry stood, held onto the fence again, and tried to calm her sizzling nerves. Too hyped up to voice her cheers, she thought them in her head instead...

Come on, sweetie. You can do it.

Zane kicked the mound, used his cleat to drag the dirt flat in front of the rubber mat. He circled to take his place, clasped the ball inside his glove, nodded at Ryder's sign. Once again, Zane moved through his pitch. Fast ball, right on target.

The batter swung with all his might. The ball snapped against leather. *Strike three.*

"Ballgame!" the umpire called.

The boys went wild. The families went crazy.

A loud "Great work, Zane," could be heard above the whooping and hollering.

Zane froze. He looked to the gate, just beside the dugout, where the parents and siblings filtered onto the field to celebrate. As the people spread out to hug and congratulate their players, the two men who'd watched every play of the game in silence came into view.

"Dad?" Zane called out. There was so much hope and love in three little letters. "Dad!"

Dropping his equipment and tossing his hat as he ran, Zane bolted toward Eddie. One step before he launched himself at the man's body, he stopped himself.

"Are you okay?" Zane whispered on a sob. "Can I hug you?"

Eddie knelt down, tears streaming down his face.

"You'd better," he answered, opening his arms to engulf Zane in an embrace.

36

───────

The most dangerous thing you can do
in life is play it safe.
Casey Neistat

Davis draped an arm over Landry's shoulders and watched the sweetest of reunions take place right there on Field #4 of the Green Hills City Park.

"Wow." She spoke softly, before resting her head against him.

"Yeah, *wow*," Davis agreed.

"That was quite a game," Landry said. "What a way to put a stamp on Opening Day."

"And there I thought the team parade this morning was going to be the highlight. Of course, the chili dogs were pretty amazing at lunch," he joked.

Landry poked him in the ribs before moving to stand in front of him.

"It'll be hard to beat this victory."

"We have a lot of games to play. I foresee a fun season ahead...some big things on the horizon."

She looked at him with a side-glance, but before she could comment or ask for details, Special Agent Michael Vela approached them.

"Hey, Landry," Michael said. "It's good to see you again." His words and his expression didn't match, one warm and welcoming, the other dark and foreboding. Then he turned his attention to Davis, every bit a high-powered law enforcer and voice of authority. "It's going down. Tonight. You coming?"

"What's going down?" Landry asked.

"I'll be there." Davis spoke over her. Literally over her as the two men looked at one another, ignoring Landry between them.

"Hello? What's going down?" she asked again.

"Sun sets at 8:30. We need to be in place well before that, so I'll pick you up at 6:15." Then Michael finally acknowledged Landry with an apologetic smile. "It really is good to see you." A light ignited in his eyes. "You know... Now that you're back from New York, maybe we can have dinner sometime." He gave Davis one of those manly nods that confirms, affirms, and bids farewell, all in one half-motion.

"Is Agent Vela spending a lot of time in Green Hills now?" Landry asked, watching the man walk to a dark SUV left idling in the middle of the parking lot by the baseball field.

"Sure hope not." Davis clipped his words and walked into the dugout to gather up equipment.

Landry scuttled to catch up, grabbing empty drink bottles and gum wrappers to throw away.

"Why not? He seems like a great guy." When Davis didn't reply, Landry kept going. "Davis, what's wrong? What happened? Are you mad about something? You were all smiles, and now you're grumpy. And what's going down? What was Agent Vela talking about?"

"Leave that," Davis ordered.

"What?"

"Leave the trash; the boys have to do that. It's the only way they learn to leave a place better than they found it."

"Oh— Okay," Landry stuttered, setting the litter back where she'd found it and moving to stand in Davis's way. "Why won't you answer my question?"

"Which one? You've asked several now. Z Man must be rubbing off on you."

If he wanted her to back down, he was sorely mistaken.

"All of them," she demanded.

She softened when dark clouds colored his sky-blue eyes. Looking closer, he hadn't relaxed his jaw since Michael Vela appeared. They seemed to get along fine, so what was the problem?

"Please?" Landry added.

Davis studied her for a long minute before exhaling a sigh.

"Fine," he relented. "I'll tell you. But not here. I'll explain everything when we get home. Come on," he said, finding his smile. "Let's go see Eddie now that he and Zane have had a little time."

The celebratory reunion continued at Davis's house.

Miss Sadie and Maree set out snacks, Zane remained glued to Eddie's side, Landry visited with Derek Macall, the other man at the baseball game with Eddie. Davis and Rhys disappeared.

Landry watched for them to reappear while listening to their new guest.

"So, you work at Parkland?" She tried to sound interested and focused, which she was... And she wasn't.

"I did," Derek said. "I grew up in Austin and attended the University of Texas. When I finished my Bachelor of Science in Nursing, I earned a degree in post-burn therapy from UT

Southwest in Dallas. From there, I accepted an offer in the burn unit at Parkland. I worked in aftercare services and discovered my calling there. After three years, I finally figured out how best to use my passion for helping burn victims. A year ago, I started Life After to counsel, train, treat, and assist burn survivors with reintegration into their communities and normal routines. And here we are today."

"He's the best— hands down," Eddie attested. "My determination to get home outweighed my common sense and ability to listen, to follow doctors' orders. Derek taught me that the fastest way to be with Zane was to slow down and let my body heal." He smiled down at Zane with an air of victory.

Fascination with Derek's work and interest in Eddie's recovery warred with nosiness. Where had Davis and Rhys gone? And what were they up to?

"I'd rather say I guided gently," Derek laughed. "The best way forward often requires adopting a new viewpoint, and that can be difficult. Life is dynamic; sometimes we must change our perspective to keep up. Life after a burn — life after *any* trauma — doesn't have to be limited by that experience. Quite the opposite, really... Life after might be better for the blessings that come with survival."

Landry couldn't be sure if Derek Macall still spoke about Eddie, or if he'd crawled into her psyche to witness her worst memories, glimpse her most frightening nightmares, and identify her most terrifying fears.

A knock at the front door rescued her from finding out.

"Excuse me," she said, avoiding eye contact with Derek.

Davis beat her to the front door by half a step.

Special Agent Michael Vela had come to call.

"Ready?" he asked.

"Rhys is coming, too. We'll be right out," Davis said. Michael returned to his SUV, and Davis closed the front door.

"Going where?" Landry refused to be ignored.

"The doctors released Mr. Armstrong. They treated him for an infection, got him some food and fluids, and his amnesia cleared. We're going to help him move some things back to his camp that were stolen from him and we found in the woods."

"Mr. Armstrong doesn't have amnesia. He has Alzheimer's disease. That doesn't *clear up* with some food and fluids. What's going on?"

Davis took Landry's arm and led her to his room, where he closed the door behind them.

"The story I just told you is what we've passed around town, planted in bars and diners throughout neighboring counties. An undercover agent posing as Walter Armstrong is going with us. We intend to flush out the gang that left Mr. Armstrong for dead, people gathering an arsenal of weapons across the southeast United States. The task force heard rumblings that those criminals plan to visit Mr. Armstrong in the woods, to finish what they started so he can't talk ever again."

Two taps rapped against his door, presumably from Rhys telling Davis to hurry.

"Please don't go," Landry asked, trying but failing not to cry. And not to beg. "This won't work. Someone's going to get hurt. Or killed."

"I love you," he said, with words as soft and tender as his touch as he traced his index finger down the side of her cheek. He repeated the cherishing gesture with the backs of his knuckles. "I've wanted to tell you — needed you to know. I love you," he said again.

"Da—" He stopped her with a gentle finger to her lips before lightly gripping her chin.

"I'm sorry. I have to go."

With the whisper of a kiss on her lips, he left.

umbfounded, she sat on the edge of his bed, which is where Maree found her a little bit later.

"Derek recommends Zane sleep here a few more nights," Maree said, sitting down beside Landry and taking her hand. Feelings and affections came easily for Maree; Landry envied her that. "Eddie needs time and space to acclimate, to establish new routines. They presented it to Zane in a way that didn't hurt his feelings. At least not too much. Although Zane still won't let Eddie out of his sight."

"I don't blame him," Landry admitted. "We all want to keep our loved ones close. Safe."

"You all right?" Maree asked.

"I must not seem like it... A lot of people have been asking that lately." Landry didn't mean to sound snarky, but her tone had a testy thread of irritability to it.

"A lot of people have been worried about you. You've undergone quite a bit in the past few months."

"Nothing compared to Eddie, or even Zane. In fact, the entire world's going through quite a bit right now," Landry pointed out.

"Like prayer requests, there's no priority list of pain and suffering. God doesn't look at one prayer as more important than another. Nor should we consider one hardship more or less valid. No matter what we are going through — big or small, happy or sad, easy or hard — it's real. It's significant, and it matters. *You* matter, Landry. To all of us." Maree continued to hold her hand as she said her piece.

"Davis just told me he loves me."

"Of course he does."

"I don't think he meant as a friend."

"No, honey," Maree laughed. "Not as *just* a friend."

"Maree, what do I do? It's like I'm teetering on the edge of a cliff, scared to go back where I came from, but equally afraid to look down and fall."

"How's the view there?" Maree asked.

"What?" Confusion muddled Landry's mind.

"What do you see from the top of that cliff? What does moving forward with Davis look like? The right relationship with the person you're meant to love is beautiful. It's still work. It requires effort, respect, give and take, forgiveness at times, and lots of understanding. But it's not drudgery. It's the kind of work that comes with huge rewards and shared victories. It results in tremendous love. The work is worth it when the love is there. So how does it look? What do you see standing on that cliff?" Maree asked again.

"Davis," Landry accepted. "I see Davis there with me."

"Who are you?" The shorter of two disgustingly filthy men shoved Agent Williams against a tree.

"Walter Armstrong," he answered, looking at the ground and feigning weakness.

"This ain't the same old man," the short, pungent guy protested, pointing a black nail at the older gentleman. "This ain't the one that's been following me, putting out my starters as soon as I leave."

"Yeah, I've been there," Agent Williams blustered. "I saw it all."

"Prove it," the nasty guy challenged. "How come you let them peoples' house burn? You put out the blaze behind them stores in town. You stole my phone and called the cops on me at that old, abandoned warehouse on the highway. I saw you trample out my practice fires, too. So, prove it. Why couldn't you stop me at that big house?" Pure evil gleamed in the man's eye. "Outsmarted you that time, didn't I? Laid a trap and you—"

"Shut up, Clive," the taller, slightly less putrid man ordered. "Answer the man. Who are you?" He approached Agent Williams while sliding a knife from a sheath on his belt.

"Like I said, Walter Armstrong. Pleased to meet you," he spat, still acting like a man recently hospitalized, but also trying to imitate a man who'd lived off the grid most of his life and wouldn't be easy to intimidate. "Now get your hands off me," he said coolly.

"Blaze, I'm tellin' you… That ain't him. Last year, I knocked him out cold — steel pipe, right across the head when he tried to save that house. No way it didn't leave a scar the size of Texas," Clive boasted obnoxiously. "Come on, Blaze—"

Blaze backhanded Clive. Blood drizzled down his face from a now-busted lip. He turned hurt eyes on the taller man.

"What'd you do that for?" Clive whined.

"To shut you up," Blaze answered. "I'll do it for good if you don't follow orders. You know I will. Go get some rope from camp and tie him to that tree. This fella's gonna see what happens to old men — no matter who they are — that interfere with the Order of Soldiers."

The Order of Soldiers? Was that the political cult Vela had mentioned? Who were they? What were they planning? Question after question popped into Davis's head. How much longer were the Feds going to wait to rescue Agent Williams? That was the most pressing of Davis's questions right then.

"I can help you," Agent Williams offered to Blaze. "I'm a soldier, too. You saw my gear… Army Ranger Walter Armstrong, 1st Battalion, 75th Infantry, combat engineer and explosives specialist, at your service."

That got Blaze's attention.

"Why you live out here? If you got all that trainin' in the military, why you homeless and livin' with the varmints?" Blaze didn't lower his knife, but potential uses for a skilled soldier piqued his interest.

"Not homeless. I live with the land, off the grid. I do so by choice, one I made a long time ago. The military used me and left me for dead. Taught me a skill, trained me to kill, and then tossed me aside. Let me put those skills to work for you. In the Order of Soldiers."

Agent Williams nearly had Davis convinced. From where they hid in the underbrush not forty yards away, they watched the wheels turning in Blaze's mind, too.

"You might be useful, old man. Kill you or recruit you? Which would show the others not to mess with me?" Blaze mused aloud.

The longer he thought, the sloppier he got. With Agent Williams no longer in the knife's trajectory, Michael Vela signaled the SWAT force to move.

Two years of arson, vandalism, pain, and destruction took less than five minutes to take down.

"*M*r. Armstrong was a hero all along." Miss Sadie said what they'd all been thinking.

"Traumatic brain injuries increase the risk of Alzheimer's disease," Landry added. "That hit over the head trying to save the Jensens' house likely escalated Mr. Armstrong's dementia symptoms."

"Will he be okay?" Zane asked, snuggled next to Eddie, who'd determined that one night at their house without Zane had been plenty to readjust. Hands full of coffee, juice, chocolate milk, and donuts, Eddie and Derek had woken everyone bright and early. Derek reported that waiting until 6:45 a.m. had been pushing it. Eddie needed to be with Zane.

"That's a hard question to answer, sweetie," Landry

replied. "From a medical standpoint, there's no cure for Alzheimer's disease. Right now, we don't even have a treatment to slow it down. So, the answer to that part is sadly no, he won't get better. But for those of faith, we know that Mr. Armstrong's pain will be over soon. He'll be honored and remembered for serving his country, for loving his community, and for fighting evil in this world. A perfect treasure awaits him, and in that way, he'll be better than okay."

"What about the Order of Soldiers?" Derek asked. "That sounds like a bad crew."

"From what Michael could tell us, they're the worst. Randall Blaze Compton and his older brother, Clive, are bottom-of-the-barrel scum. Lower-level lackies can't provide much intel, but the task force will investigate every item they found and follow up on every lead they uncover. In the meantime, city and county officials are creating a joint-agency commission with the forestry service to make sure no one abuses our land like that again." Disgust and determination strengthened Davis's explanation.

"You found the answers, cleared the accusations hovering over Mr. Armstrong, and ended the serial arson attacks. That's pretty great," Landry commended. "You accomplished all your goals, got everything you wanted."

"Almost," he said cryptically. "Almost," he said again, eyes locked on Landry.

"You don't have to carry everything in one load," Eddie told Zane, who resembled a pack mule trudging down the hall from the blue bedroom. "We live less than a mile away. We'll be back, I promise."

"Indeed, you will. Davis and Rhys want to cook out next

weekend. We can all meet here. *I'm* not cooking, but whatever Maree brings will be fabulous," Landry told them.

"Sounds like a plan," Eddie agreed. "Come on, kiddo. Let's go home."

After they left, Landry found Davis tidying up the things Zane left behind.

"I think the blue room should stay as-is," Davis stated matter-of-factly.

"Yeah, it looks good," Landry agreed, trying not to reveal the sadness in her heart.

"I guess I'll redo the green bedroom now, too."

She needed to pack her things as Zane had done. She had brought little, and while by most people's standards her load remained light, she had accumulated a few special items, mostly memorabilia and keepsakes from outings with the boys.

Her boys.

But not anymore. Zane and Eddie were back together, as they should be. Davis had plans for his house. Landry needed to make some decisions, accept or decline the job offer she'd received for that new position as a pediatric fellow, and move back to Miss Sadie's or find a place of her own. Their adventure had reached its end.

Learn to love the yo-yo.

Landry turned and walked to her room. She took clothes off hangars and folded them for her duffle.

"What are you doing?" Davis asked from the doorway.

Startled, Landry looked his way, but it hurt too much to look into his eyes. Her heartbeat turned sluggish and heavy. A tear slipped down her cheek. "Heading to Marshall Mansion, I guess."

"Why?"

"Zane's gone," she said.

"Okay?"

Davis waited for her to say something.

"What's that got to do with Miss Sadie's place?" he asked.

"That's where I live." Landry's voice broke with emotion.

"Nooo," Davis drew out, walking to close the space between them. "This is where you live. With me, the man who loves you, who wants to marry you, and wants to redo this house with you. You're welcome to move out of the green room, but only as far as the master suite."

"You love me."

"I told you that yesterday," Davis said, as though it had been nothing of consequence.

"You want to marry me?"

"Surely you've heard the song... *First comes love, then comes marriage*," he teased, setting his feet wide and bending his knees just enough so they stood eye-to-eye.

"You want to redo this house with me?"

"Come on, Eileen. I think even Mrs. Hartley would agree that some massive updating is well overdue."

Davis lifted first her left arm over his right shoulder, then her right arm over his left shoulder. Then he settled his hands on the sides of her waist.

"Doctor Stark, I love you." He emphasized each word slowly, never taking his eyes from Landry's. "Do you love me?"

She nodded without comment.

"Then let's do this; let's live life together. We'll be there for one another, to encourage and support each other. We'll focus on the good parts of life, and we'll pray through the hard parts. We'll cry together when times are tough, and we'll celebrate and rejoice together when life is good. As long as we're together, we'll face it all, take the world in stride, and enjoy every second along the way. Embrace this opportunity to grab hold of a life of love and happiness. With me," he urged.

"Learn to love the yo-yo?" she asked with a teasing smile.

"You said it," he agreed, his dazzling blue eyes alight with hope and love.

"Not yet, I haven't."

Landry stepped closer, tightened her arms around his neck.

"Okay, Daniel Davis. I love you, too," she pledged.

She lifted her lips to his, but he stood taller so she couldn't reach. She opened her eyes and looked at him in shock.

"Just to make sure I understand..." he said. "And I need to be very clear on this— The No Kissing Clause is officially, legally, *truly* no longer in effect?"

"The No Kissing Clause is no more," Landry said with a promising but coy smirk.

Davis wrapped his arms around her ribs and swung her in circles, laughing and whooping.

She laughed until she cried.

When he set her back on her feet, she gazed into his eyes, letting him see all the love and respect and desire she'd bottled up in her heart for him.

"Well, then," Davis whispered in a rough voice. "Let's take a chance on love."

Then he sealed their deal with a kiss.

———

**The best view comes after
the hardest climb.
Author unknown
(but worth repeating)**

———

 he End.

But not for long. Please enjoy this sneak peek into Book 5…

UNDEVELOPED LOVE

But to you who are listening I say:
Love your enemies,
do good to those who hate you…
Luke 6:27

Thursday, December 10, 2020

Two oak trees, full and green and immense in their girth, loomed over the entrance to Twin Oaks. They towered above the driveway and guarded the gate like fierce defenders. Blake Fisher squinted at one trunk and then at the other. Just as she'd suspected, angry faces appeared in the thick, rough bark. They'd stood watch over the Sharps' ranch for a hundred and forty years; they knew as well as Blake did exactly who belonged there — and who did not.

A work truck exited the property, providing Blake the opportunity she needed. She scooted her old but dependable FJ Cruiser through the entrance — without permission. Her impeccable timing was not a coincidence. She'd cased the ranch, tracked the comings and goings of the cowboys, staff, and family members who lived there. Her reconnaissance had paid off. Hypothetically, Blake had scaled the walls of Camelot.

She pushed aside a twinge of guilt, pretending a sense of accomplishment caused the flutter in her stomach. And really, the trespassing couldn't be helped. After months of returned letters, ignored emails, and rejected calls, the Sharps had forced Blake to take matters into her own hands.

So this is Twin Oaks.

Begrudgingly, Blake admitted — if only to herself — that descriptions and photos didn't do it justice.

She drove under a dense canopy of spindly bare branches attached to more ancient oaks that lined the brick drive. Beyond the perfectly placed trees, pipe fencing created a perimeter around rolling pastures thick with winter rye, frolicking horses, and more massive trees. The metal of the posts, painted a pristine white and radiant with the sun's bright light, projected an air of cool, clean, crisp, and stately magnificence.

The Big House, as they called it, hadn't come into view yet, but if the landscape looked snobby and off-putting, the house would be even worse. Heaven knew the family inside made stuck-up look downright gracious.

Two curves and a bridge later, Blake topped a hill and came face-to-face with all Twin Oaks's fabled and illustrious glory. Her foot lifted from the gas pedal of its own volition as her mind processed the incredible view ahead. A strong and exquisite ranch house, constructed with a perfect blend of logs, planks, rocks, and bricks, sat prominently in the middle of a brilliant clearing. That many shades of brown and such a mixture of materials should have looked disjointed. Instead, the sprawling structure looked as though it had been born of the earth on which it stood. Mimicking the impressive fence line, white shutters reflected the sun and brought the landscaping and the lodging together. An array of colorful cold-weather flowers, bright red winterberry shrubs, and ornamental foliage decorated pots and planters on the front porch. More of the same filled beds edged in low strips of aged and weathered metal, and even more foliage trailed onto the grounds, seamlessly separating the house from the fields.

Neither cold nor foreboding, Twin Oaks appeared cheerful and welcoming.

Blake knew better.

———

"Why is that rust bucket out front?"

Hudson Sharp ignored his brother's question.

"Who's the babe stepping out of it?"

Hudson Sharp ignored his *other* brother's question.

"And where has she been all my life?"

Hudson Sharp ignored his *third* brother's question.

He'd learned long ago that his best chance of finding peace and quiet came with simply *not* answering. Speaking to the boys invited more conversation, which created more noise, which Hudson abhorred. Taken one at a time, the triplets wore Hudson out; together, they functioned like a tsunami-tornado in the middle of a tropical storm . . . best to hunker down and hide until they passed through.

As hoped and expected, they meandered off when he declined to engage.

Less humored by their antics than their doting parents, Hudson wanted the nineteen-year-olds to develop a desire for something beyond girls, friends, and good times. After their freshman year of rodeoing for Tarleton State University, their grades were fine, but not great. They had done well enough to earn newcomer-of-the-year honors that season, but they had to improve if they wanted to make it to the College National Finals Rodeo.

As their older brother, Hudson had somehow assumed responsibility for their futures when he'd accepted responsibility for running the ranch. In one fell swoop, their mom and dad had announced that with the triplets gone to college, it was past time for them to start "experiencing life." They'd named Hudson president and managing member of their family corporation, bought a seventy-five-foot superyacht, and set out to spend their retirement on the water until someone provided them with a need to go home, namely grandbabies to spoil. They had made no mention of leaving their three young hellions in Hudson's charge. But someone had to keep an eye on them, and with no other volunteers vying for the role, it had fallen to Hudson to be their guardian.

In the eleven months since that big revelation last Christmas, a global pandemic had sent the boys home full-time, forcing them to take their college classes over the internet. With an endless supply of energy, a low tolerance for boredom, and one another to encourage poor decisions, the triplets were quite a handful. By Hudson's accounting, the boys were more difficult to manage than a sixty-seven-thousand-acre cattle ranch. And a horse farm. And a hobby-level goat dairy that produced milk, cheese, and soaps. And a patch of Christmas trees.

Hudson couldn't forget the Christmas trees . . . the current bane of his existence — outside his siblings, of course.

Years ago, before his Loony Aunt Juni — her chosen moniker, not of Hudson's doing — traded in her layered skirts and bohemian scarves for haute couture and thousand-dollar stilettos, Juniper Roxanne Sharp had scattered thirty handfuls of fir, pine, spruce, and cypress seedlings across thirty acres on the southeast boundary of the ranch to commemorate her thirtieth birthday. She'd put no thought into the planting, hadn't spaced the seeds, and had paid zero attention to irrigation. As a result of her haphazard behavior and indicative of Juniper's Midas touch, Twin Oaks housed one of the most bountiful Christmas tree farms in Oklahoma.

Hudson allowed the trees to be harvested only because if he did not thin them out per a soil management schedule, the acreage would suffer. He refused to sell them; instead, Hudson had worked a deal with their preacher, Mr. Mitchell, to set up a tree lot at the church. It opened the day after Thanksgiving and closed on Christmas Eve. The youth group worked the lot every year, and in exchange, the kids kept everything they earned to fund summer camps and mission trips. Best of all, Hudson kept his name completely out of the deal.

He might also have allowed the harvesting because the trees remained important to Aunt Juni, but he'd never admit such a thing in her presence. As CEO of Juniper Goat Co., a division of Sharp Enterprises, she oversaw the goat dairy. The world believed she'd abandoned her free-spirited ways, settled down in Green Hills, and burned her bangles and coins. But underneath her Harvard business degree, her fierce boardroom negotiations, and her incredible knack for marketing campaigns, his beloved Loony Aunt Juni still shared his obsession for the land, the scent of the evergreens, the neighing of horses and mooing of cows, and the pull of the soil. She still walked barefoot through the fields, dabbled in floral oils and fragrance creations for soaps and candles, and swam in the pond. Above all else, she adored Christmas.

Hudson could no more allow harm to come to those thirty acres than he could stab himself in the heart.

Which explained why he'd avoided Blake Fisher, the real estate agent blowing up his phone, his email, and his DMs on social media, like the plague. Seriously, who stalked a man over direct message, anyway?

———

Blake eased her Santa-suit-red SUV the rest of the way up the brick drive, soaking up as many details as possible . . . just in case they tossed her off the premises and banned her from returning after her first visit.

The landscape and the house were just the beginning. Multiple barns, numerous outbuildings, a chicken coop far larger than her home and office, an elegant greenhouse, and the most delightful wraparound porch Blake had ever seen accented the property with color and warmth. Everywhere she looked, something looked lovely.

Blake parked her vehicle, walked to the porch of the Big House, and stepped up to the tall double doors. Taking a deep breath to settle and steel her nerves, Blake lifted her hand to knock. Before her knuckles rapped on the intricately carved wood, one of the massive doors opened to reveal three almost-identical young men.

"Well, hello," Boy #1 greeted her with overfamiliar appreciation.

"What can *we* do for *you?*" Boy #2 asked suggestively.

"Name it, and it's yours," Boy #3 pledged with juvenile confidence.

Ah, the infamous Sharp triplets . . . living up to every wild-oat-sewing, youthfully ignorant, only-the-good-die-young description she'd heard of them since her move to Green Hills. They were precisely as she'd expected: rich and spoiled.

Blake fought the urge to wipe the smug grins off their tanned, chiseled faces.

Stay professional; everything rides on this sale.

"I'm looking for Mr. Sharp, please," she requested, holding her chin high and her shoulders back. Their wealth and entitlement did not intimidate her.

"It's your lucky day," Boy #1 said.

"You found him," Boy #2 leered.

"Mr. *Hudson* Sharp?"

"Aw, man. Why do the hot ones always want to talk to Hud?" Boy #3 grumbled.

"We'll go get him," the three boys offered simultaneously, their unified voices revealing their disappointment.

"Thank you," she called to the backs of the trio as they walked away, leaving her to peruse the foyer.

Blake ran a hand over more intricate carvings on the wall paneling beside the front doors. After absorbing the sun through the oversized windows on either side of the entryway, the smooth wood warmed her chilled skin. She admired an oil painting of a cowboy and a woman beside a stream, which hung over a set of metal hooks holding raincoats and cowboy hats. Someone had placed a large crystal vase of lush and vibrant winter flowers in the center of a round mahogany table, which was impressive in both size and quality. Had her friend Jinx Malone made the gorgeous table? Or perhaps his grandad had, when Duke could still do woodwork. Blake pressed her weight onto both hands, palms flat on the entryway table, as she leaned forward to reach the bouquet and test the flowers' perfume. Eyes closed, Blake inhaled the fresh floral fragrance. She'd just lifted onto her tiptoes to get a little closer to the heavenly scent when the authoritative clip of boot heels against the stained concrete floor alerted Blake to someone coming her way.

———

Those blasted boys would've abandoned the stranger in their foyer all night if Hudson had left it to them to get rid of her. Therefore, he had no choice but to confront the lady. Letting his steps thunder down the hall to signal he didn't appreciate the disruption, Hudson opened his mouth to roar whatever it took to make her go away when the sprite of a woman stopped him in his tracks.

Light filtering through the front doors' sidelight windows cast a glow around her, head to high-heeled toe. Bouncy waves of layered auburn hair draped to cover her face as she leaned over to smell the flowers Anita, the housekeeper's daughter, liked to put all around the house when she came to cook for them a few times each week.

Balanced on her hands, she rested her hips against the edge of the wooden table like a gymnast on the uneven bars. Both her feet dangled above the floor, one leg bent, one leg straight. After inhaling a breath so deep her shoulders lifted, she slowly lowered her feet back to the earth and shifted her weight from her arms.

With one hand, the woman ran her fingers along the tendrils hanging at her temple to hold them out of her way. As she continued the gesture, tucking her hair behind her ear, a wave of awareness and a tingle of *something* ran down Hudson's spine. When she closed her eyes for a brief pause, maybe to inhale the bouquet's fragrance one last time, or possibly shoring up patience and strength, his pulse quickened. His breath caught.

Then his enchantress looked his way, and Hudson Sharp's heart stopped completely.

BOOK 4 PLAYLIST

***Music expresses that which cannot be said
and on which it is impossible to be silent.
Victor Hugo***

Enjoy the music that helped inspire the story…

1. Flirtbird - Duke Ellington
2. Tennessee Whiskey - Chris Stapleton
3. Cigarette Daydreams - Cage the Elephant
4. Mommas - The Swan Brothers
5. Come on Eileen - Dexys Midnight Runners
6. Every Little Thing She Does is Magic - The Police
7. I Want to Know What Love Is - Foreigner
8. Be Our Guest - Angela Lansbury and Jerry Orbach
9. Just What I Needed - The Cars
10. December, 1963 - Frankie Valli & The Four Seasons
11. The Promise - When in Rome
12. Kiss Her You Fool - Kids That Fly
13. Always Something There to Remind Me -
    Naked Eyes

14. The Tide is High - Blondie
15. You've Got a Friend in Me - Randy Newman
16. Can't Take My Eyes Off of You - Ms. Lauryn Hill
17. Show Me What I'm Looking For - Carolina Liar
18. Live Like That - Sidewalk Prophets
19. Too Good to Be True - Edens Edge
20. Walking on a Dream - Empire of the Sun
21. The Night We Met - Lord Huron
22. I Melt with You - Modern English
23. Everywhere - Fleetwood Mac
24. Hold Me - Fleetwood Mac
25. Hold Me - Jamie Grace & TobyMac
26. Maybe I'm Amazed - Paul McCartney
27. Take Me Out to the Ball Game - The Andrews Sisters and Dan Dailey with Vic Schoen and his orchestra
28. Chances Are - Johnny Mathis
29. Chances - The Strokes
30. Take a Chance on Me - ABBA
31. I Choose You - Sara Bareilles
32. Everlasting Love - Carl Carlton
33. Stolen Dance - Milky Chance

Available on Spotify as
"Book 4: Take a Chance on Love
by Virginia'dele Smith"

ABOUT THE AUTHOR

Ashli Montgomery is a wife, a momma, and an author whose passion is sharing love stories, books, quilts, yoga, recipes, and all of her favorite things in life. She is quilting to mend the mind by spearheading a community of quilters through Quilt 2 End ALZ, Inc., a 501(c)(3) nonprofit she launched to use her quilting hobby as a platform to advocate for an end to Alzheimer's disease.

Ashli writes wholesome and cozy romance under the pen name Virginia'dele Smith to honor Syble Virginia Tidwell, Adele Gertrude Baylin, and Etta Jean Smith. These three cherished grandmothers were beautiful role models, teaching Ashli to love without judgment and to always put family first. Through Grandma Syble's journals and appetite for books, through Momadele's priceless cards and handwritten letters, and through many, many hours of visiting over fabric at Mema's kitchen island, Ashli also learned to treasure words.

Get to know Ashli by subscribing to her newsletter, *The Gazette,* at AshliMontgomery.com

Titles by Virginia'dele Smith

Sadie & Sam: PART 1 - Introductory Short Story (FREE)
Book 0: My Manifesto - Short Memoir (FREE)

The Davenports
Book 1: Grocery Girl
Book 2: In the Trenches
Book 3: Three Times to Make Sure
Book 4: Take a Chance on Love
The Davenports EAT — A Green Hills Cookbook

Book 5: Undeveloped Love (coming fall 2023)
A Christmas Collection Novella